Hearts Unbroken

VIVIAN BELLE

STERLING RIDGE PRESS LLC

Cover designed by Sterling Ridge Press LLC

Published by: Sterling Ridge Press, LLC www.sterlingridgepress.com

ISBN: 978-1-966093-23-7
Printed in the United States of America

First Edition: April 2025

For permissions, contact: support@vivianbelle.com or visit www.vivianbelle.com

Dedication

For all who have known loss,
yet found the courage to open their hearts again—
May you discover, as Beth and Miles did,
that sometimes the most beautiful beginnings
are woven from the threads of what was broken.
And to those still waiting in the quiet aftermath of grief:
Hope springs eternal.
Vivian Belle

About The Author

Vivian Belle is a talented author known for her sweeping **Historical Christian Romance** novels set against the untamed beauty of the American frontier. With a deep love for history and storytelling, she brings to life **resilient heroines, steadfast heroes, and faith-filled journeys** in the vast, rugged landscapes of the past.

Nestled in the **majestic mountains of northern West Virginia,** Vivian finds endless inspiration in the rolling hills, winding rivers, and boundless sky that mirror the spirit of her stories. When she's not writing, she enjoys **kayaking on tranquil waters, hiking through breathtaking mountain trails, and, of course, getting lost in a good book.**

Vivian's novels capture the heart of **faith, love, and perseverance**—where strong women and honorable men overcome life's trials to find hope, home, and happily-ever-after. Whether she's exploring the great outdoors or crafting her next frontier romance, Vivian's passion for adventure and storytelling shines through in every word she writes.

You can find out more about Vivian and her latest releases at www.vivianbelle.com or follow her on social media for updates and behind-the-scenes glimpses of her writing process. Stay connected—you won't want to miss the heartfelt stories of love and family she has in store!

Also by Vivian Belle

Where the Heart Finds Home

Faith on the Frontier

Love in Hopewell Creek

Abigail's Promise

Beneath Montana Skies

Rocky Mountain Promise

Hearts Unbroken

Contents

Chapter 1

Beth Bartlett's needle flashed in the morning light. Silver glinted against the cream linen as her fingers—nimble from years of practice—guided each delicate stitch with precision. Nearly complete now. The handkerchief needed just three more French knots to finish the small purple violets clustered along one corner. Stitch, loop, pull. Stitch, loop, pull. The rhythm was as familiar to her as her own heartbeat.

"There you are," she murmured, tying off the final knot and snipping the thread with her small silver scissors. She held up the handkerchief, examining her work with a critical eye, a ghost of a smile touching her lips. Perfect, her mother would have said, her voice a warm murmur like summer bees. But her mother wasn't here to say it. Beth's smile faded, the violets suddenly blurring through a sheen of unshed tears.

The bell above the shop door jangled, startling Beth from her thoughts. She tucked the handkerchief beneath the counter and smoothed her apron.

"Good morning, Mrs. Peterson," Beth called, offering a bright smile to the rancher's wife. "How are you today?"

"Just fine, Beth, though these summer days are getting mighty warm." Mrs. Peterson fanned herself with her hand, her round face flushed beneath her bonnet. "I'm needing fabric for new shirts for Mr. Peterson and the boys. Somethin' sturdy that won't fall to pieces after one cattle drive."

"I have just the thing." Beth moved toward the bolts of fabric lining the eastern wall of Bartlett's Dry Goods Shoppe. Her fingertips ran across the various textures, soft calicos, sturdy wools, and delicate silks, until she reached a selection of durable cotton twill. "This arrived on yesterday's train. It's strong enough for ranch work, but won't leave them scratching all day."

While Mrs. Peterson examined the fabric, Beth allowed her gaze to travel around her shop. Sunlight, thick and golden, streamed through the wide front windows, laying warm stripes across the burnished wood floor. Shelves, packed high, displayed a rainbow of ribbons, silken shimmers and sturdy grosgrain. Buttons gleaming like tiny jewels, and bolts of fabric stacked in fragrant towers: calico soft as a summer breeze, wool rough against the fingertips, silk whispering luxury. The subtle scent of beeswax candles mingled with the sharper, herbal fragrance of lavender sachets tucked between the fabric folds, a comforting, familiar perfume.

"Beth?" Mrs. Peterson's voice broke through her momentary reverie. "I asked how much I'll need for three shirts?"

"Oh! I'm sorry." Beth quickly calculated the measurements. "For Mr. Peterson and the boys, nine yards should do it. Ten if you want extra for patches."

"Ten it is. Those boys tear through clothing faster than I can make it." Mrs. Peterson chuckled, watching as Beth measured and cut the fabric.

As Beth wrapped the purchase in brown paper, she asked, "How is little Sarah feeling? I heard she had a fever last week."

"Much better, thank the Lord. That remedy Mrs. Weatherly suggested worked wonders." Mrs. Peterson's expression softened. "Sarah asked me to thank you for the doll clothes you sent over. You didn't have to do that, Beth."

Beth tied the package with twine, avoiding Mrs. Peterson's gaze. "It was nothing. Just scraps I had leftover." She didn't mention staying up until midnight to finish the tiny dresses, wanting to give the sick child something to smile about.

After Mrs. Peterson paid and left, promising to send her eldest son to collect an order of buttons later that week, Beth moved to straighten a display of ribbon spools. The shop fell into silence again, broken only by the distant sounds of horses and wagons passing outside, the persistent tick of the clock above the register, and the creak of the wooden floor beneath her feet.

In these quiet moments, Beth's thoughts drifted most freely and most dangerously. It had been just over a year since her parents had passed, victims of the influenza that had swept through Hope Springs with cruel efficiency. Occasionally, the shop seemed to echo with ghosts, the phantom sound of her father's deep laugh bouncing off the ceiling beams, or the whisper of her mother's favorite hymn drifting between the bolts of fabric. Beth would catch herself pausing, head tilted, listening for sounds that existed only in memory, then swallowing against the tightness in her throat when silence answered.

And before that... Beth's hands stilled on a spool of blue ribbon.

Before, that had been Thomas.

The memory rose unbidden, a familiar ache behind her ribs. Thomas... the sound of his laughter, warm and confident, echoing in her ears as clearly as if he were still standing beside her. She could almost feel the rough wool of his coat beneath her fingers when he'd taken her hand that day by the river, promising forever. Forever had lasted less than a heartbeat.

It had been two years since Thomas Aldridge had disappeared without a word, leaving her standing on the church steps in her wedding dress, surrounded by pitying glances and whispered condolences. Two years of wondering what she had done wrong, what flaw he had discovered about her that made him flee rather than face her.

"Stop it," Beth whispered to herself, straightening her shoulders. "That's enough of that." She physically straightened, squaring her shoulders as if to push down the rising tide of memory, forcing it back into the locked box within her heart.

She moved purposefully to the front counter and pulled out her ledger, forcing her mind to focus on numbers and inventory rather than memories. This was her life now. The shop, her customers, the peaceful apartment upstairs, and the small routines that structured her days.

It was enough. It had to be.

The familiar weight of solitude pressed against her chest—not quite pain, not anymore, but a dull pressure that reminded her of its presence with each breath. Sometimes in the quiet moments between customers, Beth would catch herself listening for her father's footsteps that wouldn't come, or turning to share a thought with her mom.

The bell above the door jingled again, pulling her from the dangerous quicksand of her thoughts, and Beth looked up to see Harriet Wells bustling in, her arms laden with books.

"These just arrived on the morning train," Harriet announced, dumping her burden onto the counter with a dramatic sigh. "Tim says the mail coach was overflowing today. You'd think people back East had nothing better to do than write letters and send packages."

Beth smiled at her friend's theatrical exhaustion. Harriet ran the bookshop next door, and her vibrant personality was as different from Beth's quiet demeanor as could be imagined. With her auburn hair often escaping its pins and her ready laugh, Harriet brought energy into any room she entered.

"New inventory?" Beth asked, picking up the top volume. "Mrs. Weatherly will be pleased. She's been waiting for this one."

"Yes, and there's something for you too." Harriet rummaged through the stack, her eyes brightening as she extracted a slim volume bound in blue, presenting it with a flourish. "The latest ladies' fashion magazine from New York. I thought you might like to see what those city women are wearing these days."

"That's thoughtful, thank you." Beth accepted the magazine, leafing through pages of elaborately dressed women with impossibly tiny waists. "Though I doubt any of my customers will be ordering bustles with three tiers of ruffles anytime soon."

Harriet perched on a stool beside the counter. "A girl can dream, can't she? I'd give anything to wear something that wasn't practical for once." She cast a sly glance at Beth. "Tim says he thinks the blue dress I wore to church last Sunday was pretty."

Beth raised an eyebrow. "Is that so? And what else does Tim Cooper say these days?"

A blush crept across Harriet's cheeks. "Nothing you need to concern yourself with, Beth Bartlett." She said as she straightened a pile of handkerchiefs that didn't need straightening. "Though he might have mentioned taking me to the harvest dance next month." Harriet's voice lilted upward, feigning casualness.

"I'm happy for you," Beth said sincerely, ignoring the brief pang in her chest. "Tim's a good man."

"He is." Harriet's expression softened before turning shrewd. "Now, if only we could find someone for you..."

"Don't start," Beth warned, turning away to arrange a basket of thread spools by color. "I'm perfectly content with my life as it is."

"Content isn't the same as happy." Harriet's voice gentled. "It's been two years since Thomas, Beth. You don't have to guard your heart quite so fiercely, you know."

Beth kept her back turned, not wanting Harriet to see the emotions crossing her face. "My heart is just fine where it is, thank you very much. Safe and sound and not causing any trouble."

"That's the problem," Harriet sighed. "Hearts aren't meant to be contained. They're meant to be given away."

The bell jangled again, saving Beth from having to respond. Mrs. Hanley entered with her youngest daughter in tow, looking for fabric for a new Sunday dress. Beth greeted them warmly, grateful for the interruption.

Harriet took the hint and gathered her remaining books. "I should get back to my shop." She paused at the door. "Think about what I said, Beth. And come by for tea later if you're not too busy."

With a quick smile that softened her words, Harriet swept out, the bell announcing her departure with the same cheerful jingle that had heralded her arrival.

Beth helped Mrs. Hanley select a pretty floral calico, measured out the required yardage, and offered suggestions for trimming that would suit the young girl's coloring. All the while, Harriet's words echoed in her mind.

Hearts aren't meant to be contained. They're meant to be given away.

Easy enough for Harriet to say, with Tim Cooper looking at her like she hung the moon. Harriet hadn't stood abandoned by her fiancée on the church steps, or watched her parents slip away within days of each other despite desperate prayers and sleepless nights of care.

"Beth?" Mrs. Hanley's voice broke through her thoughts. "Do you have any lace that would match this?"

"Yes, of course." Beth moved to the glass case where she kept the finer trimmings. "I have several patterns that would complement it beautifully."

The rest of the morning passed with a trickle of customers. Nellie Prescott collecting supplies for the quilting circle, and young Gussie Cole seeking advice on mending a torn sleeve. Beth moved through each interaction with the same warm efficiency that had earned her the town's respect and affection, her smile never faltering.

Yet behind that smile, something ached. Not the sharp grief of fresh loss, but the dull, persistent throb of loneliness that she usually managed to ignore. Harriet's visit had poked at it like a tongue probing a sore tooth.

The church bell tolled twelve times, its resonant chime rolling down Main Street like a gentle tide. Beth's stomach answered with a quiet growl as she hung the "Closed" sign in the window. She turned the key in the lock, a brass key worn smooth from years of her father's touch before hers, and retreated upstairs to her apartment. Each step carried her further from the shopkeeper and closer to just Beth, alone with her thoughts.

The space was small but neat, with simple furnishings that reflected both practicality and the occasional indulgence in beauty—a crocheted doily on the table, a vase of wildflowers on the windowsill, and her mother's quilt spread across the bed.

Beth warmed the soup left from yesterday's dinner and carried her bowl to the window overlooking Main Street. From this vantage point, Main Street unspooled below, a tapestry of sun-drenched dust and muted sounds: the creak of wagon wheels, the distant clip-clop of horseshoes on the packed earth, the murmur of voices rising and falling in the summer air. Shopkeepers exchanging greetings, children running errands for their mothers, and Sheriff Braddock tipping his hat to ladies as he made his rounds.

Two cowboys fresh from trail drives hitched their horses outside the saloon, dust coating their leather chaps and wide-brimmed hats. Across the street, Mr. Hemingway arranged a display of new steel-tipped plows in front of his hardware store, innovations that promised to break the stubborn prairie soil more efficiently than their wooden predecessors. Hope Springs was changing, growing with each new train that arrived, each new settler staking a claim to Nebraska's fertile land. Even the telegraph wires, strung just three years ago, hummed with messages from a world that seemed both impossibly distant and increasingly near.

She spotted Harriet talking animatedly with Tim Cooper. Even from a distance, Beth could see the way Tim leaned toward Harriet, hanging on her every word, and the way Harriet's hand occasionally touched his arm for emphasis. Their ease with each other made Beth's chest tighten.

"Lord," she whispered, forehead resting against the cool glass, "I know I should be grateful for what I have. The shop is doing well. I have good friends, and my health is strong. But sometimes..."

Beth's throat tightened. The words of prayer felt brittle on her tongue. To admit loneliness... it was like admitting a flaw in the careful tapestry of her self-sufficiency. A thread pulled loose, threatening to unravel everything. Her parents had raised her to be strong in faith and purpose. What would they think of her occasional yearning for a hand to reach for hers without hesitation, for laughter that wasn't just polite, or for someone to share the quiet evenings with her?

Her gaze drifted back down to Main Street, to where Reverend Weatherly stood outside the church, speaking with a tall, broad-shouldered man Beth didn't recognize. The stranger's back was to her, but something about his stance, solid and steady, caught her attention. As she watched, two small girls in matching blue dresses ran up to the man, who knelt down to their level.

Beth turned away from the window. She set her bowl of soup down and reached for her worn Bible on the bedside table, letting it fall open where the pages naturally parted. Her eyes landed on Psalm 27:14: "Wait on the Lord: be of good courage, and he shall strengthen thine heart: wait, I say, on the Lord."

Wait. Be courageous. Trust God's timing.

She had been waiting two years since Thomas. A year since her parents. Waiting for the pain to fade. Waiting to feel whole again. Waiting. Yes, she was good at waiting. Had she waited so long, so deliberately, that the space around her heart had solidified, become a shell too thick to crack, even if someone tried?

Beth closed the Bible gently and placed it back on the table. The noon hour was nearly over; customers would be expecting the shop to reopen. She rinsed her bowl, smoothed her hair, and studied her reflection in the small mirror hanging beside the door. The woman who gazed back appeared composed, serene even. A perfect shopkeeper's face that revealed nothing of the hollowness beneath. Beth had become adept at this particular needlework: stitching a smile across lips that might otherwise tremble, embroidering calm into eyes that sometimes threatened to overflow. She adjusted an errant hairpin, straightened her collar, and pinned her smile back in place before descending the stairs to the shop floor.

Downstairs, as she turned the sign from "Closed" to "Open." Beth caught another glimpse of the stranger and his daughters walking with Reverend Weatherly toward the church. The girls skipped alongside their father, one holding each of his hands, while he nodded at whatever the reverend was saying.

For a fleeting moment, Beth allowed herself to wonder who they were and why they had come to Hope Springs. Then she firmly pushed the thought away. New people came and went through town regularly. This man and his daughters were none of her concern.

The shop bell jangled as her first afternoon customer entered, and Beth turned her attention to where it belonged, to her work, her customers, and the careful rhythm of her solitary life.

"Good afternoon, Mrs. Reynolds," she greeted the midwife with a genuine smile. "What can I help you with today?"

As she guided Mrs. Reynolds to the selection of flannel for baby blankets, Beth Bartlett did what she did best. She focused on others' needs and kept her heart locked tight; the key swallowed long ago, the cost of its safety a silence that echoed louder with each passing day.

Chapter 2

The train whistle pierced the afternoon air, announcing its arrival in Hope Springs with a long, mournful wail that echoed across the prairie. Miles Donovan tightened his grip on the reins, steadying the horses as they snorted and stamped, ears flicking nervously at the mechanical beast's cry. The locomotive rounded the bend, iron wheels grinding against rails, spewing black smoke that billowed skyward like storm clouds against the merciless blue of the Nebraska sky. The acrid scent of coal smoke mingled with the sweeter smell of prairie grass baking in the sun. Hope Springs, their new beginning, was finally within sight.

"Papa, are we almost there?" Clara's small voice fought through the locomotive's roar, carrying from the wagon bed where she sat nestled among their modest belongings, all that remained of their life in Iowa. The rest had been sold, traded, or left behind, along with painful memories.

Miles glanced over his shoulder at his youngest daughter. At four years old, Clara's endless questions and boundless energy often left him struggling to keep pace. Her dark curls, so like her mother's, had escaped from their ribbon bindings after the long journey, framing a face smudged with dust and excitement.

"Yes, sweetheart. That's Hope Springs just ahead." He nodded toward the collection of buildings that made up the town's main street. "Our new home."

Beside Clara, seven-year-old Ellie sat quietly, her thin fingers clutching the worn rag doll that had been her constant companion since Charlotte's passing. Where Clara bubbled with questions, Ellie had retreated, her eyes holding a solemnity no child her age should carry.

"Will there be other children, Papa?" Ellie asked softly, her first words in hours.

Miles felt his heart constrict. "I expect so. The reverend mentioned a school when we exchanged letters."

He turned his attention back to the road, guiding the wagon past the train station where passengers disembarked and the freight was unloaded with practiced efficiency. The main street of Hope Springs stretched before them—a wide dirt thoroughfare lined with false-fronted wooden buildings, their painted facades proclaiming the businesses within. A church steeple pierced the sky at the far end. The clang of a hammer rang out from somewhere nearby. A group of men stood arguing good-naturedly outside the barbershop. Two women in calico dresses paused their conversation to stare openly at the newcomers. This wasn't just a collection of buildings; it was a living community, people bound together by necessity and choice, carrying on in this small corner of the frontier.

Miles pulled the wagon to a stop near the town square. "Wait here, girls. I need to ask for directions to our new shop."

"Can I come?" Clara was already scrambling to stand.

"Not this time. Stay with your sister. I won't be long."

He climbed down from the wagon, his boots hitting the packed earth with a solid thud. Standing at his full height, Miles rolled his shoulders, trying to ease the stiffness from the long journey. His dark hair needed cutting, and the stubble on his jaw spoke of days on the road, but there'd be time for such niceties later.

A man in a shopkeeper's apron swept the boardwalk in front of what appeared to be a hardware store. Miles approached him, hat in hand.

"Excuse me, sir. I'm looking for the blacksmith shop."

The shopkeeper paused, leaning on his broom as he studied Miles with frank curiosity. "You'd be Donovan, then? The new smithy we've been expecting?" His voice was gruff but not unfriendly.

"Miles Donovan, yes." He extended his hand. "Just arrived with my daughters."

The man's handshake was firm, his palm lined with calluses that spoke of years of honest work. "Walter Hemingway. Hardware's my business." He gestured down the street with his broom. "Smithy's at the edge of town, that way. Can't miss it, got the anvil sign hanging out front. Old Jeb passed last winter, and we've been making do with a traveling smith since. The town's been waiting patiently for your arrival."

"We made it safely. I appreciate the directions." Miles nodded respectfully. "Is there somewhere nearby my daughters and I might get a hot meal? It's been a long journey."

"Ida Frances runs the boarding house, just there." Hemingway pointed to a two-story building with a wide porch. "Best stew in three counties, if you don't mind her talking your ear off while you eat it."

Miles thanked him and returned to the wagon. As he approached, he noticed Clara had climbed onto the driver's seat and was pretending to drive the horses, making clicking sounds with her tongue.

"Clara Marie," he said, trying to sound stern despite the smile tugging at his lips. "What did I say about staying put?"

"I am staying put, Papa." Her bright eyes sparkled with mischief. "Just in a different put."

Despite the weariness that seemed a permanent part of him these days, Miles chuckled. "Scoot over, you little troublemaker. Let's go find our new home and shop, then we'll get some supper."

They traveled the remaining distance through town. A woman sweeping her porch paused mid-stroke to stare. The two men outside the barbershop halted their conversation, nodding curtly as the wagon passed. From the millinery shop window, a cluster of women made no effort to disguise their assessment of the newcomers. A small boy pointed openly until his mother swatted his hand down. Miles acknowledged each look with a polite tip of his hat, but kept the horses moving steadily forward. There would be time for proper introductions when they weren't road-weary and travel-stained.

The blacksmith shop sat at the northwestern edge of town, a sturdy structure of weathered wood with a large open-front workspace dominated by a massive forge. Miles felt a familiar comfort at the sight of it, then a stab of guilt for feeling anything resembling comfort when Charlotte wasn't here to share it. The forge would be his sanctuary and his burden. The place where he could lose himself in honest work while providing for his girls.

Next to the shop stood a small cottage, modest but solid-looking.

"Is this our house, Papa?" Ellie asked as he helped her down from the wagon.

"It is." Miles surveyed the property with a critical eye. "It needs some attention, but it'll serve us well."

Inside, the cottage smelled of disuse and wood smoke. Dust motes danced in the shafts of late afternoon sunlight streaming through grimy windows. The main room held a stone fireplace with an iron hook for cooking pots, a rough-hewn table with four mismatched chairs, and a bench covered with a faded quilt. To the left stood two small bedrooms with narrow doorways, and straight ahead was the kitchen with its cast-iron cookstove, still housing the ashes of fires long gone cold. Cobwebs draped the corners like lace, and a mouse scurried along the baseboards at their entrance, disappearing into a small hole.

"It's dirty," Ellie observed quietly, her small face solemn.

"Nothing a bit of elbow grease won't fix," Miles assured her, running his finger through the dust on the mantelpiece. "By this time tomorrow, it'll feel like it's always been ours."

Miles set about opening windows while the girls explored Clara's exclamations of discovery, punctuating the still air.

"Papa! There's a pump right outside the kitchen door!"

"Look, a shelf for my doll," came Ellie's softer voice.

Miles moved through the space, his boots echoing on the wooden floors. He ran calloused fingers along the doorframes, testing their sturdiness, and inhaled the mingled scents of dust and wood smoke that clung to the walls. Each creak and groan of the structure spoke to him of its character, its strengths and weaknesses, as he mentally cataloged what needed repair or replacement. The previous blacksmith had maintained the place well enough. It would do for them. A place to start anew.

"Girls," he called, "come help me bring in our things. Then we'll see about that supper."

They worked together, Miles carrying the heavier trunks while the girls brought in smaller bundles. When Clara struggled with a package nearly as big as herself, Miles intercepted it gently.

"Let me take that, sweetheart."

"I can do it," she protested, her small face scrunched with determination.

"I know you can." He knelt at her level. "But sometimes even strong people let others help them."

If only he could follow his own advice, Miles thought wryly as he carried the bundle inside. Since Charlotte's death, he'd shouldered everything alone, his grief, the girls' care, and the decision to leave their home in Iowa for this new start in Nebraska. The weight of it all pressed down on him like an anvil on his chest, leaving little room to breathe.

Once their belongings were inside, Miles pumped water to wash the dust from their faces and hands.

He combed Clara's wild curls and as he retied the blue ribbon that matched her dress, his fingers froze. For a moment, he couldn't breathe, couldn't think—caught in the undertow of memory. Charlotte's hands had been so deft at this task, weaving ribbons and combing curls while singing softly. His fingers were clumsy giants by comparison, better suited to bending metal than managing delicate silk. He swallowed hard, forcing down the knot in his throat that threatened to choke him. She should be beside him as they built this new life.

The fever had taken her so quickly. Days of desperate prayers while she burned hotter than his forge, her body fighting to protect the child within her. In the end, he'd lost them both—his wife of eight years and the son he'd never hold. The doctor had called it childbed fever, as if giving it a name somehow made the loss more bearable. The neighbors in Iowa had been kind, too kind, their pitying glances following him and the girls everywhere they went.

"Papa?" Ellie touched his arm, her thin face concerned. "Are you sad again?"

Miles forced a smile. "Just tired from our journey." He stroked her cheek with his calloused thumb. "Let's find that boarding house and get some supper in our bellies."

They walked back into town, Clara skipping ahead while Ellie held tightly to Miles' hand. The sun was beginning its westward descent, casting long shadows across the wide street. Several businesses were closing for the day, shopkeepers locking up and heading home.

The boarding house sat midway down Main Street, its wide porch adorned with rocking chairs and potted geraniums. A hand-painted sign swung slightly in the evening breeze: "Ida Frances Boarding & Lodging—Clean Beds, Hot Meals."

As they approached, Miles caught the mingled aromas of beef stew, baking bread, and the sharp tang of coffee. Through the windows, the warm glow of coal oil lamps pushed back against the gathering dusk. The sound of a piano being expertly played drifted from inside, abruptly stopping when Miles opened the door, all attention turning his way.

A stout woman with graying hair pulled into a severe bun that did nothing to diminish the warmth of her smile beamed up at Miles, then shifted her gaze to the girls.

"Well, land sakes!" She said. "You must be the Donovan's! We've been wondering when you'd show up. Half the town's been speculating about when our new blacksmith would arrive." She bent slightly at the waist. "And who might these lovely young ladies be?"

"Miles Donovan, ma'am." He tipped his hat. "And these are my daughters, Ellie and Clara."

"Ida Frances. I've just finished making supper, and there's plenty to spare. You poor dears must be famished after your journey."

The boarding house dining room was spacious, with three long tables set for the evening meal. A few men, railroad workers by the look of them, already occupied one table. The delicious aroma of beef stew and fresh bread filled the air, making Miles realize just how hungry he was.

As Ida led them to a table, a gangly boy of about twelve rushed in from the kitchen, carrying a stack of plates. He skidded to a halt when he saw the newcomers; the plates wobbling precariously.

"Sweet mercy, Jimmy!" Ida Frances exclaimed. "Those dishes belonged to my mother!"

"Sorry, Mrs. Frances," the boy mumbled, steadying his load. His eyes darted curiously between Miles and the girls.

"This here's Jimmy Langley," Ida explained as they sat. "He helps around the boarding house and runs messages faster than the telegraph—especially the ones nobody's told him to deliver." This last part she said with an affectionate yet pointed look at the boy.

Jimmy's ears reddened. "Pleased to meet you, sir. M-ma'ams," he added with an awkward nod to the girls. Clara giggled and waved back enthusiastically.

"Likewise, Jimmy," Miles replied. "You know your way around town well, then?"

"Yes sir. Every inch," Jimmy declared, standing straighter. "I could show you 'round sometime. If you wanted."

Miles caught the flicker of hope in the boy's eyes. "That would be a great help, thank you."

Jimmy beamed before scurrying back to the kitchen, nearly colliding with the door as he cast another glance over his shoulder.

"That boy," Ida said with fond exasperation as she served generous portions of stew and thick slices of bread. "Orphaned two years back, but the whole town looks after him. He lives here at the boarding house, does chores for his keep."

As they ate, Ida provided a steady stream of information about Hope Springs, who owned which business, which families had been there longest, and which had children close to Ellie and Clara's ages.

After supper, Miles insisted on paying, despite Ida's protests that their first meal in town would be a welcome gift. The sky was turning dusky as they made their way back to their new home, Clara now drooping with fatigue as Miles carried her.

"Papa," Ellie said as they walked, "do you think Mama can see our new house from heaven?"

The question hit him like a physical blow. Miles swallowed hard before answering. "I believe she can, Ellie. And I think she'd be happy knowing we're safe."

"I miss her," Ellie whispered, her small voice nearly lost in the evening air.

"I know, sunshine." Miles squeezed her hand. "I miss her too. Every day."

Miles studied his eldest daughter's profile in the fading light. Where Clara wore her heart openly, Ellie kept hers guarded, much like him. Of his two daughters, Ellie remembered Charlotte most clearly, and therefore felt her absence most keenly. The child seemed to be shrinking inward, her shoulders hunched as if bracing against an invisible wind. How did a man reach a heart so like his own?

Back at the cottage, he lit the lamps and helped the exhausted girls ready for bed. They'd unpack properly tomorrow, but tonight they'd make do with what they needed. He tucked them into the single bed they'd share until he could build another, listening as they said their prayers.

"God bless Papa and Clara and me," Ellie recited. "And please tell Mama we love her and miss her. And thank you for our new house. Amen."

"Amen," Clara echoed sleepily. "And God bless the horsies, too."

Miles pressed a kiss to each of their foreheads. "Sleep well, my girls."

After they drifted off, Miles stepped outside onto the small porch. The night air was cool. The sky, a vast canvas of stars stretching over the prairie. In the distance, he could see the silhouette of the church steeple against the night sky.

The crescent moon hung like a smithy's hook in the sky, as if waiting to catch and hold something precious. Stars peppered the darkness, countless pinpricks of light that had guided travelers for generations before him and would continue long after he was gone. There was something comforting in their permanence, their quiet witness to human struggles below.

He sat on the porch step, allowing himself a rare moment of still-ness. The weight of grief settled around his shoulders like a familiar cloak, heavier in these quiet moments when there were no distractions, and no little eyes watching.

"I'm trying, Charlotte," he whispered to the night. "God help me, I'm trying to be what they need."

The loss of his wife and unborn son had left a hole in his life that nothing seemed to fill. Each day, he moved through the motions of living, caring for his daughters, and working his trade, but the joy had gone out of it. Only the girls kept him anchored, their needs forcing him to rise each morning and face another day.

Hope Springs represented a clean slate. A place where no one knew him as "that poor widower," where his grief wasn't reflected back at him in every compassionate glance. Here, he could simply be Miles Donovan, the blacksmith, and father to Ellie and Clara.

He fingered the scar on his forearm absently, the raised line a reminder of his early days at the forge. So much had changed since then. The confident young man who'd courted Charlotte Fitzpatrick with songs and laughter seemed a stranger now.

From inside the cottage came Ellie's soft whimper, a sound he recognized from countless nights since Charlotte's passing. Miles rose immediately and went to his daughters, finding Ellie half-awake and reaching for comfort.

"Shhh, little one," he murmured, smoothing back her curls. "Papa's here."

"I dreamed of angels," she mumbled drowsily. "They had Mama's face."

Miles swallowed the lump in his throat. "That sounds like a beautiful dream."

"It was." Her eyes drifted closed again. "They were flying over our new house, keeping us safe."

Miles sat with her until her breathing deepened into sleep again, his calloused hand gentle against her small back. Perhaps Ellie's dream was right, perhaps Charlotte was watching over them still, guiding them toward healing in this new place.

Tomorrow would bring the real work of beginning again. Unpacking more of their meager belongings, introducing himself to community members, and establishing a routine for the girls. Tonight, though, as the prairie wind whispered around the eaves of their new home, Miles allowed himself a moment of hope, fragile as a newly forged blade before tempering.

"Goodnight, Charlotte," he whispered to the quiet house.

Chapter 3

Beth's fingers fumbled with the small pearl buttons running down the back of her dress, each one a challenge for hands more accustomed to guiding a needle through fabric than performing such backward acrobatics. Her mother used to help with these buttons every Sunday morning, accompanying the task with gentle reminders about posture or a bit of town news. Now, the weekly struggle with these buttons remained a poignant reminder of her solitude. The pale blue cotton, freshly pressed the night before, finally smoothed over her shoulders as she secured the final button. Church bells began to ring in the distance, their clear tones echoing across Hope Springs like God's own timepiece.

Beth hurried to her mirror, hastily pinning her honey-blonde hair into a careful chignon at the nape of her neck. She was going to be late if she didn't quit dilly-dallying, something that rarely happened on Sunday mornings.

She slipped her feet into polished black shoes and grabbed her Bible from the bedside table. The leather cover was worn soft from years of handling, its pages marked with pressed flowers and handwritten notes in the margins. Her father's voice seemed to whisper from those pages: Remember who you are, Bethie. A daughter of the King.

The stairs creaked under her feet as she descended to the shop below. Beth paused at the bottom, surveying the quiet space, shelves of fabric and notions standing in orderly rows. Sunday was the only day her shop remained closed, the only day she allowed herself true rest.

Outside, Hope Springs had transformed into a procession of Sunday best. Families walked along Main Street toward the white clapboard church at the end, women in pressed dresses with children scrubbed clean, and men in suits brushed free of weekday dust. Beth locked her shop door and joined the flow, nodding greetings to neighbors as she walked. This weekly pilgrimage was the heartbeat of Hope Springs—a reminder that no matter what struggles they faced individually through the week, they faced them together as a community. Like stitches in one of her quilts, separate threads woven into something stronger than any single strand could be.

"Morning, Beth!" Mrs. Peterson called, herding her four children ahead of her. "Beautiful day the Lord has given us!"

"Indeed it is," Beth replied with a genuine smile. The Nebraska sky stretched endlessly blue overhead, dotted with wispy clouds that promised continued fair weather.

The white clapboard church stood welcoming, its doors thrown wide as parishioners filed inside. Dust motes danced in the colored light filtering through the simple stained-glass windows—not elaborate biblical scenes like in the grand churches back East, but geometric patterns in amber, blue, and crimson that cast jewel-toned shadows across the worn wooden floors. Beth slipped into her usual pew, third from the front on the right side, the same spot her family had occupied for as long as she could remember. The smooth wood, polished by generations of Sunday worshipers, felt cool beneath her palms as she settled in, the faint scent of beeswax and lemon oil from yesterday's cleaning day lingering in the air.

The familiar emptiness of the pew on either side of her pinched at her heart, but she smoothed her expression as Harriet slid in next to her.

"You're cutting it close this morning," Harriet whispered, adjusting her hat.

"Just running behind," Beth murmured back, opening her Bible as the organ began to play.

Her gaze drifted across the filling church, automatically noting who was present and who wasn't, a habit formed from years of community membership. Near the back, a movement caught her eye. The stranger she'd glimpsed from her window yesterday was seating himself in the last pew, a small girl on either side of him. His dark hair was neatly combed, and he wore a proper Sunday suit. One of his daughters, the younger one with dark wild curls, wiggled restlessly while the other sat perfectly still.

"That's the new blacksmith," Harriet whispered, following Beth's gaze. Her lips curved into the satisfied smile of someone with prized information to share. "Miles Donovan. Arrived yesterday with his daughters."

"How do you know that already?" Beth asked, even as Harriet's eyes sparkled with the triumph of being first with the news. Beth suppressed a smile; Harriet collected town gossip the way others might collect pressed flowers—eagerly, thoroughly, and with particular pride in rare specimens.

"Tim told me. He delivered a telegram to Reverend Weatherly last week that stated he was accepting the blacksmith's position." Harriet leaned closer. "A widower, so I'm told."

Beth felt a sharp pang of sympathy twist in her chest. She knew too well the hollow ache of loss. How it carved out spaces inside you that nothing seemed to fill. But to face that emptiness with two young children depending on you? Her throat tightened at the thought. She'd only had to rebuild herself; this man had been tasked with rebuilding an entire family.

Before she could dwell on it further, Reverend Benjamin Weatherly stepped to the pulpit, and the congregation rose for the opening hymn.

"Shall we gather at the river, where bright angel feet have trod..."

Beth's clear voice joined the others, the familiar hymn rising toward the simple wooden rafters. As she sang, she found herself glancing again toward the back pew. Miles Donovan stood tall, the hymnal held for both his daughters to see. The smaller girl was standing on the pew to see it better, while the older one pressed close to her father's side, her thin face solemn as she mouthed the words.

After singing, Reverend Weatherly's sermon that morning centered on new beginnings, drawing from the book of Isaiah. "'Remember not the former things, nor consider the things of old. Behold, I am doing a new thing; now it springs forth, do you not perceive it?'"

The reverend's kind eyes swept across his congregation. "God constantly offers us fresh starts, beloved. Every sunrise brings an opportunity for renewal. The question is whether we're willing to step forward in faith or remain tethered to what was."

Beth shifted in her seat, suddenly feeling as though the reverend was speaking directly to her. How long had she been clinging to her pain, using it as a shield against future hurt?

In the months since the influenza had swept through Hope Springs, taking both her parents in the same terrible week, Beth had created a life of careful routine. The dry goods store her father had built, the quilting circle her mother had loved, the Sunday services they'd attended faithfully—she preserved it all like pressing flowers between Bible pages. Safe. Unchanging. Her parents' absence was a wound that had scabbed over but never truly healed, and she feared what might happen if she allowed anything—or anyone—to disturb that fragile covering.

"Loss and disappointment may shape us," Reverend Weatherly continued, his gaze sweeping across faces that had each known their measure of suffering, "but they need not define us. Just as a blacksmith reshapes metal through fire, our Lord uses our trials to forge us into something new—something stronger, more resilient, more purposeful." He paused, letting the metaphor settle. "Our Lord offers healing waters in the wilderness, rivers in the desert. We need only the courage to drink—to believe that renewal awaits, even when all we can see is scorched earth."

When the service concluded, Beth remained seated for a moment, letting the words settle in her heart. She watched as congregation members filed out, shaking the reverend's hand at the door. Miles Donovan and his daughters waited patiently, the little one bouncing on her toes while the older child held tightly to her father's hand.

"Beth, dear." Alice Weatherly's gentle voice broke through Beth's thoughts. The reverend's wife stood in the aisle, her round face creased with a warm smile. "Will you be joining us at the picnic?"

"Of course," Beth stood, gathering her Bible. "I've got the quilt squares from the sewing circle to distribute."

"Wonderful." Alice patted Beth's arm. "Benjamin and I have missed seeing you lately. Perhaps you might join us this week for dinner?"

Beth felt a flush of guilt. She had been declining invitations more frequently of late, preferring the quiet solitude of her apartment. "That would be lovely, thank you."

Outside, the churchyard bustled with activity as families prepared to walk to the picnic grounds by Silver Creek. Beth paused at the bottom of the church steps, breathing in the scent of grass warmed by the summer sun.

"Beth!" Alice called. "Come meet our newcomers."

Beth turned to see Alice beckoning her toward where Reverend Weatherly stood with Miles Donovan and his daughters. Something fluttered unexpectedly in her stomach as she approached them.

"Beth, this is Miles Donovan, our new blacksmith," Reverend Weatherly said, his hand resting companionably on the taller man's shoulder. "Mr. Donovan, Beth Bartlett, runs our dry goods shop, and she is one of Hope Springs' finest seamstresses."

"Miss Bartlett." Miles nodded politely, removing his hat. His eyes were a deep blue—not the bright summer sky above them, but something deeper, like twilight settling over the prairie. They were set in a face weathered by work and grief, lines etched at the corners that spoke of both laughter and sorrow. When he extended his hand, Beth hesitated a fraction before accepting it. His handshake was firm but gentle, his palm calloused from years at the forge, warm against her cooler skin.

"Welcome to Hope Springs, Mr. Donovan." Beth managed a smile that felt oddly stiff on her face, her pulse quickening for reasons she refused to examine. "I hope you're finding everything you need to settle in."

"Working on it, ma'am." His voice was deep, with a hint of an accent Beth couldn't quite place. "These are my daughters, Ellie and Clara."

The older girl, Ellie, kept her eyes downcast, offering only the slightest nod. Clara, however, stared openly at Beth, her dark eyes curious beneath a mop of unruly curls.

"Are you really a seamstress?" Clara asked without preamble. "Papa says I need new dresses, 'cause I keep growing like a weed."

"Clara," Miles admonished gently, though Beth caught the hint of a smile tugging at his mouth.

"It's quite all right," Beth said, kneeling to the little girl's level. "I am indeed a seamstress, and I would be happy to help with new dresses whenever you need them."

Clara beamed. "I like blue. And red. And yellow. And—"

"I think Miss Bartlett understands, sprite," Miles interrupted, placing a hand on his daughter's shoulder.

Beth glanced at Ellie, who was half-hidden behind her father's leg now. "And what colors do you like, Ellie?"

The girl looked up, surprised at being addressed. "Purple," she whispered after a moment. "And green."

"Excellent choices," Beth said. She reached into her small handbag and pulled out two fabric scraps she'd tucked in that morning, intending to show them to Nellie Prescott for the quilting circle. One was a delicate lavender print with tiny violets, the other a cheerful yellow with white dots. "Would you like these? Perhaps for your dolls?"

Ellie's eyes widened slightly. After a glance at her father for permission, she reached out and took the lavender scrap, her thin fingers tracing the pattern. "Thank you," she murmured.

Clara grabbed the yellow piece with enthusiasm. "Papa, look! It's the same color as sunshine!"

Miles met Beth's eyes, an expression of gratitude crossing his face. "That's very kind of you, Miss Bartlett."

"Please, call me Beth. Nearly everyone does."

"Beth, then." He nodded, a hint of warmth reaching his eyes. "And I'm Miles."

Reverend Weatherly clapped his hands together. "Well then! Shall we all head for the picnic? Mrs. Hanley's fried chicken waits for no man, and I intend to claim my share before Sheriff Braddock devours it all."

They walked as a group toward Silver Creek, the reverend and his wife leading the way, with Clara skipping alongside them, her questions bubbling forth like the creek itself. Beth found herself falling into step beside Miles, who walked at a measured pace to accommodate Ellie's shorter stride. The clean scent of his freshly laundered shirt floated in the breeze. Their arms nearly brushed, and Beth found herself hyper-aware of the narrow space between them, as if it were charged with the same energy that precedes a prairie thunderstorm.

"Your daughters are lovely," Beth said, searching for something to fill the silence between them.

"Thank you." Miles glanced down at Ellie, who clutched both her rag doll and the fabric scrap to her chest. "They're resilient. More than I sometimes give them credit for."

There was so much contained in that simple statement—grief, pride, worry. Beth recognized the complex emotions behind his words because she had felt them herself, struggling to rebuild after the loss.

"Children often are," she said. "And more observant than we realize."

Miles studied her for a moment. "You sound like you speak from experience."

Beth felt suddenly exposed. "I lost my parents last year to influenza. Not the same as..." she trailed off, not wanting to mention his wife.

"Loss is loss," Miles said simply. "It changes the shape of your world either way."

The path to Silver Creek meandered through wild prairie grasses, butterflies rising in clouds with each step. As they crested the gentle hill, the picnic grounds spread before them—a patchwork of humanity beneath the sheltering cottonwoods. Tables laden with food stood like altars to the community, while quilts spread across the grass created colorful islands where families gathered. Children darted about, their laughter threading through the warm air, rising above the melodic hum of conversation and clinking dishware.

"Papa, can I go play?" Clara tugged at Miles's hand, pointing to where several children were rolling hoops across the grass.

Beth saw hesitation cross Miles's face, a natural caution of a parent in a new place. "I know all the children here," she offered. "They're good-hearted. Clara would be welcome."

After a moment's deliberation, Miles nodded. "Stay where I can see you," he told Clara, who was bouncing with excitement. "And mind your manners."

"Yes, Papa!" Clara called as she darted off toward the other children, leaving Miles, Beth, and Ellie standing somewhat awkwardly at the edge of the gathering.

Ellie pressed closer to her father's side, clutching his hand. "I'm hungry," she said quietly.

"Let's find you something to eat, then." Miles looked toward the laden tables, then back at Beth. "Would you—that is—might you join us, Miss Bartlett? Beth, I mean."

The invitation surprised her. "I should help Mrs. Weatherly distribute the..."

But even as she made her excuse, Beth realized she wanted to accept. There was something about Miles Donovan that intrigued her. His steady calm, the gentle way he spoke to his daughters, and the sadness that lingered behind his eyes even when he smiled.

"Actually, I'd be happy to," she amended.

They filled plates with Mrs. Hanley's fried chicken, Ida Frances's potato salad, and slices of pie. Finding a spot beneath a spreading cottonwood, they settled on the grass, Ellie sitting close between her father and Beth.

The cottonwood's leaves rustled overhead like soft applause, casting dappled shadows that danced across their skin. Nearby, the creek burbled over smooth stones, providing a gentle backdrop to the community's cheerful commotion. The scent of sun-warmed grass mingled with the aromas of buttermilk biscuits, cinnamon, and coffee brewing in large tin pots over small fires at the edge of the gathering.

"This is delicious," Miles said after his first bite of chicken. "We didn't have gatherings like this where we came from."

"Where was that?" Beth asked.

"Iowa. Small farming town. I worked as the town blacksmith there, same as I'll do here."

"What made you choose Hope Springs?" The question slipped out before Beth could consider whether it was too personal.

Miles was quiet for a moment, his gaze finding Clara among the playing children. "After Charlotte, my wife, passed, staying there became...hard," He paused, searching for words. "Every corner held memories. Some days, those memories were a comfort. Other days, they hurt too much to bear."

Beth nodded, understanding perfectly. "So you came here for a fresh start?"

"Something like that." Miles turned his attention back to his plate. "Reverend Weatherly's cousin knew of my work and mentioned the position here was open. It seemed like providence."

"Moving is scary," Ellie's small voice surprised them both. She was looking at Beth, her dark eyes serious.

"Change is always a little frightening," she said honestly. "But sometimes it's necessary. And often, when we're brave enough to face it, we find unexpected blessings waiting for us."

Ellie seemed to ponder this, nodding slowly as she returned to her food.

They ate in companionable silence for a while, watching the community celebrate around them. Beth found herself sneaking glances at Miles, enjoying the way the sunlight caught in his dark hair, the strength evident in his shoulders, and the gentleness in his hands as he helped Ellie.

Across the picnic grounds, Clara was playing with Jimmy Langley and several other children, her laughter carrying clearly through the air. The sound brought a brief smile to Miles's face, softening the lines of worry that seemed etched there.

"She makes friends easily," Beth observed.

"Always has." Pride warmed Miles's voice. "Takes after her mother that way. Charlotte could talk to anyone, and make them feel at ease within minutes."

Beth felt an unexpected twinge at the mention of Charlotte. The woman had clearly been deeply loved, still was, judging by the way Miles spoke her name. As it should be, Beth reminded herself firmly. A good man honors the memory of his wife.

"And Ellie?" she asked, smiling at the quiet child, who was carefully arranging the remaining food on her plate.

"Ellie has always been our thinker," Miles said, his hand resting gently on his daughter's shoulder. "Observes everything, considers carefully, and then surprises you with insights beyond her years."

"I'm not very good at making friends," Ellie admitted, looking down at her plate, one finger tracing the edge in small, nervous circles.

"That's all right," Beth said, tilting her head to try to catch the girl's downcast eyes. "Quality matters more than quantity when it comes to friendships."

Ellie glanced up through her lashes, her shoulders loosening slightly, a tentative hope flickering across her face like a candle flame catching. "Really?"

"Absolutely." Beth nodded firmly, then leaned in as if sharing a precious secret. "Some of the best friendships take time to grow, like the strongest flowers in a garden. The quick-blooming ones might catch your eye first, but it's the slow-growing ones that weather the storms."

From across the picnic, Nellie Prescott waved, gesturing for Beth to join the group of women gathering for the quilt square distribution. Beth waved back, signaling she'd be there shortly.

"I'm afraid I'm needed with the quilting circle," she said, gathering her plate. "But it was lovely meeting you, Mr. Donovan... Miles. And you too, Ellie."

"Likewise, Miss... Beth," Miles corrected himself, standing as she did. He helped Ellie to her feet. "Thank you for your kindness today."

Something in his tone, sincere gratitude tinged with a hint of regret, made Beth pause. "My shop is open most days except Sunday," she found herself saying, surprised by her eagerness. "If you need anything—fabric for the house, or those dresses Clara mentioned..." She hesitated, aware she was extending more than just a business invitation. "Please stop by."

Miles studied her face for a moment, something unreadable flickering in his eyes. "We will. Thank you, Beth."

The sound of her name in his deep voice settled somewhere beneath her ribs, an unexpected weight that wasn't entirely unwelcome.

As Beth walked toward the quilting circle, she felt Miles's gaze following her. The sensation was both unsettling and oddly warming, like stepping from shade into sunlight. She hadn't expected to enjoy his company and hadn't planned to feel that tiny spark of interest that had kindled during their conversation.

Beth joined the group of women, forcing her attention to the quilt squares and patterns being discussed, but her thoughts kept drifting back to the quiet blacksmith and his daughters. To the pain they carried, so similar to her own. To the unexpected ease she'd felt in their company, despite her determination to keep her heart safely guarded.

Lord, what are You doing? She thought, while her fingers traced a pattern on a quilt square. *I'm not looking for complications. I've made my peace with my life as it is.*

But even as the thoughts formed, Beth knew peace wasn't quite the right word. She had created order from uncertainty, routine from heartbreak—but peace? That was something different. Something that had eluded her, perhaps because true peace required letting go of the past rather than merely surviving it.

Her gaze drifted back to where Miles now stood with both his daughters, Clara animated with stories of her new playmates, Ellie still quiet but leaning into her father's steady presence. Three broken hearts trying to mend themselves into something whole again.

Just like her own.

Chapter 4

CLANG. CLANG. CLANG.

The rhythm was as steady as a heartbeat, as vital as one, too. Each blow of Miles's hammer against the glowing horseshoe sent a shower of sparks cascading across the packed dirt floor—miniature shooting stars burning gold before extinguishing themselves at his feet. Sweat trickled down his temple despite the early hour, making rivulets through the fine layer of soot that had already settled on his skin. The heat from the forge washed over him in waves, a scorching tide flowing outward from the glowing heart of the blacksmith shop.

The smithy itself seemed alive around him—breathing with the bellows' wheeze, sweating beads of moisture down the stone walls, and speaking through the crackle of coal and hiss of hot metal meeting cool water. Dust motes danced in the shafts of sunlight that penetrated the soot-darkened windows, while the earthy scent of leather from hanging harnesses mingled with the metallic tang of iron and steel. Against one wall stood the tools of his trade: tongs of varying sizes hanging from iron hooks, hammers arranged by weight on a bench, and drawers containing nails, rivets, and metal stock sorted by purpose.

"Hold steady now," Miles instructed Virgil Emmett, his newly hired assistant, who gripped the tongs firmly, keeping the horseshoe in place on the anvil.

Virgil, a weathered cowboy of fifty with a salt-and-pepper mustache and hands like tanned leather, nodded without speaking, his stance showing he wasn't new to this work. Miles had found him yesterday afternoon, loitering outside the smithy with an inquiring look that spoke of both experience and need.

With three final precise strikes, Miles completed the shoe and Virgil plunged it into the water barrel. Steam hissed upward in a cloud that momentarily obscured his face.

The familiar routine anchored him, even as his thoughts threatened to drift. Each strike of hammer against metal required focus. The forge demanded all of him; it didn't allow for distraction or doubt. Perhaps that's why he'd always found solace in the work, even as a boy under his father's stern tutelage. When words failed, iron spoke, malleable beneath his hands in ways grief and fatherhood were not. Here, at least, he knew exactly what was required of him.

"That's good work," Virgil said, his voice gravelly from years of trail dust and campfire smoke. "Seen plenty of smiths who couldn't shape a shoe half as clean in twice the time."

Miles wiped his forearm across his brow. "My father believed a horseshoe done right meant a horse that could carry its rider safely home."

"Smart man, your pa." Virgil hung the cooled shoe on a rack with others finished that morning. "Looks like we got company."

Miles turned to see Sheriff Braddock leading a large bay gelding toward the open front of the shop. The horse's gait showed a slight favoring of its right foreleg.

"Morning, Donovan," the sheriff called, touching the brim of his hat. "Hear you've opened for business proper today."

"That's right." Miles stepped forward, wiping his hands on his leather apron. "What can I help you with?"

"This old boy threw a shoe yesterday while I was riding out to the Thompson place." The sheriff patted the horse's flank with affection, his weathered hand lingering on the animal's coat. "Need him back in working order, and right quick. Got word of cattle rustlers operating near the county line, and a sheriff without a sound horse ain't worth his salt."

Miles nodded and moved to examine the horse's hoof. "I can handle this. Won't take long."

While Miles worked, the sheriff leaned against a post, watching with interest. "The Town's pleased to have a smith again. We've been making do with traveling farriers since old Jeb passed."

"So I've heard." Miles selected one of the newly made shoes, checking it against the horse's hoof for size.

"Saw you at the church picnic with Beth Bartlett." There was a note of careful curiosity in the sheriff's voice. "She's a fine woman. Keeps to herself mostly, since her troubles."

Miles concentrated on his work, not rising to the bait of gossip. "She was kind to my girls."

"She is a kind woman. Heart of gold, that one."

As Miles worked the nails into the horseshoe, he found himself thinking of Beth, her gentle smile, the way she'd knelt to speak to Ellie, and the fabric scraps she'd offered so naturally. But he pushed those thoughts aside. His focus needed to remain on his daughters, his work, rebuilding their lives.

The morning passed with a steady stream of customers. Mr. Peterson bringing in a broken plow blade, Frank Hanley with a wagon wheel rim that needed repair, and Josiah Miller from the railroad with questions about making specialized tools.

By midday, Clara appeared at the open doorway, Ellie trailing behind her. They had spent the morning at the small cottage adjacent to the shop, unpacking their belongings.

"Papa, we're hungry," Clara announced, skipping into the shop despite Miles's oft-repeated warnings about keeping clear of the forge.

"Clara Marie, what did I tell you about the shop floor?" Miles set down his hammer, his voice firm but gentle.

Clara stopped immediately, pointing her toe at an invisible line near the entrance. "Stay behind the safety line unless invited." She recited the rule with the air of someone who had heard it many times.

"That's right." Miles nodded to Virgil. "Take your dinner break. I'll do the same."

Virgil hung up his apron. "Think I'll mosey over to Ida's place. Her food is worth crossing state lines for." He tipped his hat to the girls as he departed.

Miles led his daughters to the small table set in the shade beside the shop after gathering food from the house: bread, cheese, and apples.

"Did you finish unpacking your things?" Miles asked, cutting the apple into slices.

Ellie nodded. "I put my books on the shelf by the window."

"And I put my wooden animals in a line on my bed!" Clara added. "The horse is the leader because he's the biggest."

Miles smiled at his younger daughter's logic. "Very sensible."

As they ate, he noticed Ellie's quiet gaze wandering toward Main Street, where people moved about their midday business. "What are you thinking about, sunshine?"

Ellie hesitated. "Do you think Miss Beth might visit us someday?"

The question surprised him. Ellie rarely expressed interest in new acquaintances. "I don't know. I assume she stays quite busy with her shop."

"I liked her," Ellie said simply, returning to her bread and cheese.

Miles considered his daughter's words. Beth Bartlett had made an impression on both his girls, Clara with her immediate enthusiasm, and now Ellie with her quiet approval.

"Perhaps we'll see her again soon," he offered, not wanting to make promises he couldn't keep.

The midday sun climbed higher, beating down on Hope Springs with the unyielding intensity of summer. Main Street shimmered with heat, the buildings across the way appearing to waver slightly in the rising air. Miles wiped his brow, watching as Virgil returned from his meal, his weathered face glistening with perspiration.

Afternoon in the smithy would be punishing, but work awaited. Horseshoes wouldn't forge themselves.

***

Beth tugged on the metal door hinge, frowning at the way it hung askew. The door had been sticking for weeks, but this morning it had finally surrendered completely, the bottom hinge pulling free from the wooden frame with a splintering crack when Mrs. Hanley had entered.

Her father would have repaired it immediately. Joseph Bartlett had possessed an uncanny knack for maintenance, keeping their shop in pristine order with nothing more than a few simple tools and his patient hands. Beth's own attempts at repairs often fell short. These moments of failing infrastructure brought home how much she still depended on others—a reality that both chafed at her pride and emphasized her solitude.

"Everything all right, dear?" Harriet asked, peering over from where she was helping Beth arrange a new shipment of buttons by color and size.

"This door has given up the fight," Beth sighed, kneeling to examine the damage more closely. "The metal has bent, and the wood is splintered where the screws pulled free."

Harriet joined her, surveying the damage with a critical eye. "You'll need to get that fixed before closing time, or you won't be able to lock up properly."

Beth ran her fingers along the damaged wood. "I know. I was hoping to patch it myself, but..."

"You need the blacksmith," Harriet said.

"I'm sure Mr. Donovan is quite busy getting his shop established," Beth protested, though she knew Harriet was right. The door needed professional attention.

"Nonsense. It's his job to fix these things." Harriet straightened up, brushing dust from her skirt.

Beth stood, smoothing her apron. "I suppose I could ask him to look at it when he has time."

"No time like the present." Harriet glanced at the clock. "Now go on. I'll watch the shop while you're gone."

The blacksmith.

Miles Donovan.

Just his name brought warmth to her cheeks.

Beth hesitated a moment longer before untying her apron. "Very well. But only because the door genuinely needs repair."

"Of course," Harriet's smile was entirely too knowing for Beth's comfort.

The walk to the blacksmith shop took less than five minutes, but it gave Beth ample time to regret her decision. What would she say? Would Miles think she was making up an excuse to see him? Was she making up an excuse to see him?

No, she told herself firmly. *The door needed fixing, and Miles was the blacksmith. It was purely practical.*

As she approached the smithy, she saw Miles sitting at a small table with his daughters, sharing what appeared to be a simple midday meal outdoors. The sound of their quiet conversation carried on the warm breeze, punctuated by Clara's bell-like laughter.

She slowed her steps, suddenly reluctant to interrupt. Perhaps she should come back later when he was working.

Before she could retreat, Clara spotted her. "Miss Beth!" The little girl waved enthusiastically, nearly knocking over her cup in her excitement.

Miles turned, surprise evident on his face as he registered her presence. He stood, wiping his hands on a cloth. "Miss Bartlett. Beth, I mean."

Beth. Just the sound of her given name on his tongue felt too familiar, too forward. He hoped he hadn't sounded like a fool. He wiped his hands again, though they weren't truly dirty. Her presence had a way of making him feel slightly off balance, pleasantly so.

"I'm sorry to interrupt your meal," Beth said, clasping her hands in front of her. "I can come back later."

"Not at all." Miles gestured toward the table. "Would you care to join us? There's plenty."

"Oh, no, thank you. I've eaten." Beth took a few steps closer. "I actually came to ask if you might be able to repair my shop door. The hinge has pulled free from the frame, and it's bent."

Miles nodded. "I can take a look at it."

"Papa can fix anything that's broken," Clara piped up, her dark eyes serious.

Beth couldn't help but smile at the child's confidence. "Is that so?"

"Mostly anything," Miles corrected, a faint flush coloring his tanned cheeks. "Let me gather my tools, and I'll come take a look."

Ellie, who had been tracing patterns on the wooden table with her fingertip, looked up with unexpected eagerness. "Can we come too?" she asked, her voice still soft but with a thread of hope running through it. Her eyes met Beth's directly for the first time. "I'd like to see your shop."

Beth's heart warmed at the request from the shy child. "I'd be delighted to have you visit."

Miles hesitated, glancing toward the smithy. "Virgil should be back soon, but I don't like leaving the forge unattended..."

"I don't mind waiting," Beth assured him. "Please, finish your meal with your daughters."

Miles considered for a moment, then nodded. "Thank you. I won't be long."

Beth retreated a few steps, giving the family privacy to finish. As she waited, she observed Miles with his daughters. He listened attentively when they spoke, his focus complete despite his awareness of Beth's presence nearby. When Clara knocked over her cup, Miles cleaned up the spill without scolding, his large hands surprisingly deft with the task.

Virgil returned, and after a brief exchange, Miles gathered a leather tool satchel and spoke quietly to his daughters. They nodded, seeming to accept whatever instructions he had given.

"We're ready," Miles announced, approaching Beth with the girls trailing behind him.

The walk to Beth's shop was filled with Clara's chatter about everything she had seen in Hope Springs thus far. Ellie remained silent, though Beth noticed the girl's observant gaze taking in the details all around her.

When they arrived, Harriet was helping Mrs. Prescott select buttons for a new shirt. Her eyebrows rose slightly at the sight of Miles and his daughters, but she wisely made no comment.

"It's this door," Beth said, gesturing toward the entrance with a hint of embarrassment. "The bottom hinge finally gave up the ghost this morning."

Miles knelt to examine the damage, his fingers tracing the splintered wood with the reverence of a man who understood craftsmanship. "Been troubling you for some time, hasn't it?" he asked, glancing up at her.

"How could you tell?" Beth asked, surprised.

"The Wood's worn here," he pointed to subtle indentations in the frame. "From being forced closed when it didn't want to align." He ran his thumb along the bent metal strap. "Metal's fatigued, too. It's been holding on through sheer stubbornness."

"I'll need to forge a new strap," he continued, returning his attention to the door. "And this wood—" he tapped the splintered section gently, "—needs reinforcing if you don't want to be facing the same trouble come winter."

"Can it be repaired today?" Beth asked. "I'm worried about securing the shop overnight."

Miles nodded. "I'll take measurements now and forge the new piece this afternoon. I can install it before closing time."

Beth felt relief wash over her. "Thank you. I appreciate your promptness."

"It's my job," Miles said simply, though his eyes held something warmer than professional courtesy.

While Miles took measurements of the door frame, Clara wandered into the shop, her eyes wide at the colorful array of fabrics and notions.

"Look, Ellie!" she exclaimed, her voice dropping to a whisper of wonder as she pointed to a display of ribbons. "They're like rainbows! Mama would've loved these, wouldn't she? She always said pretty things make sad hearts happy again."

"They're pretty," she admitted.

"Would you like to see how they're made?" Beth asked, seizing the opportunity to connect with the reserved child.

Ellie nodded, her expression brightening slightly.

Beth led the girls to a shelf where spools of thread were arranged by color. "These threads are woven together to make ribbons and fabric. Different patterns create different designs."

"Like Papa's work," Ellie observed. "He says every hammer strike makes a pattern in the metal."

Beth smiled, touched by the comparison. "That's very insightful, Ellie. Your father shapes metal, and I shape fabric or ribbons, but we're both creating something useful from raw materials."

"Papa says useful things can be beautiful too," Clara added, running her fingers lightly over a bolt of blue calico.

"Your Papa is very wise," Beth agreed, her gaze drifting to where Miles was carefully noting the dimensions of her door in a small notebook. She quickly looked away when he glanced up.

Miles finished his measurements and packed away his tools. "I'll return before closing with the new hinge strap," he promised.

"Thank you." Beth walked him and the girls to the door. "What do I owe you for this work?"

Miles hesitated. "Let's settle that when the job is complete."

After they departed, Harriet materialized at Beth's side, her expression speculative. "My, my. The new blacksmith certainly is...capable."

"Yes, he appears to be," Beth said firmly, returning to the counter.

"He has such adorable children," Harriet continued, undeterred. "That little Clara is a spark of life, isn't she? And Ellie seems sweet, if a bit withdrawn."

"They've been through a lot," Beth said, her tone softening. "Losing their mother and now moving to a new town."

"A bit like someone else I know," Harriet observed quietly. "Though you lost different loved ones."

Beth busied herself arranging thread spools, unwilling to pursue that line of conversation.

"The shop is getting low on muslin. I should reorder soon."

Harriet allowed the subject to change, though her knowing smile remained.

***

True to his word, Miles appeared an hour before closing time, a leather apron still tied around his waist and a newly forged metal strap in his hands. Soot darkened his forearms, and a sheen of honest sweat gleamed on his brow.

"As promised," he said, holding up the metal piece. It was functional, but not without beauty. The metal curved gracefully at the ends, and a simple pattern had been hammered into its surface.

"It's lovely," Beth said with genuine appreciation. "You didn't need to make it decorative."

"A door this fine deserves proper hardware," Miles replied, his eyes taking in the carefully maintained shopfront. "My father always said there's no reason useful can't also be pleasing to the eye."

Beth thought of Clara's earlier words. Papa says useful things can be beautiful too, and smiled at the consistency between Miles's philosophy and what he taught his daughters.

"Where are Ellie and Clara?" she asked as Miles set down his tools.

"With Virgil. He's showing them how to curry the horses properly." Miles positioned the door so he could work on it. "They took a liking to him right away, despite his gruff manner. Or perhaps because of it."

"Children often see past our carefully constructed fronts," Beth said, stepping back to give him room to work.

Miles nodded, already focused on repairing the door. "Ellie talked about your shop all afternoon. The ribbons and fabrics made quite an impression."

Something warm unfurled in Beth's chest, like a flower turning toward unexpected sunshine. "She's welcome anytime," she said, surprised by the eagerness in her voice. "Both of them are."

Minutes passed in comfortable quiet, broken only by the soft rasp of sandpaper against wood and the occasional metallic tap of hammer meeting nail. Outside, the street bustled with afternoon commerce, women calling greetings, children running errands, a wagon rattling past, but inside the shop, time seemed to slow around Miles's methodical movements. Beth found herself mesmerized by his hands, so large and clearly powerful, yet capable of such precision. Each motion was economical, nothing wasted. There was artistry in his work, a quiet confidence that spoke of years mastering his craft. The same confidence, she realized, that showed in how he parented his daughters, firm yet gentle, structured yet kind.

"You're good at this," she said without thinking.

Miles glanced up, a hint of a smile softening his features. "You sound surprised."

"Not surprised." Beth searched for the right words. "Impressed, perhaps. There's care in your work."

"As there is in yours," Miles replied, nodding toward a dress displayed in the shop window.

The observation struck Beth more deeply than Miles likely intended. Her mother had always insisted that a person's character revealed itself in their handiwork—in the unseen seams of a dress as much as in its visible embellishments. "Shortcuts in stitching become shortcuts in living," Marianne Bartlett would say while inspecting Beth's early attempts with a critical but loving eye. Beth had carried that lesson into adulthood, believing that how one crafted their work reflected how they crafted their life.

By that measure, what did Miles's careful, thoughtful repair work say about the man himself? The way he'd reinforced the weakened wood rather than simply covering it spoke of integrity. The decorative yet functional design of the metal strap suggested someone who found value in beauty without sacrificing practicality. Even the careful cleanup of wood shavings showed respect for her space.

Small things, perhaps. But telling.

Beth felt her cheeks warm. "Different skills, same dedication."

"Indeed." Miles returned to his task, but the air between them felt somehow lighter, more comfortable than before.

When he finished, Miles stepped back to let Beth inspect his work. The door now hung perfectly, swinging easily on its hinges without the sticking that had plagued it for weeks.

"It's perfect," Beth said, genuine appreciation in her voice. "How much do I owe you?"

Miles seemed to consider for a moment. "Five dollars should cover the materials and time."

Beth knew it was a fair price, perhaps even less than the work was worth. She counted out the money and handed it to him. "Thank you again. I was worried I'd have to leave the shop unlocked overnight."

"Glad I could help." Miles pocketed the payment and began gathering his tools. As he worked, Beth noticed a long scar running along his forearm, visible where he had pushed up his sleeve.

"That looks like it was painful," she said, nodding toward the scar.

Miles glanced down, as if surprised to see it exposed. "Early lesson in smithing. Wasn't paying proper attention and caught a piece of hot metal. My father wasn't pleased, not about the mistake, but because I tried to hide how badly I was hurt."

"Pride can be dangerous that way," Beth said. "Keeping pain to ourselves doesn't make it less real."

Their eyes met. Something vulnerable flickered in Miles's gaze before he looked away, closing his tool satchel with careful precision.

"True enough," he acknowledged quietly.

A moment of silence stretched between them, heavy with unspoken understanding—two people who recognized the shape of each other's pain without needing words to map its contours. Beth was the first to break it, her fingers finding a loose thread on her cuff to worry between thumb and forefinger. She stepped back behind the counter, the familiar barrier of commerce between them like a fortress gate closing against too much vulnerability.

"Will I see you and the girls at church on Sunday?" she asked, her tone deliberately light.

Miles nodded, seeming grateful for the shift in conversation. "We'll be there. Clara is already asking if there will be another picnic."

"Yes, we have them every Sunday after church throughout the summer." Beth smiled at the thought of the enthusiastic child. "The Weatherly's believe in bringing the community together whenever possible."

"They seem like good people." Miles picked up his tool satchel, ready to depart. "Well, I should get back. Virgil's patience will only extend so far, and Clara can be... energetic."

"Of course." Beth walked him to the door and held it open. "Thank you again for your prompt attention to this."

"My pleasure, Beth." Miles tipped his hat slightly before stepping out onto the boardwalk.

Beth watched him walk away, his tall figure cutting a distinct silhouette against the late afternoon light. His gait was steady, purposeful, a man who knew his direction even when the path might be difficult. Only when he disappeared around the corner did Beth close the door. It shut with a satisfying solidity, the latch clicking into place with the decisive sound of something made right again.

Useful things can be beautiful too. The thought lingered as she returned to her counter, trying to focus on the ledger she had been updating before Miles arrived.

Chapter 5

"You should have seen his face when I told him I'd never read Moby Dick," Harriet said, her laugh bubbling up like creek water over stones as she unwrapped her sandwich. Her eyes sparkled with mischief and that unmistakable glow of a woman being courted. "He looked positively scandalized! As though I'd admitted to never having seen the sunrise!"

Beth smiled, settling into the worn leather chair tucked between bookshelves in the corner of Wells' Bookstore. The lunch hour had just begun, and she'd closed her shop temporarily to share a meal with Harriet, as they occasionally did.

"And then what happened?" Beth asked, taking a bite of her apple.

"Then—" Harriet leaned forward conspiratorially, her auburn curls bouncing with the movement, "—he promised to read it aloud to me, a chapter each Sunday after church." Her cheeks flushed pink with pleasure. "Can you imagine? Tim Cooper reading Herman Melville just for me?"

"He's quite taken with you," Beth observed, genuinely happy for her friend.

"Oh, Beth." Harriet sighed dreamily, resting her chin on her hand. "When he looks at me, it's like I'm the only person in the world. Yesterday he brought me wildflowers, just because! Said they reminded him of the ribbon in my hair last Sunday."

The bookstore surrounded Beth with a symphony of sensations—the crisp rustle of pages being turned, the creaking of the old oak floorboards beneath their feet, the distinctive aroma of paper and leather bindings mingling with the sharper notes of lemon oil Harriet used to polish the shelves. Afternoon sunlight filtered through wavy glass windows, giving the entire shop a dreamy, amber-tinted glow. Books lined every available surface—stacked precariously on tables, wedged into shelves until their spines bulged outward, and even piled in corners like literary towers waiting to topple. All were organized in Harriet's uniquely chaotic system that somehow made perfect sense to her alone, where Dickens might neighbor with a farmer's almanac because both, according to Harriet, "had something important to say about winter."

"I'm truly happy for you," Beth said, meaning it. "Tim's a good man."

Harriet studied Beth's face, her expression softening. "You know, there are other good men in Hope Springs." She paused meaningfully, tracing the rim of her water glass with one finger. "Including certain newcomers who happen to be skilled with metal and have two adorable daughters."

Beth busied herself with re-wrapping the remainder of her bread and cheese, her fingers fumbling slightly with the cloth. "I'm perfectly content with—"

"With your quiet life and your shop and your solitude." Harriet finished for her, rolling her eyes. "Yes, you've mentioned that approximately eight hundred times." She leaned forward, lowering her voice. "But I saw how you looked when Mrs. Peterson mentioned seeing him at the mercantile yesterday. Your ears practically perked up like a cat hearing a milk bottle open."

"They did not," Beth protested, heat rising to her cheeks.

"Contentment isn't the same as happiness, Beth," Harriet said, her teasing tone giving way to something gentler. "And it isn't betraying anyone to admit you might want more."

"Happiness isn't guaranteed in this life," Beth countered quietly. "The Lord promises joy and peace, not perpetual bliss."

"True enough." Harriet conceded the theological point. "But He didn't create us to be alone, either. 'It is not good for man to be alone'—or a woman, I'd wager."

Beth smiled at her friend, truly pleased with Harriet's happiness. Yet beneath her genuine joy lurked a twinge of something she hesitated to name. Not jealousy—never that—but perhaps a quiet mourning for a path she'd convinced herself was closed to her forever. She'd built a life without romance, without partnership, without the gentle brush of a hand seeking hers in quiet moments. Had she been so determined to protect herself that she'd walled away possibilities along with pain?

"You deserve every happiness, Harriet," she said, meaning every word despite the hollow ache behind her ribs.

The bell above the bookstore door jingled. Ida bustled in, her ample figure filling the narrow space between bookshelves as she made her way to the counter.

"Afternoon, girls!" she called cheerfully. "Just need today's newspaper, Harriet dear. The one from Lincoln, if you've got it."

"Fresh off the morning train," Harriet confirmed, rising to retrieve it from behind the counter.

Ida's sharp eyes surveyed the store, landing on Beth. "Beth Bartlett! Just the person I wanted to see. Hear you spent some time with our new blacksmith at the church picnic."

Beth kept her expression neutral. "Reverend Weatherly introduced us, yes."

"Such a shame about his wife." Ida shook her head, clucking sympathetically. "Those poor little girls without a mother! The younger one—Clara, is it?—stopped by the boarding house yesterday. Bold as brass, asking questions about everyone in town."

"She seems like a spirited child," Beth acknowledged.

"Spirited indeed!" Ida laughed. "Asked me if I was old, then wanted to know why I wasn't married if I wasn't that old yet!"

Beth smiled. Clara's directness was refreshing in a town where politeness sometimes covered deeper truths.

"And the father," Ida continued, leaning against the counter as Harriet handed her the newspaper. "Handsome man, isn't he? Reminds me of my second cousin's husband. The man hardly said ten words together, but when he spoke, everyone listened."

"Your newspaper, Mrs. Frances," Harriet interrupted pointedly. "Anything else you need today?"

"Just a bit of conversation," Ida replied with a wink. "Best part of running a boarding house, hearing all the news. Miss Gussie, you know, the new schoolteacher, she says Mr. Donovan came by yesterday to enroll Ellie for the fall term. Says the girl hardly spoke two words, but her penmanship was beautiful for a child her age."

Beth absorbed this information silently, picturing solemn Ellie carefully writing her name in a school register. Had the child been frightened? Nervous? Had Miles's steady presence comforted her?

Harriet, ever protective, steered the conversation elsewhere. "Speaking of news, I heard Mrs. Hanley's planning something special for the harvest festival later this year. Something about a play?"

Ida immediately took the bait. "Oh yes! Eleanor's got notions of putting on a real theatrical production. Trying to convince her husband to build a proper stage and everything."

While Ida expounded on the festival plans, Beth caught fragments of conversation from two women browsing nearby.

"...blacksmith fixed Jacob's plow yesterday, when everyone knows Jacob can barely pay for seed this season. Wouldn't take more than half payment, said the rest could wait until after harvest..." Mrs. Collins whispered behind a leather-bound volume.

"...girls are sweet enough, I suppose, but that older one seems sickly. Pale as milk and quiet as a ghost..." Alexandra replied.

"...wonder how long before the widows start calling with pies and casseroles? Felicia Wilson's already asking if he prefers apple or cherry..." Mrs. Collins giggled. "Though some unmarried shopkeepers might have the inside track, if you catch my meaning..."

Beth's fingers tightened around her lunch pail. The older one—Ellie—wasn't sickly; she was grieving. And the speculation about widows and unmarried shopkeepers made her stomach clench.

Beth stood abruptly. "I should get back to the shop."

"So soon?" Harriet glanced at the clock. "You've hardly touched your lunch."

"I'll finish it later." Beth gathered her food, suddenly eager to escape.

Just as she reached the door, it swung open, revealing Tim with his telegraph messenger bag slung across his chest.

"Miss Bartlett," he greeted with a tip of his hat. "Leaving just as I arrive?"

"Yes, I have a shop to mind," Beth explained with a smile. "But I believe Harriet will be pleased to see you."

Tim's gaze immediately sought Harriet across the store, his face brightening. "I've got a fifteen-minute break. Thought I might spend it where the view is the prettiest in all of Hope Springs."

The naked adoration in Tim's expression, the way his eyes softened at the corners, how his breath caught visibly in his throat, made something behind Beth's ribs contract painfully. She pressed her hand briefly against her sternum, as though to hold something in place, before slipping past him into the sunlight. Harriet's delighted greeting followed her out, the sound both sweet and somehow sharp, like biting into fruit not quite ripe enough.

Outside, the afternoon sun beat down on Main Street, pulling the scent of sun-warmed wood from the boardwalk planks. Beth paused, blinking as her eyes adjusted from the bookstore's dimness. Main Street hummed with activity. Mr. Hemingway swept the boardwalk in front of his hardware store with rhythmic strokes that matched the tempo of distant hammering from the new construction at the edge of town. Sheriff Braddock made his usual rounds, the star on his chest catching sunlight as he nodded to passersby. Two women compared purchases outside the general store, their voices rising and falling like birdsong, while a wagon loaded with lumber creaked past, its wheels cutting fresh ruts in the dusty street.

The normality of it all steadied her. This was her world—practical, predictable, and safe.

As Beth walked next door to her shop, she noticed the smithy's sign swinging in the breeze at the far end of the street. Smoke rose from the forge, indicating Miles was at work. Was Clara playing nearby while he shaped iron into useful tools? Was Ellie reading quietly in a corner, watching her father work?

Why did she care?

She shouldn't care. It was foolish to be curious about a newcomer, especially a widower with two young daughters. It was safer to keep to herself, to maintain the walls she'd so carefully built. Walls that had protected her since that awful day Thomas had left her standing alone at the altar, her white dress suddenly feeling like a shroud for her dreams.

But the thought of Miles Donovan shaping metal at his forge, his daughters nearby... it was a picture that held a strange kind of warmth, a quiet pull. Like iron to a lodestone, her thoughts kept returning to him, and that frightened her more than she cared to admit. The last time she'd allowed such thoughts, they'd led to heartbreak. Was she truly foolish enough to risk that again?

Beth had positioned herself carefully in Hope Springs—involved enough to be respected, distant enough to remain invulnerable. She participated in church functions, contributed to community needs, and provided essential services through her shop. But she kept parts of herself locked away, like fine china reserved for guests who never came.

That careful balance had served her well until now. The Donovan's, with their grief and their own needs, somehow threatened that equilibrium. Especially Miles, whose quiet strength and obvious devotion to his daughters resonated with something deeply buried in her heart.

Beth unlocked her shop door with more force than necessary, irritated by her curiosity. Miles Donovan was simply a new resident of Hope Springs, a widower doing his best for his daughters. His affairs were none of her concern.

The tiny bell above the door jangled sharply, its cheerful tone at odds with her tumultuous thoughts. Inside, the shop waited—fabrics arranged by color and type, buttons sorted in glass jars, and thread spools stacked in neat pyramids. Order. Control. Predictability.

Everything she had cultivated in her life since Thomas had shattered her trust, and her parents' deaths had fractured her security.

The familiar scents of cotton, wool, and the lavender enveloped her like a comfortable shawl. This was her domain, where she knew every item, every price, and every purpose. This was safe.

The afternoon passed in a flurry of customers and tasks, each interaction a welcome distraction from her unsettled thoughts. Mrs. Reynolds arrived with fabric for baby blankets. She was expecting her first grandchild come winter. Mr. Hemingway needed buttons replaced on his Sunday shirt. Eleanor Hanley stopped by to discuss fabric for costumes for the harvest festival play, full of plans and enthusiasm.

By closing time, Beth had managed to push thoughts of the Donovan's to the back of her mind, focusing instead on cutting patterns, totaling accounts, and ordering inventory for the coming month. As the sun began its westward descent, she locked the shop door, turning the sign to "Closed" with a sense of accomplishment.

Upstairs in her apartment, Beth changed into a simpler dress, her fingers working the buttons with practiced efficiency. She lit the lamps against the gathering dusk; the match flaring bright in the silence before settling to a steady flame.

She warmed a bowl of stew left from yesterday's dinner and carried it to the window overlooking Main Street. The chair creaked beneath her weight, the cushion perfectly molded to her form after countless solitary evenings.

The view from her window offered a perfect vantage point of Hope Springs settling into evening. Across the street, the Hanley family gathered on the boardwalk, children's laughter drifting upward. Through the mercantile's second-floor window, she could see the Peterson's at their dinner table, heads bowed in prayer, five places set.

Gas lamps were being lit along Main Street, the lamplighter moving from post to post with practiced efficiency. His long pole extended upward, bringing each glass-enclosed flame to life against the purpling sky. The saloon at the far end had already lit its colored lantern, a beacon of red light that her father had always called "the devil's welcome mat." The last freight wagon of the day rumbled past, heading for the livery stable, where it would rest until morning.

In the distance, the railroad line cut a straight path through the rolling prairie, steel rails gleaming in the last light. Progress, her father had called it, though he'd worried about how the trains would change their small town. He'd been right to worry. Hope Springs was growing with each passing month, new faces arriving on nearly every train.

Faces like Miles Donovan's.

Beth's spoon clinked against the side of her bowl, the sound loud in the quiet room. On her small table sat a single plate, a single cup, a single napkin—pressed and folded with precise corners. How many meals had she eaten alone at this window? How many evenings had she spent with only her needle and thread for company?

Beth set aside her bowl and reached for her mending basket. Atop her pile of work sat a small square of linen she'd been embroidering with a verse from Psalms: "Wait on the Lord; be of good courage, and He shall strengthen thine heart." The words had comforted her through many difficult nights.

As her needle moved through the fabric, Beth's thoughts drifted to the church picnic. To Miles sitting beside her on the grass, to quiet Ellie carefully arranging food on her plate, and to Clara's infectious laughter carrying across the clearing. There had been an ease in their conversation that day that had surprised her, an unspoken understanding between two people acquainted with loss.

The realization that she'd enjoyed his company disturbed her hard-won equilibrium. After Thomas's abandonment, Beth had rebuilt her life carefully, brick by brick, creating sturdy walls around her heart. Now, hairline cracks had appeared in that protection.

"This is foolishness," she whispered to herself, knotting her thread with unnecessary force. "One conversation at a church picnic means nothing."

Yet, she couldn't deny the flutter of interest she'd felt, or how his deep voice had stayed with her, or how his gentle treatment of his daughters had touched something long dormant within her.

Dormant. Yes, that was it. Like a seed long buried, something within her was stirring, unfurling in the unexpected warmth of his presence.

It was disconcerting, unsettling, and... undeniably intriguing.

Beth set aside her embroidery and moved to kneel beside her bed. The floorboards were cool beneath her knees, worn smooth in this exact spot from countless nights of prayer. Outside, a whippoorwill called into the gathering darkness, its lonely song a counterpoint to her racing thoughts.

"Lord," she began softly, her fingers interlacing until her knuckles whitened, "I don't understand what You're doing. I've made my peace with being alone. I've accepted Your plan for my life." She paused, honesty compelling her forward as she pressed her forehead against her clasped hands. "But my heart is restless tonight in ways I don't welcome. It feels like standing at the edge of a swift current, afraid of being swept away."

Outside, a distant peal of laughter floated through her partially open window—perhaps from the boarding house where travelers and residents often gathered in the evening.

"I don't want to be hurt again," Beth continued, her voice barely audible. "I don't want to open my heart only to have it shattered. Thomas taught me that lesson well."

The memory of her wedding day—standing alone while whispers of pity circulated through the gathered guests—still had the power to sting.

"Yet You tell us to trust, to hope, to believe. Father, give me wisdom. If these feelings are from You, help me navigate them with grace. If they're merely my own loneliness speaking, grant me the strength to overcome them."

A sense of peace gradually settled over her as she prayed, not answers, but the quiet assurance that she wasn't alone. Whatever happened, God remained constant, His purposes unfolding in His timing, not hers.

"Your will, not mine," she whispered, rising from her knees. "Give me courage to follow wherever You lead, even if the path frightens me." Her fingers brushed the embroidery she'd set aside—the words about waiting on the Lord and being of good courage stood half-finished, needle still piercing the cloth. How often had she stitched words of bravery while her heart cowered behind its defenses?

"Thy will be done," Beth whispered again, a prayer and a surrender and perhaps, though she scarcely dared admit it, a hope. She rose and moved to close her window, pausing as her gaze caught a final glimpse of activity at the far end of Main Street—a tall figure locking the smithy door, a smaller hand clasped in his. Even at this distance, she recognized Miles and Ellie.

The sight stayed with her as she readied for bed, like an image pressed between the pages of her heart—a picture not quite her own, yet somehow calling to her all the same.

Chapter 6

"Higher, Papa! Higher!"

Clara's demand rang across Silver Creek's grassy banks, her voice carrying the unquestioning confidence of a child who believed her father capable of anything—even touching the clouds if she asked earnestly enough. Sunday sunlight gilded her small frame as Miles swung her in ever-widening circles, her legs dangling in midair, tiny button boots flashing. Her dark curls, so like Charlotte's, flew outward, catching the summer breeze as her laughter scattered like silver coins across the picnic grounds.

Sunday hymns still echoed in Miles's ears as he gave his daughter the flight she craved. "Shall We Gather at the River," they'd sung in church, and here they were, gathered indeed, the entire town spread along Silver Creek's gentle curve in their Sunday best. The Lord's day stretched before them, hallowed by morning worship and now sanctified by community and shared food—a ritual as old as faith itself.

"Any higher and you'll fly away like a bird," Miles teased, setting her down with exaggerated care. He pretended to stagger backward, pressing a hand to his brow. "My strong girl! You've worn your poor papa to exhaustion."

Clara giggled, her round cheeks flushed with excitement. "If I could fly, I'd go up and up and up!" Her arms stretched skyward. "Then I could see everything at once!"

"And who would help me if you flew away?" Miles knelt, bringing himself to her eye level. He smoothed a wayward curl from her forehead, his calloused finger gentle against her soft skin.

He straightened, still smiling at his daughter's infectious joy. Then, as he surveyed the bustling picnic grounds—the colorful blankets spread across the grass, the groups of townspeople clustered in conversation—his gaze snagged on a familiar figure.

Beth.

Even from a distance, she seemed to possess a quiet grace, a serene stillness amidst the lively chaos of the picnic. The sight of her hit him like an unexpected blow to the chest—not painful, but forceful enough to momentarily halt his breath. His hand rose unconsciously to straighten his collar; he ran his palm over his freshly trimmed beard. The days of passing her shop with fabricated errands, of rehearsing casual greetings that never felt quite casual enough, condensed into a single moment of recognition: he looked forward to seeing her in a way that went well beyond neighborly courtesy.

The Sunday picnic after church at Silver Creek bustled with activity around them. Quilts and blankets dotted the grassy bank in a patchwork of faded calicos and homespun wool, each laden with covered dishes that released tantalizing aromas—fried chicken, sweet potato pie, fresh-baked bread still warm from morning ovens. The air was perfumed with wildflowers and sun-warmed grass, occasionally cut through with the sharp tang of lemonade being poured from sweating glass pitchers.

Children splashed in the shallow parts of the creek, their joyful shrieks punctuating adult conversations as they hunted for smooth skipping stones and minnows. The creek itself provided a constant musical backdrop, water burbling over smooth-worn rocks and fallen cottonwood branches. Honeybees buzzed lazily between wildflowers and open jars of preserves, while meadowlarks called from nearby fence posts.

Nearby, Sheriff Braddock and Frank Hanley were setting up targets for horseshoe pitching, the metallic clank of iron shoes being sorted cutting through the softer sounds as they good-naturedly argued about proper distances. Their voices carried the distinctive Nebraska prairie cadence—slightly flattened vowels and clipped endings, shaped by generations of speaking against prairie winds.

Miles scanned the crowd again. He spotted Ellie, sitting quietly at the edge of the gathering with her doll clutched to her chest, watching the other children play with obvious longing.

"Go see what your sister is doing," Miles urged Clara. "Maybe she'd like to play too."

As Clara skipped off, Miles continued his survey of the picnic grounds. The entire town seemed to have turned out. Ida supervised a table overflowing with food, directing traffic with the authority of a general. Jimmy and several boys his age were constructing some sort of dam in the creek, their pants rolled up to their knees. Reverend Weatherly stood in animated conversation with Walter Hemingway and several other men, occasionally punctuating his points with broad gestures.

And there, with Harriet and Tim, was Beth again.

She wore a simple dress of pale green that complemented her eyes. Her honey-blonde hair flowed freely around her shoulders and framed her face, softening her appearance. She carried a covered basket, laughing at something Harriet said as they made their way toward the food tables.

Miles realized he was staring only when Virgil appeared at his side, offering a tin cup of lemonade.

"Mighty pretty view," the older man remarked dryly, following Miles's gaze. He scratched at his salt-and-pepper mustache, eyes crinkling at the corners.

Miles accepted the cup, clearing his throat. "It's a fine day for a picnic."

"Wasn't talking 'bout the weather, son." Virgil's voice rasped like a file against rough iron, decades of prairie dust embedded in every syllable. "Miss Bartlett cleans up real nice, doesn't she?"

"Mind your manners, Virgil," Miles admonished, though without heat. "She's a respectable businesswoman."

His words felt flimsy even to his own ears. It wasn't just the respect he felt. It was... admiration. And something more personal. He quickly averted his gaze, hoping Virgil hadn't seen the heat rising in his cheeks.

"And you're a respectable blacksmith." Virgil took a long swig from his cup, adam's apple bobbing beneath weathered skin. "Been around long enough to know respectability ain't never stopped spring fever. Or summer fever, for that matter." He winked. "Don't see why those two facts can't coexist peacefully."

Miles shook his head, unwilling to dignify the observation with a response. Over the past weeks since repairing Beth's shop door, he'd found himself making excuses to pass by Bartlett's General Dry Goods. Small errands, casual greetings. Nothing improper or forward. Just... awareness.

"Papa!" Clara's voice pulled him from his thoughts. She tugged at his hand, pointing toward the creek. "Jimmy says they're going to have races and games with prizes! Can we play?"

"Of course you can, sprite." Miles smiled down at his daughter. "Where's Ellie?"

"Over there with Miss Beth!" Clara pointed toward a patch of wildflowers at the edge of the picnic grounds.

Sure enough, Beth was kneeling beside Ellie, examining something the child held cupped in her small hands. The sight of them together, heads bent close in shared discovery, caused a curious tightening in Miles's chest.

"Well, I'll be," Virgil murmured. "Your quiet little one's taken to the seamstress quite well."

Yes, she had. And it was a good sign. Ellie didn't easily offer her trust. Beth's gentle nature was clearly reaching his reserved daughter, and for that alone, he felt a surge of gratitude towards the woman.

And, perhaps, something more than just gratitude—a realization that sent a wash of guilt through him. Charlotte's image rose in his mind, her laugh echoing in his memory. He'd promised her forever, had whispered it against her hair as she faded. Was noticing another woman's kindness, her gentle smile, her way with his girls a betrayal of that promise? He rubbed absently at the phantom weight of his wedding band, removed months ago but still leaving its mark on his finger and his heart.

"Ellie's selective about whom she trusts," Miles said. Since Charlotte's death, his older daughter had retreated into herself, speaking less and observing more. To see her actively engaging with Beth, a woman she'd met only a few times, was remarkable.

Clara tugged his hand again. "Come on, Papa! The games are starting!"

Miles allowed himself to be led toward the creek, though his gaze lingered on Beth and Ellie for a moment longer.

Chapter 7

"See how the petals fold?" Beth traced the delicate structure of the wildflower Ellie had brought her. "This is called a prairie gentian. They're quite special. They only bloom for a short time each summer."

Ellie nodded seriously, her dark eyes intent on the purple blossom. "It matches the fabric you gave me."

"So it does." Beth smiled, touched that Ellie remembered their first meeting. "You have a good eye for color."

"Mama used to say that too." Ellie's voice grew quiet. "She made all our dresses."

Beth's heart squeezed at the mention of Charlotte Donovan, a woman she'd never met but whose absence shaped the lives of the three Donovan's so profoundly.

"I'm sure she was very talented," Beth said gently.

Ellie studied the flower for another moment before offering it to Beth. "You can have it if you want."

"Thank you, Ellie. That's very kind of you." She carefully tucked the bloom into her hair above her ear. "How does it look?"

"Pretty," Ellie pronounced with a shy smile. "It's the exact same color as your eyes."

"Beth! There you are!" Harriet's voice called from nearby. She approached with Tim in tow, both carrying plates heaped with food. "They're announcing the games, and you promised you'd participate."

Beth's stomach tightened. She had indeed made such a promise. One she'd hoped Harriet might conveniently forget.

"I was just admiring Ellie's wildflower knowledge," Beth explained, rising to her feet. Her fingers fluttered to her collar, adjusting it unnecessarily before moving to smooth nonexistent wrinkles from her skirts. She tucked a loose strand of hair behind her ear, then untucked it, then tucked it again. "I'm not sure if I'm dressed for games, Harriet." She glanced down at her well-made but decidedly ungame-like attire, a flicker of panic crossing her features at the thought of tumbling across the grass in view of the entire town.

Tim laughed good-naturedly. "Nobody's dressed for games, Beth. That's half the fun of it."

"Miss Beth! Miss Beth!" Clara came rushing over, nearly colliding with Beth in her excitement. "Are you going to play in the games? Papa says he will if you will!"

Beth blinked, startled. "He said what?"

"He didn't exactly say that, sprite," Miles corrected, appearing behind his daughter with an apologetic look at Beth. "I said I might participate in some of the games, and you announced that Miss Beth should be my partner."

Clara nodded enthusiastically. "For the three-legged race! Jimmy says you need a partner, and Papa doesn't have one, and you don't have one, so you should be partners!"

Beth met Miles's gaze, seeing the same mixture of amusement and embarrassment she felt reflected there. Before either could respond, Reverend Weatherly's voice rang out across the picnic grounds.

"Ladies and gentlemen, children of all ages! The games will commence in five minutes! All participants gather by the big oak!"

"See? It's starting!" Clara grabbed both their hands, attempting to drag them toward the gathering crowd. "Hurry!"

Beth glanced at Miles, who shrugged with a small smile. "I'll participate if you will," he offered.

"That sounds suspiciously like what Clara claimed you said in the first place," Beth pointed out, unable to suppress a smile. The sunlight caught in her eyes, turning them to amber.

Miles watched that smile transform her face, cracking the careful composure she typically maintained. Her unexpected playfulness tugged at something in his chest.

"She may have been partially correct, then," he admitted, the corners of his eyes crinkling. "My daughter seems to know my mind before I do these days."

"Oh, very well." Beth allowed herself to be pulled along by Clara's insistent tugging. "But I warn you, Mr. Donovan, I haven't run a three-legged race since I was a little girl."

"That makes two of us," Miles replied dryly. "Though in my case, I've never run one as a girl."

The unexpected joke startled a laugh from Beth. Perhaps this wouldn't be so terrible after all.

The first few games were for the children, sack races, egg-and-spoon relays, and a contest to see who could stay in the shallow creek water longest without splashing. Jimmy Langley emerged victorious in the latter, earning a slice of Mrs. Hanley's prize-winning apple pie.

When it came time for the adult games, Beth was increasingly drawn into the spirit of the occasion. She cheered alongside Harriet as Tim competed in the horseshoe pitching contest, laughed as Frank Hanley's wife Eleanor demonstrated surprising skill at the ring toss, and applauded when Maggie Reynolds outperformed everyone in the archery competition.

"I didn't know you were such a marks woman, Maggie," Beth said when the midwife rejoined the spectators with her small carved wooden trophy.

"My father believed every woman should know how to hunt if necessary," Maggie explained with a wink. "Said you never know when menfolk might be too busy talking about hunting to actually bring home dinner."

This elicited laughter from the surrounding women and good-natured protests from several of the men.

"Three-legged race participants, to the starting line!" Sheriff Braddock called out, standing at the edge of a flat stretch of grass where Tim was marking the course with small flags.

Beth hesitated, suddenly self-conscious. "I'm not sure—"

"A promise is a promise, Beth Bartlett," Harriet reminded her, already moving toward the starting line with Tim.

Looking around, Beth saw several couples lining up. Harriet and Tim, the Weatherly's, the Hanley's, and other townsfolk. Miles stood slightly apart, watching her with a question in his eyes. Clara and Ellie had joined the other children on the sidelines, Clara jumping up and down in anticipation.

Taking a deep breath, Beth walked over to Miles. "I believe we've been volunteered as a team."

Miles's expression brightened. "So we have." He accepted a length of cloth from Sheriff Braddock. "Shall we?"

They moved to the starting line, where Miles knelt to tie their adjacent legs together—his right to her left. Beth placed a hand on his shoulder for balance, acutely aware of the sturdy strength beneath her palm.

"Not too tight?" Miles asked, looking up at her with those startlingly blue eyes.

"It's fine," Beth assured him, though her heart had picked up speed for reasons that had nothing to do with the impending race.

"Racers ready?" Sheriff Braddock called. "The course runs to the oak tree and back. First team to cross the finish line wins!"

Beth and Miles positioned themselves, standing close together with their bound legs between them. Beth tentatively placed her arm around Miles's waist, and he did the same, his hand resting lightly at her side.

"The trick is to count steps," Miles murmured. "Inside legs together, outside legs together. One, two, one, two."

"On your mark!" Sheriff Braddock raised his arm. "Get set... GO!"

The race began with a chorus of shouts and laughter. Beth and Miles lurched forward, immediately out of sync. She stumbled against him, and his arm tightened around her waist to keep her upright.

"Inside leg!" Miles reminded her, steadying their stride. "One, two, one, two."

They found their rhythm, moving down the course as the cheers of the townspeople urged them on. Beth was acutely conscious of Miles's arm around her waist, the solid warmth of him against her side, the slight roughness of his palm through the thin fabric of her dress. Her heart raced from more than just exertion, her breath catching whenever their hips bumped together. She couldn't remember the last time she'd been this close to anyone, let alone a man. The scent of him—leather and clean sweat with hints of iron and soap—enveloped her with each synchronized step, startlingly intimate and not unwelcome.

It struck her, in that moment of synchronized movement, how life continued to surprise her. The Beth of a year ago would never have imagined herself here—breathless with laughter, partnered with a man she barely knew, and surrounded by the cheers of neighbors. Loss had taught her to expect endings, to brace herself against them. Yet here she was, in the midst of something that felt remarkably like a beginning, unexpected and unplanned.

"We're gaining on Tim and Harriet," Miles noted, a competitive edge entering his voice. "Can you go faster?"

Beth nodded, matching her steps to his longer stride. "One, two, one, two!"

They rounded the oak tree neck-and-neck with Harriet and Tim, who were laughing too hard to maintain proper form. Beth felt a bubble of unexpected joy rise in her chest as she and Miles turned back toward the finish line.

"We might actually win this," she gasped, picking up speed.

"Not if I can help it!" Tim called, making a valiant effort to coordinate with Harriet.

The race ended in a jumble as both teams crossed the finish line nearly simultaneously, collapsing onto the grass amid cheers and applause.

"I believe we have a tie!" Sheriff Braddock announced, to good-natured protests from both teams.

Beth lay on the grass beside Miles, their legs still bound together, both breathless with exertion and laughter. The wildflower clung precariously to her hair, somehow surviving their tumbling race intact—a small purple miracle. When she turned her head, she found him looking at her with an expression that made her catch her breath for entirely different reasons.

"That was..." Miles began.

"Undignified?" Beth suggested, suddenly aware of how disheveled she must look.

"Wonderful," Miles corrected softly.

Before Beth could respond, Clara and Ellie descended upon them, Clara bouncing with excitement.

"You almost won, Papa! You and Miss Beth were so fast!"

"Help us up, sprite," Miles requested, reaching for the knot binding him to Beth. "Before Miss Beth decides never to race with me again."

Once freed, Beth smoothed her skirts, tucking loose strands of hair behind her ears.

"Your flower stayed," Ellie observed quietly.

"So it did." Beth touched it gently. "It must be special indeed."

Beth couldn't remember the last time she'd laughed so freely or felt so unburdened. The race had broken something loose inside her—a knot of reservation she hadn't realized had grown so tight.

As shadows lengthened across the grass, the picnic transitioned from boisterous games to mellower entertainments. Someone produced a fiddle from beneath a wagon seat, its varnished surface catching the golden afternoon light. Another person pulled a harmonica from a pocket, and soon the air filled with the lilting strains of 'Buffalo Gals' and 'Oh! Susanna.' Couples formed on a flat stretch of grass, skirts swirling and boots stomping in time to the music.

Beth declined several invitations to join the dancers, the exhilaration of the race giving way to her more customary reserve. She settled beside Maggie Reynolds on a blanket at the edge of the gathering, content to watch as Clara attempted to teach her father a complicated skip-step.

"The Donovan girls seem taken with you," Maggie observed, nodding toward them.

"They're sweet children," Beth replied, watching as Clara demonstrated the pattern again with exaggerated movements.

"And their father seems taken with you as well," Maggie added with the directness that was her hallmark.

Beth felt heat rise to her cheeks. "Maggie, really. We barely know each other."

"Sometimes that's all it takes, a few meaningful moments." The woman's eyes softened. "My William and I courted for only six weeks before marrying. When you know, you know."

"There's no courting happening," Beth protested, though her eyes strayed to where Miles now stood speaking with Reverend Weatherly and Sheriff Braddock. "We're merely... friendly acquaintances."

"If you say so, dear." Maggie patted her hand. "Though I've never seen friendly acquaintances look at each other quite the way you two do."

Before Beth could respond, she felt the first drop of rain on her cheek—cool and startling against her flushed skin. Looking up, she was startled to see dark clouds gathering overhead, their approach having gone entirely unnoticed while she'd been caught in Miles's steady gaze. The previously clear sky now churned with purple-tinged clouds, as if the heavens themselves were responding to the unsettling shift in her emotions.

"The Weather's turning," Maggie observed, rising to her feet with the unhurried movements of someone who'd seen countless prairie storms come and go. "Summer shower coming on fast. Like most things worth noticing—they catch you unaware and leave you changed." The older woman's knowing glance between Beth and Miles wasn't lost on either of them.

As if on cue, Reverend Weatherly's voice rose above the crowd. "Looks like we're in for a bit of rain, folks! Gather your things!"

The first few raindrops quickly became a steady shower. People scrambled to collect blankets and baskets, children squealed with delight at the unexpected excitement, and the musicians hastily covered their instruments.

Beth jumped up to help Clara and Ellie gather their things, but the rain intensified rapidly, fat drops pelting down with increasing urgency.

"Under the trees!" Miles called, appearing beside them. He scooped up Ellie with one arm and grabbed Clara's hand with the other. "Beth, this way!"

Beth grabbed the small basket containing her contribution to the picnic and followed Miles toward a massive oak tree whose thick canopy offered some protection from the sudden downpour. Several other picnickers had the same idea; the Weatherly's, Sheriff Braddock, and elderly Sam Atwater were already huddled beneath its sprawling branches.

"Summer storms," Reverend Weatherly chuckled, making room for them. "The Lord's way of keeping us humble in our planning."

"And of watering His garden," Alice added with her customary cheerfulness. "The flowers will be grateful even if our picnic is dampened."

Beth wrung water from her skirt, grateful for the relative dryness beneath the oak. Clara immediately began speculating about whether rainbows would appear afterward, while Ellie pressed close to Miles's side, watching the rain with wide eyes.

"Are you cold?" Miles asked Beth, noticing her slight shiver.

"A little," she admitted. Her dress offered little protection against the sudden chill that accompanied the rain.

Without hesitation, Miles shrugged out of his jacket. "Here."

"Oh, I couldn't—" Beth protested.

"Please," Miles insisted.

The jacket carried his scent, iron and leather and something uniquely him. Beth pulled it closer despite herself, touched by the simple gesture of chivalry.

As the rain continued to fall in earnest, their small group beneath the oak settled in to wait out the shower. Water dripped through the canopy in rhythmic patterns, occasionally finding paths down collars and sleeves despite their shelter. Sam Atwater, who'd arrived in Nebraska Territory back in '54 with nothing but a Springfield rifle and a copy of the Farmer's Almanac, began regaling them with tales of far worse weather.

"This ain't nothing but a lady's tears," Sam declared, adjusting the suspenders that had supported his trousers since before the War Between the States. "Should've seen the blizzard of '62. Snow so deep, we tunneled between buildings like prairie dogs. Had to hang ropes between the general store and the livery, so folks wouldn't get lost in the whiteout and freeze solid."

Sheriff Braddock, fingering the Colt Navy revolver that never left his hip even at church functions, contributed a few hair-raising adventures involving a flash flood during the spring of '71 that had swept away half the Kearney stagecoach road. Beth suspected the tales were embellished for the wide-eyed benefit of Clara and Ellie, particularly when he described lassoing a floating piano to save a family's prized possession.

"What about you, Donovan?" Sheriff Braddock asked, eventually. "Surely, you have a weather tale or two."

"Nothing so dramatic as Sam's cyclone, that lifted three cows and deposited them unharmed in the next county."

"Now, I never said they were unharmed," Sam protested with mock indignation. "Just that they gave the best butter for a year after!"

Laughter rippled through their shelter as the rain drummed steadily on the leaves above.

"There was once," Miles began hesitantly, "when we were traveling through Missouri. The girls were smaller. Clara was just a baby. A thunderstorm caught us on the road, miles from town."

He glanced at his daughters, who were listening with rapt attention. "Lightning struck a tree not twenty yards ahead of our wagon. Split it clean down the middle. The horses panicked, and nearly overturned us."

"What did you do, Papa?" Clara asked.

"Your mother..." Miles paused, swallowing visibly. "Your mother had the presence of mind to throw a blanket over the horses' heads while I fought the reins. Charlotte always kept her wits about her, even when I was losing mine. She calmed both the horses and me with that steady voice of hers—the same one she used when girls had fevers as babies." His eyes softened at the memory. "She got us to an abandoned barn, then made a game of counting lightning strikes with you, Ellie, while I tended the horses. Said we might as well enjoy nature's fireworks since we had front-row seats."

"Mama wasn't scared of anything," Ellie said quietly.

"No, she wasn't," Miles agreed, his voice gentle. "Charlotte always faced things head-on. Said there was no point borrowing trouble by worrying, but no wisdom in ignoring trouble once it arrived."

Beth nodded, understanding the quality he was describing. "She sounds like a remarkable woman."

"She was." Miles's gaze held hers for a moment longer than necessary. "Much like others I've been fortunate enough to meet."

The air between them seemed to thicken, charged with unspoken meaning. Beth became acutely aware of the others around them, of Miles's jacket still draped around her shoulders, and of the steady rhythm of rain creating a private world beneath the oak's canopy.

The moment was broken by Clara's excited exclamation. "Look! It's stopping!"

The downpour had gentled to a light sprinkle. Sunlight pierced the clouds, creating dappled patterns through the oak's leaves.

"And there's your rainbow, Clara," Reverend Weatherly pointed toward the eastern sky, where a vibrant arc of color was forming against the retreating storm clouds. "The Lord's promise after every storm."

"See, Ellie?" Clara grabbed her sister's hand, her face alight with vindication. "I told you there'd be one!"

Beth watched the colors strengthen against the darkened sky—violet melting into indigo, then blue, green, yellow, orange, and finally red. A covenant of renewal, of beauty after destruction. She glanced at Miles, who was watching his daughters with tenderness evident in every line of his face. Perhaps some storms weren't meant to be weathered alone. Perhaps, after the deluge, new growth was not only possible but inevitable.

As people started emerging from various hiding places across the picnic grounds, Beth reluctantly removed Miles's jacket.

"Thank you for the loan," she said, handing it back to him. "It was very kind of you."

"I'm glad I could be of service." Miles accepted the jacket with a slight bow.

They joined the general exodus as people prepared to return to town. The brief shower had cooled the air pleasantly, leaving everything refreshed despite the damp.

Beth collected her things. As she prepared to join Harriet and Tim for the walk back to town, Clara appeared at her side.

"Miss Beth? Can you walk with us?" The little girl looked up hopefully.

Beth glanced at Harriet, who made a shooing motion with her hands, clearly encouraging the arrangement.

"I'd be happy to," Beth told Clara, falling into step beside her.

They formed a small procession, Clara skipping ahead, Ellie walking quietly beside Beth, and Miles bringing up the rear.

"Did you enjoy the picnic, Ellie?" Beth asked.

Ellie nodded. "I liked the music. And the races were funny."

"I agree on both counts." Beth smiled down at her. "Perhaps next time you might join in on more of the children's games? I noticed several girls your age playing all afternoon."

Ellie considered this seriously. "Maybe," she allowed. "If you'll watch."

"I'd be honored," Beth said.

They walked on as Clara chattered about her plans to build a fort. The path widened as they approached town, and Miles moved up to walk beside Beth.

"Thank you for being so kind to my girls," he said.

"It's no hardship. They are delightful," Beth assured him.

"They are, aren't they? Even on their most difficult days." He glanced at Beth. "You're good with them. Natural."

"I've always loved children. My mother used to say I was born knowing how to comfort babies."

"Do you desire a large family?" Miles asked.

"Yes," Beth admitted quietly, her fingers working at the damp folds of her skirt. "Thomas, my former fiancé, and I had talked of having at least four children." She looked away toward where Clara was splashing through a puddle. "Two boys and two girls was what we'd planned." The old ache was still there when she mentioned Thomas, but duller now, more like a bruise than an open wound.

"I'm sorry," Miles said simply. "For bringing up painful memories."

"No need to apologize." Beth squared her shoulders slightly, meeting his gaze with quiet dignity. "It's part of my story, that's all. Just as Charlotte is part of yours."

Miles studied her face, the set of her jaw, the way her eyes held his without flinching or seeking pity. "Different paths than we'd planned, but paths nonetheless." His voice carried the weight of shared understanding—that they both navigated landscapes neither had chosen, maps redrawn by loss.

"Yes." A single word, but in it Beth acknowledged what remained unspoken between them: that perhaps these unexpected paths had led them to this moment, walking side by side through mud-slicked grass, with his daughters skipping ahead.

They reached the edge of town, where the path divided—one fork leading toward Main Street, the other toward the blacksmith shop and the Donovan home.

"Will I see you at church Sunday?" Miles asked, seeming reluctant to end their conversation.

"Yes, of course." Beth smiled. "I'll save room in my pew if you'd like to join me."

"We'd like that," Miles replied, his expression warming. "Wouldn't we, girls?"

Clara nodded enthusiastically, while Ellie offered a small but genuine smile.

As Beth continued toward her shop, she realized she was still smiling—not the careful, measured expression she typically offered the world, but a real smile that reached her eyes and warmed her heart like summer sunshine after a long winter. The rainbow still arched across the eastern sky, bridging the rain-washed blue expanse with improbable colors.

The day had brought unexpected pleasures: the silly, breathless joy of the three-legged race with Miles's steady arm around her waist; the intimate camaraderie beneath the oak tree during the rain shower, where strangers had become friends in the space of shared stories; the simple pleasure of walking and talking with Miles and his daughters, their footprints overlapping in the damp earth.

Something had shifted within her, like a bolt of fabric unfolding to reveal an unexpected pattern beneath—one she wasn't yet ready to examine too closely, but couldn't quite refold to its original state. The wildflower Ellie had given her was still tucked behind her ear, its delicate petals beginning to wilt but still holding their color, much like the long-dormant hope that had begun, against all expectation, to bloom again in her heart.

Chapter 8

The iron fought him today. Miles could feel its resistance with each hammer strike, the metal sullen and uncooperative beneath his blows. Like it knows, he thought, driving the hammer down with particular force. Like it can sense I'm distracted. Sweat trickled down his back as he worked the bellows harder, stoking the forge until the coals transformed from merely hot to a furious, hungry orange-white. Heat blasted his face as he thrust the rod back into the heart of the fire, willing it to surrender, to yield, to forget its nature and become something new. The metal gradually surrendered, its stubbornness glowing with inner light, finally ready to be shaped into a flat-blade shovel head.

"That order for Mr. Peterson?" Virgil asked from the doorway, the older man's knife moving in easy, practiced strokes across a piece of cedar. Wood shavings curled at his feet like pale question marks.

Miles nodded, inspecting his work before plunging the metal into a water barrel. Steam hissed upward in a furious cloud, momentarily obscuring his face. "He needs it by Monday. Ground's hard, and his old one cracked clean through."

"You've taken on more work this week than three men could handle," Virgil observed, his weathered face creased with concern. "Been at it since before dawn most days." He paused, then added with careful nonchalance, "Saw the seamstress looking this way yesterday when I was mending the fence. Pretty woman. Seemed like she might've been considering a visit."

Miles's hammer faltered mid-strike. "Miss Bartlett has a shop to run. I doubt she spends time thinking about visiting a blacksmith."

"If you say so." Virgil's knife continued its steady rhythm against the wood. "Funny thing, though. When I chatted with her yesterday, I mentioned you might be working yourself into an early grave. She asked if you ever took a day off."

Miles reached for a rag to wipe his brow, hoping the forge's heat disguised the warmth in his face. "Work keeps the mind occupied and food on the table."

"And a man from thinking too much?" Virgil's knowing look made Miles turn back to the forge. "Or feeling too much?"

Thinking too much. Thinking about Beth, about her kindness, her quiet strength, her unexpected presence in his life. He pushed the thoughts aside, focusing on the metal, on the task at hand. Work was his refuge, his anchor in this new life.

His hammer struck the iron with more force than necessary. These feelings toward Beth—they felt inappropriate and disloyal. The wedding band might be off his finger, but the promises he'd made still bound him. Didn't they? And yet...each time he saw Beth with his daughters, something long dormant stirred to life. The guilt that followed was almost as powerful as the longing.

"The girls need new shoes before winter," Miles said, instead of acknowledging Virgil's point. "And Clara outgrows her dresses faster than I can blink."

Virgil tucked his knife away. "Speaking of the little sprites, it's near noon. Shouldn't you be checking on them?"

Miles glanced at the position of the sun through the shop's open front. He'd promised to return to the house for the midday meal, and here he was, losing track of time again. He set down his hammer with a sigh.

"I'll finish this later. Can you bank the fire?"

Virgil nodded. "Go on."

Miles untied his leather apron and hung it on its peg. The short walk from the smithy to his cottage gave him time to transition from blacksmith to father. The cottage came into view, its simple frame structure still desperately needing the fresh coat of paint he'd promised himself he'd apply weeks ago.

Through the open window, he heard Clara's high, excited voice and Ellie's quieter responses. At least they seemed content today. He paused at the door, taking in the scene within.

Clara sat cross-legged on the floor, arranging wooden animals in elaborate formations. Her dark curls had escaped their ribbons again, forming a wild halo around her small face. Ellie sat at the table, carefully mending a tear in her doll's dress with inexpert stitches.

"Papa!" Clara bounded up when she spotted him. "I made an animal kingdom! The horse is still king because he's the tallest, but now the cow is queen."

Miles scooped her up, ignoring the dirt on his clothes. "A horse and cow ruling together? Quite progressive."

"What's 'progressive' mean?" Clara asked, wrinkling her nose.

"It means new and different," Miles explained, setting her down to wash his hands at the basin.

Ellie looked up from her mending. "I'm fixing Dolly's dress," she said. "But it's hard without a thimble. I keep pricking my fingers."

Miles crossed to her, examining her work. The stitches were uneven but determined, evidence of her careful concentration. "That's good work, sunshine. Maybe we could ask Miss Beth if she has a child-sized thimble next time we see her."

Ellie's face brightened at the mention of Beth. "I'd like that"

Miles moved to the iron stove nestled against the far wall, stoking the banked coals beneath until they glowed orange through the grates. He lifted the lid on a cast-iron pot, releasing a cloud of savory steam that carried the earthy scent of root vegetables and beef into the room. He stirred the stew and gathered mismatched but carefully scrubbed bowls from the pine shelf.

He turned to glance around. The cottage was spare but meticulously tidy, with wide-plank floors swept clean enough to eat from. Afternoon light slanted through unadorned windows. No curtains softened the windows' stark lines, no cushions adorned the straight-backed chairs, no tablecloth graced the scrubbed wooden table. The walls held only practical items: a calendar from the general store, a small mirror with a crack running along one edge, and a single framed tintype photograph of a woman with eyes that matched Ellie's. Charlotte would have added feminine touches—the little graces that transformed shelter into sanctuary. Without them, the space felt like a pause between breaths, functional but incomplete, waiting.

"Papa, you're frowning again," Clara observed, tugging at his pant leg. "Are you sad about Mama?"

Miles's heart caught. His younger daughter's directness still caught him off guard. "Just thinking, sprite. Now, who's hungry?"

They settled around the table, Miles saying grace before serving the stew. Clara immediately launched into a detailed account of how she'd organized her animals, while Ellie ate quietly, her eyes occasionally drifting to the window.

"What's on your mind, Ellie?" Miles asked during a rare pause in Clara's monologue.

Ellie hesitated, stirring her stew. "Miss Beth had pretty flowers in her shop window yesterday when we walked past. I wish we had flowers."

Miles looked around their bare yard through the window. He'd been so focused on getting the forge operational and earning a living that beautifying their surroundings had fallen far down his list of priorities.

"We could plant some," he suggested. "There's that patch of ground beside the porch."

"Really?" Ellie's eyes widened. "Could we make a garden like Mama's?"

The mention of Charlotte's garden back in Iowa brought a pang of remembrance. Charlotte had loved her flowers, spending hours tending them with Ellie at her side.

"We could try," Miles said. "Though I don't know much about gardening."

"Miss Beth might know," Clara piped up. "She has pretty flowers behind her shop in a garden. I saw them when Jimmy showed me the alley shortcut."

"When were you in the alley behind the shops?" Miles asked, momentarily sidetracked by this revelation.

Clara suddenly became overly interested in her stew. "Jimmy was showing me where the best hide-and-seek places are."

Miles made a mental note to have a word with Jimmy Langley about appropriate places for a four-year-old girl to play. "Well, we don't need to bother Miss Beth about our garden. I'm sure we can manage."

"Too late," Clara said with a mischievous smile, pointing out the window. "She's coming right now!"

Miles turned to look, nearly knocking over his water cup in surprise. Sure enough, Beth Bartlett was walking up the path to their home, carrying something in her hands.

Beth. Walking up his path. With a pie. It was a scene so domestic, so...wife-like, that the thought took him completely by surprise. She looked lovely, her blue dress highlighting the warmth in her eyes, her hair catching the sunlight. He felt a sudden tightening in his chest.

"Land sakes," Miles muttered, taking in the state of their home with new eyes. The sparse furnishings, the undecorated walls, the half-unpacked crate in the corner he'd been meaning to deal with for weeks.

Clara was already racing to the door. "Miss Beth! Miss Beth!"

Miles rose quickly, straightening his shirt and running a hand through his hair, belatedly realizing it was probably standing on end from working at the forge. Before he could stop her, Clara had thrown open the door and was bouncing on her toes with excitement.

"We were just talking about you!" Clara announced.

"Clara Marie," Miles admonished gently, reaching the door behind her. "Let Miss Beth at least greet us properly."

Beth stood on their threshold, sunlight catching in her golden hair neatly pinned back, wearing a simple blue dress that brought out the flecks of azure in her eyes. She held a pie in her hands, the buttery crust still warm enough that the sweet scent of apples, cinnamon, and nutmeg wafted toward them like a promise. Miles caught a hint of lavender water too—subtle and feminine—so different from the coal dust and iron that clung to his skin.

"I hope I'm not intruding," she said, a hint of uncertainty in her eyes. "I baked this morning and thought perhaps you might enjoy some."

Miles was speechless, struck by the domesticity of the moment. Beth at his door with a freshly baked pie, and his daughters are eager for her attention.

"You're not intruding at all," he finally managed. "Please, come in."

"A pie!" Clara exclaimed, practically dancing with delight. "Is it apple? That's Papa's favorite!"

Beth laughed, her eyes meeting Miles's over Clara's head. "Yes, it's apple."

Miles stepped back to allow her entry. "I apologize for the state of things. We're still settling in."

"No need for apologies," Beth assured him, stepping inside. Her eyes took in the room with interest rather than judgment. "It's a lovely home."

Lovely? He glanced around the bare room, seeing only its emptiness. But through Beth's eyes, perhaps it could be lovely, could become a home again. Her simple words were a balm, a surprising kindness.

Ellie had risen from the table and now stood shyly by her chair. "Hello, Miss Beth."

"Hello, Ellie." Beth's smile was gentle. "I hope I'm not interrupting your meal."

"We've just finished," Miles said, taking the pie from her hands. The brief contact of their fingers sent an unexpected warmth through him. "Would you care for some tea? It's the least we can offer in exchange for this kindness."

"Tea would be lovely," Beth answered, removing her light shawl.

Miles busied himself with the kettle, watching from the corner of his eye as Beth interacted with his daughters. Clara immediately showed off her animal kingdom, while Ellie hesitantly displayed her doll's repaired dress.

"These stitches are very well done," Beth said, examining Ellie's handiwork with serious attention. "You have natural talent, Ellie."

The girl's thin face glowed with the praise. "Papa said maybe you might have a thimble I could use. I keep pricking my fingers."

"I certainly do," Beth responded. "In fact, I have a small sewing kit I've been putting together with some scraps and notions. Perhaps you might like to have it?"

Ellie's eyes widened. "For me?"

"If your father approves." Beth glanced at Miles, seeking permission.

He nodded, touched by her thoughtfulness. "That's very generous of you."

The kettle whistled, and Miles poured the boiling water into the teapot, adding the precious tea leaves he saved for special occasions. As the tea steeped, he cut slices of Beth's pie, the golden crust flaking perfectly under his knife.

They gathered around the table. Miles noticed how naturally Beth fit into their small circle, pouring tea with graceful movements and responding to Clara's rapid-fire questions with patient humor.

"Miss Beth, do you know about gardens?" Clara asked, her mouth full of pie.

"Clara, don't speak with your mouth full," Miles reminded her.

Beth laughed. "I know a little about gardens. My mother kept a lovely one behind our store, and now I do the same."

Ellie perked up. "We want to make a garden like Mama's," she said. "With flowers. But Papa doesn't know how."

Miles felt heat rise to his face. "I'm afraid my talents lie with metal, not growing things."

"Papa can fix anything, but he can't make flowers grow," Clara added helpfully, earning a stifled laugh from Beth.

"Well, gardens aren't terribly difficult to start," Beth said. "You mainly need good soil, seeds, and regular watering."

"Would you help us?" Ellie asked, hope shining in her dark eyes. "Please?"

Miles started to intervene, not wanting to impose on Beth's kindness, but she spoke first.

"I'd be happy to," she said, meeting Miles's gaze. "If your father doesn't mind."

Something about the way she said, "your father" rather than "Mr. Donovan" or even "Miles" struck him, as if she were consciously acknowledging his role, respecting his position in his daughters' lives.

"I'd be grateful for the help," Miles admitted. "Flowers would certainly brighten the place."

After they finished their tea and pie, Beth insisted on helping clear the dishes, despite Miles's protests. The simple domestic activity, Beth washing while he dried, felt both foreign and right, a rhythm they fell into without awkwardness.

"The pie was delicious," Miles said as they worked. "You didn't need to go to such trouble."

Beth handed him a dripping plate. "It was no trouble. Baking helps me think."

"And what were you thinking about?" The question slipped out before he could consider its propriety.

Beth paused, her hands still in the water. "The future, I suppose. The shop needs new inventory for fall, and I've been considering what patterns will sell best."

It wasn't the entire truth. Miles could see that in the slight lowering of her eyes, but he didn't press. Everyone was entitled to their private thoughts.

"Papa!" Clara called from the doorway. "Can we show Miss Beth the forge? Please?"

"I'd love to see where you work a little more," Beth added, drying her hands on a towel. "If you wouldn't mind showing me."

"It's nothing special," Miles demurred, though pride in his craft made him stand a little straighter.

They walked the short distance to the smithy, Clara skipping ahead while Ellie stayed close to Beth's side.

The forge was quiet now, the fire banked to glowing coals. Tools hung in orderly rows on the walls, and the scent of hot metal and coal dust permeated the air. Miles stepped in first, re-lighting several lanterns to better illuminate the space.

He began explaining his work, showing Beth the different tools and their purposes. Her genuine interest encouraged him, and soon he found himself demonstrating how he shaped horseshoes, carefully manipulating metal tongs to remove a prepared piece from near the coals.

"These are my striker tools," Miles explained, gesturing to an organized rack of implements with handles worn smooth from use. "Fuller, swage, drift pin." He pointed to each in turn. "I apprenticed under my father, and he insisted every tool has its place. 'A cluttered forge makes cluttered work,' he'd say." Miles ran his hand along the edge of his anvil, a 129-pound piece of hardened steel. "This anvil's voice tells me more about the metal than my eyes ever could. Each ring, each note—whether it's high and clear or dull and flat—speaks to how the iron's responding." He demonstrated with a light tap that produced a bright, sustained tone that hung in the air between them. "A good smith listens as much as he looks."

Beth watched him as he spoke, clearly interested as he spoke.

"The heat makes the iron malleable," he explained, placing the metal on the anvil. "Then with the hammer, I can shape it however it's needed."

"It's like fabric," Beth observed, watching his hands with an intensity that made him suddenly conscious of every callus and scar. "Different under your hands, depending on how you treat it. Demanding respect for its nature."

"I never thought of it that way," Miles admitted, impressed by the comparison. "But you're right. Each piece has its own character, its own way of responding to work." He hesitated, then added, "Sometimes what seems most unyielding only needs patience and the right approach to reveal its true potential."

"Is that what draws you to it? Finding that potential?"

Miles considered seriously, setting down his tools and turning to face her fully. "Partly. There's satisfaction in making something useful from what others might see as just crude metal. In taking something broken and making it whole again, or giving it a new purpose. I imagine you feel something similar about your sewing."

Beth nodded, her eyes meeting his with a recognition that transcended mere craft. "Exactly that. Creating something needed from fragments and pieces. Something that will bring comfort or utility." She trailed her fingers along the edge of his workbench. "Though occasionally, I wonder if what I'm really trying to mend are things that can't be fixed with needle and thread."

The confession hung between them, neither fully acknowledged nor dismissed.

Miles became acutely aware of how close they were standing, how the lantern light softened Beth's features, and how her eyes reflected his movements with interest. Clara and Ellie were examining a collection of horseshoes hung on the far wall, momentarily distracted.

"Beth, I—" Miles began, then stopped. The lantern's glow painted her features in amber and gold, softening the careful composure she usually maintained. A smudge of coal dust had somehow found its way to her cheek, and he lifted his hand and wiped it away.

What did he mean to say? Thank you for being kind to my daughters? For bringing a pie? You're lovely? Stay? The words felt too forward, too presumptuous. He was a blacksmith, a widower with calloused hands and responsibilities etched as deeply as the lines on his face. She was Miss Bartlett, a respected businesswoman with delicate fingers and dreams he couldn't presume to understand. A woman who deserved... what? He didn't even know what he wanted, only that he didn't want this moment to end.

"Yes?" Her voice was soft.

The air between them seemed to hold its breath. Miles found himself drawn forward by some invisible force.

"Papa, can you make a horseshoe for Dolly's horse?" Ellie asked.

The moment broken, Miles stepped back. "Of course, sunshine. A tiny horseshoe for a tiny horse."

They spent another quarter-hour in the forge, the girls asking questions and Beth admiring several decorative pieces Miles had created. As the afternoon waned, Beth reluctantly mentioned she should return to the shop.

"Thank you for the pie," Miles said as they walked back toward the house. "And for indulging the girls with your time."

"It was my pleasure," Beth replied. "They're wonderful children."

Inside the house, Clara insisted on showing Beth one last thing, a drawing she'd made of their family, including a figure with yellow hair that she proudly proclaimed was "Miss Beth."

"You drew me in your family picture?" Beth asked, her voice catching slightly.

Clara nodded vigorously. "Because I like you."

"That's a great honor, Clara. Thank you." Beth knelt at the child's level. "I'll look forward to helping with your garden next time I visit."

"When will that be?" Clara asked immediately.

"Clara," Miles warned gently.

"Soon," Beth promised, rising to her feet. "Perhaps next Saturday, if that suits your father."

"It does," Miles said, perhaps too quickly. "We'd be honored."

As the lengthening shadows signaled Beth's departure, an unexpected flurry of motion caught everyone's attention. Ellie, who rarely acted impulsively, had darted out of the house to the side of the blacksmith shop. She returned moments later, her hands cupped carefully around something hidden, her expression a mixture of determination and shyness.

"For you," she said, unfolding her fingers to reveal a small blue wildflower, its stem carefully wrapped in a damp cloth the child must have prepared beforehand. "Because you gave us pie. And because..." she hesitated, glancing at her father before continuing in a near-whisper, "because it matches your eyes sometimes."

Beth knelt to accept the gift, her throat tightening at the gesture's significance from this quiet child who measured words as carefully as Miles measured metal. "Thank you, Ellie," she managed, her voice wavering slightly. "I'll put it in water as soon as I get home and think of you each time I see it."

At the door, Miles hesitated, his hand resting on the weathered wood frame, torn between proper decorum and the desire to extend this unexpected afternoon that had somehow shifted something fundamental in their small household. "Thank you again for coming by."

"Thank you for welcoming me," Beth replied, her eyes meeting his with a warmth that lingered. With a final smile to the girls, she stepped onto the path leading back to town.

Miles watched her walk away, the afternoon sunlight catching in her hair. Clara and Ellie waved enthusiastically beside him, and Beth turned once to wave back before continuing on her way.

"I like Miss Beth," Ellie said. "She remembers things I tell her."

"And she makes good pie," Clara added, practical as always. "Can she come live with us?"

Miles nearly choked. "Clara Marie Donovan, what a question."

"Well, can she? Jimmy says people get married when they like each other, and you smile different when Miss Beth is here. So that means you like her."

"Grown-up relationships are complicated, sprite. Miss Beth has her own home and her own shop to run."

"But she likes us," Clara insisted with a child's straightforward certainty. "I can tell. And you smile like you used to when she's here."

Used to. The words hung in the air between them, a dividing line separating the life they'd had with Charlotte to whatever this new existence would become. Miles knelt at his daughter's level, his hand gentle on her shoulder as he searched for the right words.

"I'm sure she does like us," Miles agreed, wondering when his youngest had become so perceptive—and when she had started measuring time in the same way he did, with that invisible line dividing everything into before and after. "Now, who's going to help me find a spot for this garden we're apparently starting?"

The girls raced off to inspect the yard, Clara's voice carrying back as she pointed out possible locations, Ellie following more cautiously in her sister's wake. Miles watched them, these daughters who carried pieces of Charlotte in their movements, their expressions, their very essence. Yet, they were changing, growing, becoming more themselves with each passing day. Adapting to this new life in ways he sometimes struggled to match.

As the girls debated the merits of various garden locations with increasing enthusiasm, Miles found his thoughts returning to Beth and the unexpected warmth she'd brought into their home. To the way she'd knelt to examine Ellie's stitches with genuine interest. To how she'd laughed at Clara's endless questions with patient delight rather than exhaustion. To the quiet understanding in her eyes when she'd looked at the photograph of Charlotte, not with jealousy or dismissal, but with respect for what had been lost.

Beth.

The name echoed softly in his mind like the ring of a hammer on cooling metal. Her measured kindness, her gentle smile, the way she'd fit so easily into their small world, not filling the empty space Charlotte had left, but creating something new alongside it. Something that might, with careful tending, grow into its own kind of beauty.

Like a garden where there had only been bare earth before.

***

Beth walked slowly back toward Main Street, the wildflower from Ellie tucked carefully in her hand. With each step, she felt herself reluctantly leaving behind the warmth that had enveloped her in the Donovan home. The afternoon had not gone as she'd planned—it had gone better in ways that both comforted and unsettled her. She'd meant only to deliver the pie, a simple neighborly gesture that would allow her to see Miles and his daughters briefly. Instead, she'd spent hours in their company, the conversation flowing as naturally as a stream finding its path, feeling more at home in their modest cottage than she sometimes did in her own apartment. The realization sent a shiver of both anticipation and caution through her.

What was happening to her carefully ordered life?

"Lord, guide my heart," Beth whispered as she walked. "I don't want to be foolish again."

But it didn't feel foolish. It felt... right. The way Miles had shown her his forge, his hands strong and capable as he shaped metal, his eyes lit with passion for his craft. The quiet pride in his voice when he spoke of his work. The tender patience he showed his daughters.

The girls. Beth smiled, remembering Clara's exuberance and Ellie's shy gift. They had carved out spaces in her heart with remarkable speed.

As Beth reached her shop, she paused at the door, looking back toward the edge of town where the Donovan's lived. She had promised to return next Saturday to help with the garden and suddenly, it seemed a very long time to wait.

"There you are!" Harriet's voice broke into her thoughts. Her friend stood in the doorway of the bookshop, arms crossed. "I was beginning to wonder if you'd run away."

Beth felt heat rise to her cheeks. "I was simply delivering a pie."

"To our blacksmith? For three hours?" Harriet's eyebrows rose significantly.

"The girls wanted to show me things," Beth defended, unlocking her shop door. "And we had tea."

Harriet followed her inside. "And what else?"

"Nothing else," Beth insisted, though the memory of standing close to Miles in the forge, the lantern light playing across his features, made her heart beat faster. "He showed me his forge, that's all."

"His forge," Harriet repeated with suggestive emphasis. "How very... intimate."

"Harriet Wells!" Beth scolded, though she couldn't entirely suppress a smile. "You have a scandalous mind."

"And you," Harriet retorted, "have a brilliant smile on your lovely face that I haven't seen in years." Her expression softened. "It looks good on you, Beth."

"I've simply had a pleasant afternoon. Nothing more."

"If you say so. Just remember what I told you before: hearts aren't meant to be safe. They're meant to be given away."

Entering her empty shop, Beth placed Ellie's wildflower in a small glass jar of water on her worktable. The blue petals seemed to glow in the late afternoon light filtering through the front windows. She trailed her fingers over a bolt of indigo cotton—almost the exact shade of Miles's eyes. The fabric shop had always been her sanctuary, the place where she felt most capable and content. Today, though, it felt strangely hollow after the warmth of the Donovan home.

Beth moved to her cutting table, automatically straightening pins and notions, though they were already in perfect order. The systematic organization that had once brought her such satisfaction now seemed a poor substitute for the joyful chaos of Clara's animal kingdom or the shy gift of Ellie's flower. When had order become more important than connection? When had she decided that avoiding pain meant avoiding joy as well?

"This is foolishness," she murmured to herself, attempting to regain her practical perspective. "They are simply neighbors in need of kindness." But even as she said it, the memory of Miles standing in his forge, hands strong and capable as they shaped unyielding metal, sent a flutter through her that had nothing to do with neighborly concern.

Chapter 9

The shop bell jangled with unusual violence as Mrs. Peterson burst inside, the door slamming behind her with enough force to set fabric bolts trembling on their shelves. Her normally immaculate coiffure had surrendered several pins to the wind, gray strands escaping to frame her face like wisps of smoke.

"Land sakes, Beth! Have you seen the sky?" Mrs. Peterson's knuckles whitened around her market basket, clutching it as if it might anchor her against whatever approached. The woman who'd never missed a Sunday service in forty years or appeared in public with an unpolished button looked genuinely frightened.

Beth looked up from the ledger she'd been updating. The shop had darkened as if evening had arrived hours early, casting her careful columns of numbers into shadow. Thread spools on the wall seemed to absorb rather than reflect the strange, filtered light.

She moved quickly to the front of the store, breath catching at the view. Main Street lay transformed beneath a sky turned malevolent. The morning's cheerful blue had surrendered to something unnatural—a sickly green-gray that cast everything in a corpse-light pallor. To the west, clouds churned not like gentle wool but like something alive and hungry, their underbellies glowing with a brassy hue that made her think of battlefield illustrations from Harper's Weekly during the war. Birds had vanished. Even the summer insects had gone silent, as if all of nature was holding its breath before the onslaught.

"That doesn't look good," Beth said, a familiar tightness forming in her chest, the instinctive reaction of anyone who had lived long enough on the prairie to recognize the signs.

"Sheriff Braddock is riding up and down Main Street telling everyone to prepare," Mrs. Peterson continued. "The Train station's telegraph received reports of a severe storm system moving this way from the west."

Through the windows, Beth watched as Hope Springs transformed into a hive of activity. Shopkeepers nailed protective boards across their windows. Parents hurriedly collected children from play. Men worked to secure loose items that might become dangerous in high winds.

"Will you be okay?" Mrs. Peterson asked.

"I'll be fine upstairs. The building is solid." The words came automatically, her practiced self-sufficiency rising like a shield.

"Don't be foolish, girl." Mrs. Peterson's expression softened with maternal concern. "No one should be alone during a prairie tempest. I believe I'll head to the church. It doesn't look like I'll have time to make it home before this storm hits."

"I've weathered storms before," Beth insisted gently.

After Mrs. Peterson departed, Beth began her preparations. She closed the heavy wooden shutters over the display windows, securing them with iron hooks that had held firm through many previous storms. She filled every available container with fresh water, gathered lanterns and candles on the counter, and moved valuable fabric bolts away from the windows in case rain found its way inside.

As she worked, her mind drifted to Miles and his daughters. Their small homestead sat on relatively open ground near the edge of town, far more exposed than her sturdy shop building on Main Street. Would the girls be frightened?

Beth paused in her work, one hand still clutching a bolt of calico she'd been moving to safety. Through the partially shuttered window, she watched the sky darken further as a gust of wind sent a flurry of papers tumbling down the street outside. A woman's bonnet cartwheeled past, followed by a wooden crate that shattered against the hitching post.

Perhaps she should check on them before the storm arrived in earnest. The thought formed before she could dismiss it, surprising in its intensity.

"Don't be silly," she chided herself aloud, her voice sounding thin in the empty shop. "Miles Donovan is perfectly capable of looking after his family."

Still, concern nagged at her as she continued securing her shop against the approaching tempest.

***

Miles studied the western sky with growing unease. Years of working outdoors had taught him to read weather patterns, and everything about the approaching storm sent warning signals through his body. The unnatural stillness, the greenish tint to the clouds, the distant rumbling that vibrated in his chest rather than his ears, all pointed to something far worse than a typical summer thunderstorm.

His grandfather, a veteran of the War of 1812, had called such skies "battlefield heavens"—claiming they mirrored the eerie calm before cannons roared at Lundy's Lane. The old man's weather wisdom had saved their family farm more than once, and Miles had learned to heed such ancestral warnings. This sky held violence in its very color.

"Papa?" Ellie stood in the doorway of their home, Clara hovering anxiously behind her. "Is it going to rain?"

Miles turned toward his daughters, forcing calm into his voice. "Yes, sunshine. A big storm's coming. We need to prepare, just like we did back in Iowa."

Inside, Miles moved with purpose, gathering blankets, lanterns, and his small medical kit while instructing the girls to fill water jugs. Through the western window, he could see dust and debris beginning to spin in small vortices across the yard as the wind strengthened.

"Will we go to the cellar?" Ellie asked, her small face solemn with understanding beyond her years.

"We will," Miles confirmed, kneeling to her level. His pulse quickened at the distant rumble that vibrated through the floorboards, but he kept his face composed, smoothing the worry lines from his brow. "Just as a precaution." He forced a smile, the kind he'd practiced in front of Charlotte's mirror a hundred times after her passing when the girls needed reassurance. He couldn't genuinely feel. "We'll make an adventure of it, like a camping trip underground."

The cellar door was in the corner of the kitchen on the floor, leading to a small but sturdy refuge beneath the house. Miles had inspected it thoroughly when they first arrived, reinforcing weak spots and ensuring the heavy door would hold. Now he opened it and the earthy scent of the underground space filled the kitchen as he lit a lantern.

"Ellie, take these blankets down and spread them in the corner," he instructed, handing his oldest daughter a stack of bedding. "Clara, help your sister while I get the rest of our supplies."

As the girls descended the ladder-like stairs, Miles gathered food and additional light sources. A violent gust of wind rattled the windows, and for a moment, his thoughts flickered to Beth, alone in her shop on Main Street. Would she seek shelter with neighbors? The Weatherly's perhaps, or Harriet?

Miles shook the thought away, focusing on his daughter's safety. Beth was sensible and resourceful. She'd lived in Hope Springs her whole life and surely knew how to weather a storm.

A particularly powerful gust slammed something against the side of the house with a splintering crack. Clara's frightened yelp echoed from the cellar below.

"It's all right, Clara," Miles called down. "Just the wind getting frisky."

He peered out the window once more. The sky had darkened to a threatening bruised purple, and the air felt charged with electricity. In the distance, a flash of lightning illuminated the prairie, followed seconds later by a deep roll of thunder that shook the floorboards beneath his feet.

Miles gathered the remaining supplies and closed the cellar door behind him, joining his daughters in the earthen sanctuary below. Clara immediately pressed against his side, her small body trembling slightly.

"Will our house blow away, Papa?" she whispered.

Miles wrapped his arm around her shoulders. "Houses are strong, sprite. They're built to withstand prairie weather." But even as he offered reassurance, doubt gnawed at him. This storm felt different, its approach more menacing than any he'd witnessed before.

Ellie sat perfectly still on the blankets, clutching her doll to her chest, her eyes fixed on the cellar ceiling as the wind's howl grew steadily louder above them.

"Let's pray together," Miles suggested, gathering both girls close. "Prayer brings comfort in a storm."

As they bowed their heads, the first truly powerful gusts slammed into the house above, and Miles tightened his protective embrace around his daughters.

"Dear Lord," he began, his voice steady despite the tremor in his chest, "watch over us in this storm as You have watched over us in all storms of life..."

***

Tim Cooper burst into the sheriff's office, face flushed from running the length of Main Street.

"Emergency wire from Lincoln!" he gasped, thrusting a yellow paper toward Sheriff Braddock, who stood studying a map spread across his desk. "Tornado spotted twenty miles west, moving straight for Hope Springs!"

Sheriff Braddock scanned the message, his weathered face grim. "How long?"

"Not long," Tim replied, catching his breath. "The station agent said the barometer's falling faster than he's ever seen."

The sheriff rolled up the map with decisive movements. "Sound the church bell—three long rings, three short. Everyone knows that's the tornado signal." He grabbed his oilskin slicker from the peg by the door and checked his pocket watch—a railroad timepiece his father had carried through the Mexican War. "Tell Mason to ready the horses. We'll need to check the outlying homesteads after this passes."

"What about the new telegraph line to Grand Island?" Tim asked. "Should we warn them?"

"If the wires stay up," the sheriff replied grimly. "But this storm might take down every pole between here and there."

Tim nodded and rushed back out into the strengthening wind. Within minutes, the church bell's urgent pattern rang out over Hope Springs, its warning clear to every resident: seek shelter immediately.

Beth heard the bell from her shop. Its meaning registered instantly, sending a chill through her despite the muggy heat. A tornado warning. The most dreaded alert on the prairie.

She rushed to the window, scanning the western sky. The clouds had formed a solid wall now, roiling and churning like a pot about to boil over. Lightning flashed continuously within the mass, and the air felt strangely pressurized, making her ears pop.

Without further hesitation, Beth hurried upstairs to her apartment. Despite her reassurances to Mrs. Peterson, fear fluttered in her chest. She had weathered many storms alone in this building, but tornadoes were different. Deadly different.

From her window, she could see people hurrying toward storm cellars or substantial buildings. The Weatherly's stood on the church steps, beckoning townsfolk inside the sturdy stone basement. Harriet and several others ran toward them, hunched against the wind.

Beth's gaze automatically traveled to the edge of town, toward Miles's homestead. From this distance, she could make out only the general outline of buildings, now obscured by dust and debris, carried on the strengthening gale. Had they taken shelter? Did they have somewhere safe to go?

A rational voice in her mind insisted that Miles would know what to do, that he would protect his daughters. Yet worry persisted, tightening around her heart like a vise.

She should stay put. Going out now would be foolish, dangerous. But the thought of Miles and those sweet girls facing this monster storm in their small home at the edge of town...

Chapter 10

The world above the cellar had become chaos.

Miles huddled with his daughters in the farthest corner as the storm's full fury descended upon their homestead. The cellar door rattled violently in its frame despite the heavy bar he'd placed across it. Overhead, the house shuddered and groaned.

"Tell us a story, Papa," Clara begged, her voice barely audible above the storm's roar. "A happy one."

Miles tightened his arms around both girls. "Once there was a brave princess named Clara and her wise sister, Princess Ellie," he began, raising his voice to be heard above the howling wind. "They lived in a beautiful castle with their father, the king..."

He continued the improvised tale, describing magical gardens and friendly dragons, even as his eyes remained fixed on the cellar door. The girls' bodies gradually relaxed against him, the familiar comfort of his voice providing a counter-rhythm to the storm's terrifying symphony.

A tremendous crack suddenly split the air, louder than thunder, more final than lightning. The entire cellar seemed to shudder as a terrible wrenching sound filled the air above them.

"Papa!" Ellie cried, burying her face against his chest.

"Hold tight to me," Miles commanded, pulling both girls beneath him as a thunderous roar surrounded them, a sound like a thousand freight trains bearing down at once.

The pressure in the cellar changed abruptly—a crushing weight followed by a vacuum pull that made their ears pop painfully. The lantern flame stretched horizontally like a golden pennant, then extinguished with a soft pfft, plunging them into absolute darkness. Miles felt Clara's scream against his chest more than he heard it as the roar became all-encompassing.

For thirty terrifying seconds, the world consisted only of chaos. First came a sound like a thousand wagon wheels grinding across gravel, then a high-pitched keening that reminded Miles of metal being torn at his forge. Dirt and small objects rained down through the floorboards above—tiny pebbles, dirt, and splinters. The very air seemed to fight against their lungs, too thick, then too thin. The smell of earth and ozone and fear filled the darkness. Miles pressed his daughters to the earth floor, silently praying words that were torn away by the maelstrom before they could fully form in his mind.

Then, as suddenly as it had arrived, the roaring began to recede. The pressure eased. The violent shaking subsided to intermittent tremors.

In the new silence, Clara's whimpers seemed impossibly loud.

"Shh, now, we're safe," Miles whispered, though his heart still hammered against his ribs. "We're safe now."

He fumbled for the matches in his pocket, hands shaking as he struck one against the box. The small flame illuminated tear-streaked faces and wide, frightened eyes. Miles lit the lantern that had been knocked to the floor but miraculously remained intact.

"Is it over?" Ellie asked, her voice small and trembling.

"The worst is," Miles answered, unsure if he spoke truth but needing to calm their fears. "We'll wait a little longer to be certain."

As if in answer, rain began to fall, not in gentle drops but in a sudden deluge that drummed against... Miles looked up, frowning, as he noticed water begin to drip down from the ceiling of the cellar. The sound was wrong. Rain on a roof had a particular rhythm, a familiar pattern. This sounded different. More direct.

With growing dread, Miles approached the cellar stairs, holding the lantern high. The cellar door was still in place, still barred, but around its edges he could see not the expected darkness of the kitchen but a strange, gray light.

"Stay here," he instructed the girls firmly. "Don't move until I come back for you."

Climbing the steps carefully, Miles pushed against the cellar door. It resisted, then gave way suddenly, releasing a small avalanche of debris, splintered wood, broken glass, and soaked earth. Rain poured in through the opening, falling directly on him.

Miles pulled himself up and out of the cellar, then stood frozen in shock, the rain plastering his shirt to his skin as he surveyed what remained of his home.

There was nothing.

Where their small house had stood, only the foundation remained. A rectangular outline of stone. Everything else—walls, roof, furniture, possessions—had been swept away by the tornado's violent hand. The smithy shop stood in partial ruin, its roof torn off and walls partially collapsed. Their barn was completely gone, as if it had never existed.

Scattered across the surrounding land lay the broken pieces of their life. Shattered furniture, torn clothing, and splintered timbers. The rain washed over it all, turning the earth to mud that pulled at Miles's boots as he stood immobilized by the totality of the destruction.

"Papa?" Ellie's voice called from below. "Can we come up?"

Miles snapped back to awareness. "No, sunshine. Stay where you are. It's still raining." He couldn't let them see this, not yet. Not until he'd processed it himself.

Everything they owned, gone. Their home was destroyed. The security he'd worked so hard to build swept away in minutes.

Miles ran his hand over his face, the rain mixing with the dirt and tears. First Charlotte, now this. How many times could a man start over? The bitter taste of failure coated his tongue despite knowing no amount of preparation could have prevented this. He'd promised the girls stability when they'd come to Hope Springs—promised himself he could provide it—and now they stood homeless. The weight of responsibility pressed down harder than the heaviest anvil he'd ever lifted.

Miles sank to his knees beside the cellar opening, rain streaming down his face and mingling with tears he hadn't realized he was shedding. What would they do now? Where would they go?

"Lord," he whispered, the word half prayer and half plea, "help us."

The rain began to slacken, and through a break in the clouds to the west, a shaft of light illuminated the devastated homestead. The sun hadn't set yet. There were hours of daylight left to salvage what could be found, to make a plan, to move forward.

Miles took a deep breath and descended back into the cellar where his daughters waited. They had each other. They were alive. And somehow, they would rebuild.

He would be strong for them now, and later, in private, he would wrestle with the loss that threatened to overwhelm him.

"Papa, why are you all wet?" Clara asked as he reached the bottom of the stairs.

Miles knelt before his daughters, taking their small hands in his. "Girls, the storm was very strong," he began gently. "Our house is... damaged. We can't stay here tonight."

"Did it blow away?" Ellie asked, her perceptive dark eyes searching his face.

Miles nodded, deciding that honesty, carefully delivered, was best. "Yes, sunshine. The wind took our house. But God protected what matters most, you and Clara and me. We're safe, and that's what's important."

"Where will we sleep?" Clara's bottom lip trembled.

"We'll find a place," Miles assured her, praying silently that his words would prove true.

He looked around the cellar, the blankets, the lantern, and Ellie's precious doll. Miles tried to focus on practicalities rather than the devastating loss above.

The rain had stopped completely when Miles finally led his daughters up the cellar stairs and into the fading daylight. He had prepared them as best he could, describing the damage in simple terms, yet their small gasps of shock as they emerged tore at his heart.

"Our house is gone," Clara whispered, clutching Miles's hand tightly. "All gone."

Ellie said nothing, her face pale as she surveyed the devastation, but her grip on her father's other hand was painfully tight.

"Look there." Miles pointed to where a child's wooden horse lay remarkably intact amid the debris. "Some things survived. We'll find more."

The girls looked unconvinced, their eyes wide with shock and uncertainty. Miles knelt between them, pulling them close.

"Home isn't just a building," he said softly. "Home is where we're together. We'll build a new house, and it will be home because we're in it together. Do you understand?"

He thought of Charlotte then, of how she'd always maintained that possessions were just things—useful, sometimes beautiful, but ultimately replaceable. "The things that matter can't blow away," she'd told Ellie once after a treasured doll was lost during their travels. Miles hadn't fully understood what she meant until this moment, kneeling in the mud surrounded by destruction, his children's hands in his—the only treasure that truly mattered.

They nodded solemnly, though he could see the fear still lingering in their eyes. Miles stood, scanning the horizon. The storm had passed to the east, leaving a strangely peaceful sky in its wake.

"Let's gather whatever we can that survived," he said with a confidence he didn't entirely feel.

As they began picking carefully through the debris, Miles spotted a flash of movement on the road leading to their property. A figure was approaching rapidly, someone running with purpose despite the mud and debris littering the path.

Miles shielded his eyes against the sun, then felt his heart jump with recognition as the visitor's identity became clear.

Beth running toward them, determination in every step, her face a portrait of concern that transformed to shock as she took in the devastation before her.

"Miles!" she called. "Miles! Ellie! Clara!"

She reached them breathlessly, her eyes wide as she surveyed the destruction. "Oh, merciful heavens," she whispered.

"We're unharmed," Miles said quickly, seeing the fear in her eyes. "We were in the cellar when it hit."

Beth's gaze moved from him to the girls, then back to the ruined homestead. Relief and horror warred in her expression.

"I was so worried," she admitted, hands twisting the damp fabric of her skirt. "When I heard the tornado warning, all I could think was that you three were out here alone, and I..." She stopped, color rising to her cheeks despite the situation. "I couldn't bear not knowing if you were safe a moment longer."

Their eyes met, words unspoken hanging between them. Miles felt something shift within him—a door long closed creaking open just enough to let in a sliver of light.

"You shouldn't have come," he said softly, even as gratitude flooded through him. His hand moved toward hers, then faltered, dropping back to his side. "But I'm glad you're here."

"Everything's gone," Clara said, her voice unnaturally adult. She pointed to the empty foundation. "Our house flew away, like in the story about the pig and the wolf. 'Cept we didn't build it with bricks." Her matter-of-factness made the tragedy somehow more poignant as her small fingers tightened around her father's.

Beth knelt before the child, her eyes gentle. "Houses can be rebuilt, Clara. The important thing is that you and Ellie and your papa are safe."

"That's what Papa said," Ellie murmured. "But we don't know where to sleep tonight."

Beth straightened, a determined set to her jaw. "Well, that's easily solved. You'll come with me. I have a second apartment above the shop."

"We couldn't impose—" Miles began.

"It's not an imposition," Beth cut him off firmly. "It's what neighbors do. It's what friends do." Her eyes met his, steady and certain. "Please, Miles. Let me help."

In that moment, looking at Beth's resolute expression and feeling his daughters' small hands in his, Miles recognized something important. Pride had no place in this situation. Accepting help wasn't weakness, it was wisdom, and perhaps even strength of a different kind.

"Thank you," he said simply. "We accept."

Relief softened Beth's features. "Good. Let's gather what we can now, and we'll return tomorrow with more help to salvage the rest."

As they worked together, collecting the scattered remnants of their lives, Miles felt a curious mixture of devastation and gratitude. Their home was gone, their possessions scattered across the prairie like dandelion seeds in a summer breeze. Their future, which had seemed so carefully plotted just hours before, now stretched before them unwritten.

Yet, his daughters were safe. And in the midst of the chaos, Beth had appeared like an answer to his unfinished prayer—her unexpected presence a reminder that some foundations couldn't be uprooted by any storm. Charlotte had always told the girls that God worked in patterns too large for people to see up close. Perhaps this destruction was part of a design still taking shape, threads being unraveled, only to be rewoven into something stronger.

Miles watched as Beth knelt to comfort Clara, who clutched a mud-spattered book they'd recovered. The sunlight caught in Beth's hair, creating a halo of amber light around her bent head. Some ruins, he thought, might be clearing the ground for new beginnings.

Chapter 11

Rain pattered against the windows of the dress shop as Beth led the Donovan's up the narrow back staircase. Their footsteps echoed in the silence—Beth's confident stride, Miles's heavier tread, and the irregular patter of Clara's curious steps. Ellie, cradled in her father's arms, made no sound at all, her head lolling against his shoulder.

Lantern light threw their shadows against the faded floral wallpaper.

"Is this it?" Clara asked, her small voice bouncing off the walls as Beth paused before the door at the end of the corridor. Water dripped from her bedraggled curls onto the polished floorboards, forming tiny puddles like scattered tears.

"Yes, this is it," Beth replied, her hand hesitating on the doorknob. The brass felt cool beneath her fingers, unused for over a year. Behind this door lay her parents' former living quarters, untouched since the fever had claimed them both. A preservation of the past she'd maintained through monthly dustings but could never bring herself to dismantle or inhabit.

Miles noticed her hesitation, shifting Ellie's weight in his arms. "Beth?"

Beth squared her shoulders and turned the key with a decisive click. "This was my parents' living space."

The door swung open with a soft creak. Beth's lantern cast dancing shadows across the room as she stepped inside, illuminating the furniture draped in white sheets like silent ghosts frozen mid-waltz. The air was stale but not unpleasant—carrying faint traces of her mother's fragrant sachets, and the lingering ghost of pipe tobacco that clung to her father's armchair by the window. The floorboards whispered beneath their feet, remembering footsteps from happier days. A clock on the mantel stood stopped at 3:17, marking the moment Beth had ceased winding it after the funeral.

"It's just a bit dusty," Beth said, trying to keep her voice steady as memories flooded back. Her father reading by that window. Her mother humming at the stove. Family suppers around the table that now sat shrouded and silent. "We'll have it a proper home in no time."

Home.

Such a simple word for something so complex. Beth had struggled to feel at home in this building since becoming its sole occupant. The dress shop below, with its familiar rhythms of commerce, creation, and conversation, had become her only sanctuary. Yet now, watching Clara's curious exploration and Miles's protective hover over Ellie, the apartment seemed to stir from its slumber, remembering its purpose. Walls meant to embrace a family, chairs designed for conversation, a stove built to nourish bodies and souls alike.

"It seems bigger than our house was," Clara whispered, reaching out to touch a sheet-covered chair.

Beth set her lantern on a side table and quickly lit several more around the room, chasing away the deepest shadows. "Let me get these sheets off and open some windows. The fresh air will help, even with the rain."

Miles gently set Ellie down on a chair Beth had uncovered. "What can I do to help?"

"There's some firewood stacked by the stove. A fire would take the dampness out of the air." Beth moved efficiently around the room, pulling more sheets off furniture to reveal her parents' comfortable, if modest, possessions. A sturdy oak dining table. Four cushioned chairs. A settee by the fireplace. A rocking chair her father had built for her mother when they were first married.

As Miles built a fire in the stove, Beth opened the windows just enough to allow fresh air without letting in rain.

The cast-iron stove, a Sunshine model her father had proudly purchased from a traveling salesman in '69, soon radiated welcome heat. Beth lit the kerosene lamp with the etched glass shade, a wedding gift from her mother's sister in St. Louis. Its warm glow revealed the practical elegance of the room. The braided rag rug her mother had made during the harsh winter of '67, the daguerreotype portraits of stern-faced ancestors on the wall, the leather-bound Bible on the side table. Family births and deaths meticulously recorded on the frontispiece in her father's precise hand. Each object carried history, each corner held memories that both comforted and stung.

"What's this?" Clara asked as she pointed to a wooden box on a shelf.

"My mother's sewing kit." Beth ran her fingers across the carved lid. "She taught me everything I know about needlework."

"Did she make pretty dresses like you do?"

"The prettiest," Beth said, her throat tightening. "Even prettier than mine."

Miles watched Beth's face in the lantern light. The vulnerability there, the grief still evident beneath her composure, made his chest ache. "Thank you for this," he said quietly. "I know it can't be easy."

Beth met his eyes across the room. "Some things are worth the difficulty." She turned away quickly, focusing on Ellie, who sat unnaturally still. "Are you hungry, Ellie? I have soup in my apartment that I had planned to have for dinner."

The girl nodded slightly, her face pale in the lamplight.

"I'll fetch it," Beth said.

As Beth headed for the door that connected to the hallway leading to her apartment, Clara called after her, "Can I come too? I want to see where you live!"

Beth hesitated, glancing at Miles, who nodded permission. "Alright."

Clara scampered to Beth's side, slipping her small hand trustingly into Beth's.

Inside her own familiar space, Beth moved with purpose, hands trembling slightly as she opened the cedar chest. Memories hit—her mother's careful folding, her father's insistence on "keeping good linens for guests." These blankets, saved for visitors who never came after her parents' passing, had waited like patient sentinels for a purpose. Beth ran her fingers over the embroidered edges her mother had worked during long winter evenings, then decisively gathered them into her arms. This was what they were meant for—comfort, warmth, shelter. Not preservation in a dusty chest, but service to those in need.

"Your room is pretty," Clara declared, spinning in a small circle. She stopped abruptly, tilting her head to study the neatly arranged hairpins on Beth's dresser and the photo of her parents. "Where's your mama and papa?"

Beth stilled, the child's innocent question landing like a pebble in still water. "They're in heaven now, with your mama."

"Do you think they're friends? Your mama and mine?" Her voice carried no sadness, only genuine curiosity, as though heaven were just another town a day's ride away.

"I'd like to think so," Beth said softly, surprised by how comforting the idea felt. "I'm sure they have a lot in common."

"Like what?" Clara perched on the edge of the bed, swinging her legs, her expression suddenly scholarly.

"Well, they both made pretty dresses. And they both loved their families very much."

Clara nodded, her brow furrowed in serious contemplation, before her face brightened. "And they both know how to make good soup," she added, sniffing the air appreciatively. "Papa says Mama's soup could make grumpy Mr. Carter smile, and he never smiled at anything 'cept his dog!" She patted Beth's arm conspiratorially. "Your soup might make Papa smile, too. He doesn't do that enough since Mama went to heaven."

Beth laughed, the sound unexpected even to her own ears. "Let's get that soup for your sister. She needs warming up."

They returned to find Miles kneeling before Ellie, his large hands gently rubbing warmth into her small ones. The stove crackled with a newly built fire, casting a warm light across the room.

"I've brought soup and blankets," Beth announced, setting down her burden. "Clara, would you like to help me set the table?"

Soon they were seated around the dining table, steam rising from bowls of vegetable soup. Beth had added extra water to stretch the portion, but there was bread to fill any gaps left by the thin broth.

"This is good," Miles said after his first spoonful.

"Papa burns soup," Clara informed Beth matter-of-factly. "And bread. And eggs."

"I'm not quite that hopeless," Miles protested, though his lips quirked in a small smile.

"You are," Ellie spoke for the first time since their arrival, her voice barely audible. "Remember the time you made the kitchen so smoky we had to eat outside?"

Miles pretended to look wounded. "You said you liked picnics."

"Not in winter," Ellie murmured, the ghost of a smile touching her lips before fading. She took another sip of soup, then set down her spoon, her bowl still half full.

"Aren't you hungry, sunshine?" Miles asked, concern creasing his brow.

Ellie shook her head. "My throat and my head hurt."

Beth leaned across the table and gently placed her palm against Ellie's forehead. "You're warm," she said with a frown.

"Let's get her tucked into bed. Rest is what she needs most."

Beth showed them to the bedroom her parents had shared. The large bed dominated the room.

"You and the girls can sleep here," she said to Miles as she put fresh linens on the bed. "My parents' clothes are still in the dresser drawers, and you're welcome to them."

Miles swallowed hard, the full weight of their situation pressing down on his shoulders like an anvil. Just this morning, they'd had a home—modest but theirs. Now he stood as a charity case in a stranger's bedroom, about to wear another man's clothes. Pride and necessity battled within him, but one glance at his daughter's faces settled the matter. His children needed shelter, and his own feelings would have to be set aside.

"No, I couldn't take your parents' bed," Miles protested. "The girls and I can make do with the settee."

"Nonsense," Beth countered firmly. "Ellie needs proper rest, and you're all exhausted. This bed hasn't been slept in for nearly a year. It's time it served someone again."

While Miles helped Clara change into the oversized nightdress Beth had found in the dresser, Beth tended to Ellie. The girl's limbs were pliant as a rag dolls as Beth guided them through the sleeves of the nightgown, her usual quiet dignity replaced by something that chilled Beth to the bone. This wasn't just Ellie's careful reserve—it was an absence. Her eyes, usually bright with thoughtful observation, had dulled to flat pools. Her skin, beyond the slight fever's flush, had a translucent quality, like fine china held up to light. When Beth asked if the nightgown was comfortable, Ellie's head moved in what might have been a nod, but her gaze remained fixed on some invisible point beyond Beth's shoulder.

"There we go," Beth said, tucking the blankets around Ellie's thin form. "Warm as toast now."

"Will the storm come back?" Ellie whispered, her dark eyes wide with fear.

Beth smoothed the hair back from the child's forehead. "No, sweetheart. That storm has moved on far away from here."

"Promise?"

"I promise." Beth sat on the edge of the bed. "Would you like me to read you a story before you sleep? I think I still have some of my old storybooks."

Clara, already settled on the other side of the bed, bounced up to her knees. "Yes, please! A story about princesses!"

"Or animals," Ellie suggested softly.

Beth found an illustrated volume of fables on the bookshelf in the living room and returned to sit between the girls. Miles leaned against the door frame, watching as Beth opened the book to a story about a clever rabbit outsmarting a fox.

Her voice rose and fell with the narrative—booming for the fox, twitching her nose playfully for the rabbit—a performance she hadn't given since reading to Mrs. Weatherly's grandchildren last Christmas. Clara clutched her borrowed nightgown to her mouth to stifle her giggles when the fox fell into the stream, her eyes bright with delight. In the doorway, Miles's shoulders had lost some of their rigid tension, the lines around his eyes softening as he watched. Ellie fought against her heavy eyelids, determination in the way she blinked rapidly to stay awake, not wanting to miss a word even as fever painted twin flags of color high on her cheeks.

When Beth finished, Clara immediately begged for another, but Ellie's eyes had drifted completely closed.

"I think one is enough for tonight," Beth said gently. "It's been a long day, and you both need rest."

"Can we pray first?" Clara asked. "Papa always prays with us at bedtime."

Beth glanced up at Miles, unsure if she was overstepping. He nodded encouragingly from his position by the door.

"Of course, we can pray," Beth said, taking each girl's hand in hers. Clara's was warm and eager, Ellie's hot and limp.

"Dear Heavenly Father," Beth began, "thank You for keeping Miles, Clara, and Ellie safe during the storm today. Thank You for giving us shelter and food and each other's company. Please watch over Ellie and help her feel better soon. And please give Clara sweet dreams without any storms in them. Help us all to rest peacefully in Your care. Amen."

"Amen," Clara echoed, then added, "and thank You for Miss Beth's soup and her pretty house. Amen again."

Beth smiled, tucking the blankets more securely around them both. "Sleep well, little ones."

As Beth leaned over to adjust Ellie's pillow, the child's breath hitched, then quickened into shallow pants. Perspiration beaded across her forehead despite the cool evening air from the partially opened window. Ellie's eyes fluttered open for a moment—glassy and unfocused—before closing again. Beth and Miles exchanged a worried glance over the bed, the shared concern forming an unexpected bridge between them.

She rose from the bed, dimming the lamp to a soft glow before joining Miles in the doorway. They stepped into the main room, leaving the bedroom door ajar.

"You're good with them," Miles said quietly. "Natural, like you've been caring for children all your life."

"I've always loved children," Beth replied, busying herself with straightening the items on the table to avoid meeting his gaze. "But Ellie worries me. That fever came on quickly."

Miles ran a hand through his hair, still damp from the rain. "She's always been the frailer of the two. Takes sick easier than Clara."

"If you need me throughout the night, I'm a light sleeper, so just call out."

"You've done enough already," Miles objected, his voice rough with emotion. "Taking us in, feeding us, giving up your parents' home—"

"It's not being used," Beth interrupted, avoiding his gaze by smoothing an invisible wrinkle from the tablecloth. "Hasn't been since they died. Perhaps it's time it sheltered a family again."

"Beth, I don't know how to thank you properly." His tone carried more than gratitude—a vulnerability that made her heart quicken.

"You don't need to thank me at all." Her fingers twisted the fabric of her apron. "Anyone would have done the same."

"No." Miles shook his head firmly, stepping close enough that she could smell the rain and earth still clinging to him. "Not everyone would open their home and their heart this way. You're..." He paused, and Beth found herself holding her breath, waiting for words she both yearned for and feared. "You're a good person, Beth."

The simplicity of it—so much less and somehow more than what she'd anticipated—sent heat flooding to her cheeks. She stepped back, the sudden proximity overwhelming. "I should get you some dry clothes," she managed, her voice not quite steady. "You'll catch your death in that damp shirt."

What remained unspoken hung between them like the charged air before lightning strikes.

She fetched one of her father's shirts, holding it out to Miles. Their fingers brushed as he took it, sending a small shiver up her arm that had nothing to do with the cool night air.

"There are extra blankets in the chest if you need them," she said. "My pantry in my apartment is stocked, and I'll gather some basics and bring them by in the morning."

"Beth." Miles caught her hand gently as she turned to leave. "Thank you. Truly."

"You're welcome," she said. "Try to get some rest, Miles. Tomorrow we can assess what you've lost and what more can be salvaged."

The hallway seemed longer somehow as Beth made her way back to her own rooms, each step widening the distance between the borrowed family tableau behind her and the solitude that awaited. The clock in the shop below chimed eleven mournful notes as she closed her door, leaning against it momentarily before lighting her lamp.

In her apartment, Beth's practiced composure finally crumbled. Her hands trembled as she poured herself a cup of cold tea, the liquid sloshing over the rim onto her fingers. She didn't bother to wipe it away. At the window overlooking Main Street, she pressed her forehead against the cool glass. The rain had dwindled to a gentle patter that drummed a lullaby on the awnings below. Moonlight bathed the town in silver whenever clouds parted, revealing scattered debris that would be cleared away tomorrow. Hope Springs remained standing, its wounds superficial. While the Donovan home lay in splinters across the prairie, as thoroughly destroyed as if it had never existed at all.

Beth's fingers found the locket at her throat—her mother's locket—clutching it so tightly the edges bit into her palm. Her breath fogged the window as she closed her eyes, lips moving in a silent prayer of gratitude that Miles and his daughters had been spared. Her free hand pressed against her midriff, trying to still the cold, twisting sensation that took root there when she imagined what might have been—three more graves in the cemetery on the hill, three more names for the town to speak in hushed, sorrowful tones on Decoration Day.

Beth closed her eyes, offering another silent prayer of gratitude that Miles and his daughters had been spared.

"They're safe," she whispered. "I'll help them rebuild." The promise felt like a seed planted in freshly turned soil—painful in the breaking, hopeful of the possibility.

Chapter 12

B eth knocked on the apartment door, balancing a wooden crate of provisions against her hip, her knuckles rapping a second time when no one answered. She shifted the weight of the box, about to knock again, when the door swung open.

Miles stood before her, hair tousled from sleep, wearing her father's slightly too small shirt and pants. The fabric strained across his shoulders, exposing several inches of wrist. Dark shadows hollowed his eyes, and a day's worth of stubble darkened his jaw.

"I'm sorry," Beth said. "Did I wake you?"

"No, I've been up." His voice rasped like a file against wood, each word seeming to require effort.

"How are Ellie and Clara?" Beth asked, unable to keep worry from her voice.

"Ellie's fever broke quickly just after midnight," Miles said, relief evident in the softening of the lines around his eyes. His large hand ran unconsciously through his disheveled hair. "Clara is fine—bouncing off the walls since sunrise."

"Thank the Lord," Beth breathed, genuinely relieved, though a remnant of concern lingered. Fevers could return as quickly as they departed, especially in children already weakened by trauma. She'd seen it too many before.

"Here, let me take that," Miles said.

Their fingers brushed as he lifted the crate from her. She followed him into the apartment, where morning light filtered through the windows she'd opened the previous evening.

"I brought some essentials," Beth explained as Miles set the crate on the kitchen table. "Coffee, eggs, bacon, bread, flour, sugar, some apples... and a few other things I thought might be useful."

Miles examined the contents, lifting out a small cloth pouch with a questioning look.

"Willow bark tea," Beth explained. "For Ellie, if the fever returns."

A small sound drew their attention to the bedroom doorway where Clara stood, drowning in the oversized nightdress, her dark curls a wild tangle around her face.

"Miss Beth!" The little girl ran across the room and wrapped her arms around Beth's waist. "Last night I dreamed you made pancakes!"

Beth laughed, smoothing Clara's unruly hair. "Well, dreams sometimes come true. I brought everything we need for pancakes."

Clara beamed up at her. "Can we make them now? Please?"

"First, let's check on your sister," Beth suggested gently.

They entered the bedroom together where Ellie lay curled beneath the quilt, her breathing even, dark lashes resting against pale cheeks. Beth approached quietly, laying her palm against the child's forehead.

Ellie's eyes fluttered open at Beth's touch. "Miss Beth?" Her voice sounded small and fragile.

"Good morning, sunshine," Beth said softly. "How are you feeling?"

"Better," Ellie murmured, though her usual reserve seemed amplified by vulnerability. "Is the storm still gone?"

"All gone," Beth assured her. "The skies are clear today."

"Our house isn't coming back, is it?" Ellie asked, her dark eyes meeting Beth's with troubling adult understanding.

Beth sat carefully on the edge of the bed. "No, sweetheart. But I'm going to help your papa find what can be saved."

Miles knelt beside the bed, his large hand gentle as he brushed hair from Ellie's forehead. "We'll build a new home, sunshine. A stronger one."

"Will it look the same?" Ellie's fingers worried at the quilt edge.

"Maybe not exactly the same," Miles admitted. "But it will be ours."

"Can we help pick how it looks?" Clara piped up, climbing onto the bed beside her sister.

"Of course," Miles promised.

"Can I have a special place for Dolly?" Ellie asked.

"Yes, we will figure out a special place for Dolly," Miles confirmed seriously.

Beth watched this exchange, her heart expanding with emotion. These three who had lost nearly everything still had what mattered most, each other.

"Now," Beth said brightly, standing up. "Who would like pancakes?"

Clara's enthusiastic "Me!" overlapped with Ellie's more subdued, "I would, please."

"Then pancakes it is," Beth declared. "Clara, would you like to help mix the batter?"

In the kitchen, Beth guided Clara through measuring flour and milk, while Miles set the table with the mismatched ironstone dishes.

Beth adjusted the damper on the cast-iron stove to maintain even heat. The morning sunlight filtering through the windows caught in the suspended flour dust, creating motes of dancing gold in the air around Clara's curls.

Beth reached for the precious tin of baking powder—a recent luxury that had revolutionized her morning baking compared to the sourdough starter her mother had religiously maintained—and added a careful pinch.

"My turn to stir?" Clara asked hopefully, eyeing the wooden spoon.

"Three times around, no more," Beth cautioned with mock severity, handing over the implement. "Too much stirring makes for tough pancakes."

"I've decided to keep the shop closed today," Beth mentioned as she poured the first ladle of batter onto the hot griddle, where it sizzled and bubbled. "I thought I might help you salvage what you can from your home."

"You've already done so much," Miles said

"I want to."

Their eyes met across the small kitchen, gratitude and understanding, and something more tender passed between them.

"Will you come too, Ellie?" Clara asked her sister, who had shuffled quietly into the kitchen and settled at the table.

Ellie's eyes widened with apprehension. "Is it scarier there now?"

Miles sat beside his daughter. "It will look the same as it did last night. But there's nothing to fear."

"I'll stay with you the whole time," Beth added. "Sometimes, facing what frightens us makes it less frightening."

Ellie considered this wisdom, then nodded slowly. "I'll come."

Breakfast transformed the mood in the apartment. Clara chatted animatedly between bites of pancake drizzled with precious maple syrup Beth had brought. Even Ellie managed several small portions before declaring herself full.

"These are even better than Mama's," Clara announced, then immediately looked stricken. "I didn't mean—"

"It's all right," Miles said gently. "Your mama would be happy you're enjoying your breakfast."

"She would," Ellie agreed unexpectedly. "Mama always said food tastes better when someone makes it with love."

Beth felt her cheeks warm at the implication. "That's very true, Ellie. My mother said the same thing."

After breakfast, they faced the challenges of the day. Beth helped the girls dress in clothes she'd found in the church donation room this morning. Clothing slightly too large for Ellie, slightly too small for Clara, but clean and serviceable.

"We'll need a wagon," Beth said practically, turning her attention to the day's tasks. "Sheriff Braddock might lend us his. And some crates for what we can salvage."

The streets of Hope Springs buzzed with activity as they made their way to the sheriff's office. Shopkeepers swept debris from boardwalks; men hammered loose shingles back into place; women exchanged reports of damage while talking on the boardwalk. The tornado had clipped the edge of town, leaving most buildings intact but a few untouched.

"Looks like Mrs. Peterson lost her chicken coop," Beth observed as they passed the widow's small house.

"Lost more than that," Sheriff Braddock's voice called from his office porch. "Storm took half her garden and scared her Rhode Island Reds so bad they haven't laid an egg since."

By mid-morning, they were making their way toward the ruined home. Sheriff Braddock had indeed provided his wagon, along with firm instructions to be careful of loose debris and unstable structures. Beth drove the team, with Ellie beside her in the seat and Miles and Clara in the wagon bed with empty crates and burlap sacks.

The morning sunlight revealed the tornado's destructive path more clearly than the previous evening's chaos had allowed. A jagged swath of devastation cut across the prairie like a giant's footprint, where trees had been uprooted and fences shattered. Scattered belongings dotted the landscape—a chair perched inexplicably atop a distant rise, a cooking pot embedded in soil, and tattered fabric fluttering from broken branches like surrender flags.

Birds called from undamaged trees beyond the destruction, their ordinary morning songs seeming almost offensive against the tableau of ruin.

As they approached what remained of the Donovan property, Beth felt Ellie tense beside her. The child's fingers dug into the wagon seat until her knuckles whitened.

"It's all right," she murmured to the child, covering the small hand with her own. "Remember, buildings can be rebuilt."

Miles jumped down as Beth halted the wagon at what had been the edge of their yard. He lifted his arms to help Ellie down, then Clara, before offering his hand to Beth. His palm was warm and calloused against hers, steadying her as she descended.

"Where do we begin?" Beth asked, surveying the wreckage spread as far as the eye could see across the muddied earth.

They worked methodically through the morning, picking carefully through the debris. Clara quickly turned the somber task into a treasure hunt, squealing with delight whenever she discovered an intact possession. Ellie stayed close to Beth, holding a small burlap sack in which she carefully placed found items, a wooden button, a bent spoon, and, miraculously, an unbroken teacup.

"Look!" Clara called, pulling something from beneath a splintered board. "Mama's music box!"

Miles crossed to his daughter, his steps quickening despite the exhaustion that had slowed his movements all morning. He took the small wooden box with reverent hands, thumbs brushing away mud from its carved surface. The lid was cracked, but when he carefully opened it, the delicate mechanism inside still functioned, releasing a few notes of a gentle melody before falling silent.

Miles's breathing hitched. His shoulders curved inward as if against a sudden chill, and for a moment, Beth thought he might crumble like the remnants of his home. When he spoke, his voice emerged as a whisper.

"Charlotte loved this," he said, the muscle in his jaw working. "Her grandmother gave it to her." His calloused thumb traced the hairline fracture across the lid, over and over, like a man reading braille.

Beth touched his arm lightly, feeling the tension beneath the fabric. "A precious find, then."

"More than you know," Miles agreed, carefully closing the lid before Clara could see the moisture gathering in his eyes.

They continued working, the wagon slowly filling with salvaged items, kitchenware, a few tools, and clothing that had somehow escaped destruction or could be mended. Beth discovered an iron cook pot half-buried in mud, perfectly intact except for a dented lid.

"This can certainly be used again," she declared, cleaning it as best she could with the hem of her apron.

Ellie tugged at Beth's sleeve, pointing silently toward what had been the smithy. The structure's partial walls still stood, though the roof was entirely gone. "Papa's special hammer might be in there."

"His special hammer?"

"The one with the cross on it," Ellie explained.

Beth nodded, understanding. "Let's look, but carefully. Some of those boards might not be stable."

They picked their way to the smithy's entrance, stepping over fallen beams and scattered metalwork. Inside, the forge stood remarkably intact, though filled with debris and rainwater. The anvil remained bolted to its base, its polished face now dulled with ash and moisture. Scattered across the ground lay the specialized implements of a smith's trade—tongs with curved jaws for gripping hot metal, swages for shaping rounded grooves in horseshoes, a half-faced hammer whose peen end bore the unmistakable markings of Miles's careful craftsmanship.

Ellie moved toward a corner where a workbench had partially collapsed. "It was here," she said, pointing to the wreckage. "In a wooden box with his other special tools."

Ellie hesitated, then reached for Beth's hand. Her small fingers wrapped around Beth's with surprising strength. "Mama always helped Papa find things," she whispered, her dark eyes searching Beth's face. "She said he'd lose his head if it wasn't attached."

She squeezed Ellie's hand gently. "Then we'll have to do our best to find these tools, won't we?"

Beth began carefully moving smaller pieces of wood aside. "Like this one?" she asked, lifting a dirt-smudged wooden container.

Ellie's face brightened. "That's it!"

Together, they opened the box to find several specialized blacksmith tools nestled inside—a set of carefully maintained punches for decorative work, a small hammer with a leather-wrapped handle for delicate shaping, and a larger one with a small cross carefully etched into its handle, the mark of both Miles's faith and his craftsmanship.

"We found it, Ellie." Beth smiled at the child's obvious relief. "Your papa will be so pleased."

"Found what?" Miles appeared in the doorway, Clara perched on his shoulders.

"Your special tools," Ellie said, pride evident in her voice. "Miss Beth helped me."

Miles set Clara down and crossed to them, genuine emotion crossing his features as he took the box. "I thought these were gone for certain." His fingers traced the cross on the hammer's handle. "My father gave me these when I completed my apprenticeship."

"Ellie remembered exactly where they were," Beth told him.

Miles knelt at his daughter's level. "Thank you, sunshine."

A shout from outside interrupted them. "Donovan! You out here?"

They emerged from the smithy to find Sheriff Braddock dismounting from his horse, accompanied by a wagon carrying several men from town—Frank, Reverend Weatherly, Tim, and Virgil.

"Thought you could use some help," the sheriff called, surveying the destruction with a low whistle. "Twister sure did a number on your place."

"We've come to see what can be done," Reverend Weatherly added, climbing down from the wagon. "The Lord instructs us to bear one another's burdens."

Miles stepped forward to shake the men's hands. "I'm grateful for any assistance."

"Figured we could clear the worst of it," Frank said, practical as always. "See what foundation's left of your home? Might get a new frame up quicker than you think."

"I can't pay for lumber just yet," Miles admitted. "I need to get the smithy functioning first."

"Already taken care of," Tim announced with a grin. "A telegraph came through this morning. The railroad's sending materials free of charge in exchange for exclusive service on their equipment when they come through next month."

"And the church fund will cover the rest," Reverend Weatherly added.

Beth watched emotions play across Miles's face, surprise, gratitude, and something like embarrassment at needing such help.

"I don't know what to say," he finally managed.

"Don't need to say anything," Virgil drawled, already rolling up his sleeves. "Just point us where to start."

Another wagon approached, this one carrying Eleanor, Alice, Harriet, and several other women from town, each bringing baskets of food and additional helping hands.

"We thought you all might need sustenance," Eleanor called cheerfully. "And more help sorting through whatever can be saved."

The property quickly transformed into a hive of activity. Men cleared larger debris, while women helped sort and rescue what could be salvaged. Jimmy Langley appeared with several other children, eager to assist in whatever way they could.

"The whole town's here," Clara marveled, watching wide-eyed as people she barely knew worked together.

"That's what community means," Beth explained, guiding the child toward a flat area where a meal was being laid out. "Helping each other when it's needed most."

Miles looked overwhelmed, his expression a mixture of gratitude and disbelief.

"I never expected this," he said, his calloused fingers clenching involuntarily at his sides.

Beth noticed the tension in his jaw, the way his shoulders stiffened even as gratitude washed over his features. "You would do the same for any of them," she pointed out.

"Still." Miles gazed around at everyone working so diligently, the muscle in his cheek working as he swallowed hard. All his life, he'd been the one other leaned on—first his parents, then Charlotte, then his daughters. The reversal of roles cut deeper than he cared to admit. "It's humbling."

"Pride is a luxury sometimes," Beth said gently, her voice barely carrying above the cheerful commotion of helping hands. "Accepting help when truly needed isn't weakness. It's wisdom."

Miles studied her face. "How did you become so wise, Beth Bartlett?"

"Hardship teaches lessons," she replied simply.

Eleanor approached them, wiping her hands on her apron. "Frank and the men have been talking. With everyone pitching in, they believe they could have a simple structure up within three weeks. Not fancy, mind you, but solid walls and a roof."

"Three weeks?" Miles repeated, astonished.

"Sooner if the weather holds, and the railroad delivers materials as promised." Eleanor smiled. "Meanwhile, you'll need lodging, of course."

"They're staying with me," Beth said quickly, the words tumbling out before she could measure them. "Above my shop, in my parents' old apartment."

Eleanor's eyebrows rose slightly, but her smile remained kind. "How thoughtful of you, Beth." A meaningful pause stretched between them, filled with unspoken social calculations. "Though I'm sure others would be happy to—"

"The arrangement suits us well," Miles interrupted politely but firmly. "Beth has been extraordinarily generous."

Eleanor's gaze flicked between them, the assessment softening to something warmer. "Well then," she said, patting Beth's arm, "that settles it. But don't hesitate to ask for help, my dear. No need to shoulder everything yourself."

As Eleanor moved away to help organize the communal meal, Miles turned to Beth, his voice lowered for privacy. "You're certain about this? Having us underfoot for potentially weeks?" His eyes searched hers, offering an escape from a commitment made in the heat of crisis. "The girls can be... lively."

"Completely certain," Beth assured him, surprising herself with her conviction. The thought of returning to her quiet, ordered life—of empty rooms and meals for one—suddenly seemed unbearable. "The apartment has stood empty too long. It should be filled with life again."

"Thank you," he said.

Ellie's appearance at Beth's side. The child slipped her small hand into Beth's with a newfound ease that warmed Beth's heart.

"Mrs. Weatherly says it's time to eat," Ellie reported. "And Jimmy found more of Papa's tools under the big trees in the backyard."

"Wonderful news," Beth smiled down at her. "Shall we go see what everyone's brought for lunch?"

The community meal was spread across improvised tables made from salvaged boards and saw horses. The women had brought an abundance of food—golden-brown fried chicken glistening in the sunlight, biscuits still warm enough to melt the butter pats nestled inside them, crumbly corn bread scenting the air with its sweet aroma, pots of beans seasoned with salt pork and molasses, and even several pies with lattice crusts bubbling with berry juice.

As everyone gathered to eat, Reverend Weatherly asked for a moment of prayer. They stood in a large circle, hands joined, heads bowed beneath the clear prairie sky that stretched endless blue above them, as if yesterday's violence had never occurred.

"Heavenly Father," the reverend began, "we thank You for Your merciful protection of the Donovan family during yesterday's terrible storm. Though material possessions have been lost, lives were spared, for which we are deeply grateful. We ask Your blessing upon our efforts to rebuild what was destroyed, and we thank You for the spirit of community and Christian love that brings us together today. May this work of our hands honor You. Amen."

"Amen," echoed around the circle.

Plates clattered, utensils clinked, and laughter rippled across the gathering—a stark contrast to the destruction surrounding them, yet somehow perfectly fitting. Life continuing despite loss. As people began filling plates, Sam Atwater approached Miles with a weather-beaten face creased in a smile.

"Seen three twisters in my lifetime and one of them took my home too," the old man announced without preamble. "Built it back stronger and better."

"Three twisters?" Clara asked, eyes wide with wonder.

Sam nodded seriously. "First time, I was about your papa's age. Lost everything but my dog, my family, and the clothes we had on. Neighbors came, just like today. Had a new roof over my head before the month was out. The other two twisters, God spared me and my family, and we only had minor damage to my home both times."

"Were you scared?" Ellie asked quietly.

"Terrified each time," Sam admitted candidly. "But fear doesn't rebuild or fix houses. Hard work and good neighbors do that."

"And faith," Reverend Weatherly added, joining their conversation. "Faith that God provides, even in our darkest hours."

"Like He provided Miss Beth to us," Clara piped up, reaching for Beth's hand with sticky fingers. "And pancakes. And all these people." Her face brightened with the uncomplicated certainty of childhood. "Mama always said God works in mys-ter-i-ous ways," she pronounced carefully, clearly quoting a phrase she'd heard many times.

"Your mama was a wise woman," Reverend Weatherly said gently.

Clara nodded solemnly. "That's why God needed her in heaven. Papa says the wisest people get called there first." She turned questioning eyes to her father. "Right, Papa?"

Miles swallowed hard, his hand coming to rest on his daughter's curls. "Sometimes that seems to be the way of things, sunshine."

As the meal continued, plans formed more concretely. The men would start preparing the foundation of the home. The women organized a schedule for providing meals to the workers and arranged for additional clothing and necessities for the Donovans.

Beth found herself in conversation with Alice Weatherly, helping serve slices of berry pie to the children.

"It's very generous of you to open your home to Miles and his daughters," Alice said, her kind eyes assessing Beth carefully.

"It seemed the natural thing to do," Beth replied, handing a plate to Jimmy. "The apartment was sitting empty."

"Still, people might talk," Alice cautioned gently.

Beth hadn't considered the potential for gossip, but now realized how her impulsive offer might appear to others. A single woman housing a widower and his children could certainly raise eyebrows.

"Let them talk," she said with more confidence than she felt. "There's nothing improper about helping neighbors in need."

Alice patted her hand. "Of course there isn't, dear. But perhaps Benjamin and I should stay in your apartment with you for a few days, just to quiet any potential rumors."

"That's very thoughtful, but unnecessary," Beth assured her. "They're in my parents' apartment, not mine. There are proper walls and doors between us."

Alice studied her face. "You've grown fond of them."

It wasn't a question, and Beth didn't deny it. "They're easy to care about."

"Yes," Alice agreed. "Particularly Miles, I imagine."

Beth felt heat rise to her cheeks. "I admire his strength and devotion to his daughters."

"Admiration is an excellent foundation," Alice said, her smile knowing. "Far better than mere attraction."

Beth felt heat rise to her cheeks. The perceptiveness in Alice's eyes unsettled her. Was she so transparent? She'd spent years building walls around her heart, telling herself that independence was protection. Now three people had walked through those walls as if they didn't exist, and the thought terrified her almost as much as it warmed her. "I admire his strength and devotion to his daughters."

"And what happens when their home is rebuilt?" Alice asked, her voice too low for others to hear.

The question struck Beth like a physical blow. She hadn't allowed herself to think that far ahead, hadn't considered how empty her building would feel once they were gone. Before she could formulate a response, Ellie appeared at her side, plate in hand.

Ellie appeared at her side, plate in hand. "May I have more pie, please?"

"Of course you may," Beth answered, grateful for the interruption.

By late afternoon, remarkable progress had been made. The wreckage had been sorted into piles—salvageable materials, items to be discarded, and possessions to be restored. The foundation had been partially cleared, and measurements taken for rebuilding.

Frank sketched a simple floor plan on the back of a feed store receipt, discussing options with Miles. "Two bedrooms here, living area there. We can add more later when you're settled. We should put a priority on fixing your shop as well. You'll need income."

"And the community needs a blacksmith," Tim added, joining the conversation. "Town doesn't function proper without one. My plow blade's been needing attention for a month."

Sheriff Braddock joined them, wiping sweat from his brow with a bandana. "Virgil says he can rig up a temporary forge behind the livery until yours is rebuilt. Wouldn't be ideal, but you could take on basic work."

"That's generous of him," Miles said, surprise evident in his voice.

"Man needs to work," the sheriff said simply. "Especially a man with children to support."

"We're commanded to bear one another's burdens," Reverend Weatherly reminded them. "When one member suffers, all suffer together. When one rejoices—"

"—all rejoice together," several voices finished in unison, the familiar scripture flowing naturally from lips that had recited it many times.

Beth watched the scene unfold, struck by the living embodiment of words often spoken in church pews but not always carried beyond the sanctuary doors. Here, faith took physical form in sweat-stained shirts and blistered hands, in women who'd emptied their pantries and men who'd abandoned their own pressing work. This was the gospel made visible—not in platitudes, but in present help.

As the sun began its descent toward the horizon, people gradually packed up to return to their homes, promising to return in the morning. Beth gathered the girls, who were showing signs of exhaustion despite their determination to help.

"Time to head back," she told Miles, finding him securing rescued tools in a crate. "These two need rest, and so do you."

Miles nodded, his fatigue evident in the slump of his shoulders. "You're right. We've accomplished more today than I ever imagined possible."

Reverend Weatherly overheard them as he helped his wife into their wagon. "The Lord works through willing hands, Miles. Never forget that."

As they prepared to leave, Miles paused for a moment, gazing at the cleared area where his home had stood just yesterday. Beth stood beside him. The girls already settled in Sheriff Braddock's borrowed wagon.

"It will stand again," she said softly.

Miles turned to look at her, his blue eyes intense in the golden hour light.

"Beth... thank you," he finally said, voice rough with emotion. "Not just for the shelter, but for..." He gestured vaguely, words failing him.

"You would do the same," Beth replied, meeting his gaze steadily despite the flutter beneath her ribs.

"Yes," Miles agreed, his eyes never leaving hers. "I would."

As they drove back toward Beth's shop in the golden evening light, Clara's head nodded against Miles's shoulder, and Ellie leaned quietly against Beth's side. The day of hard work and emotional recovery had exhausted them all.

"We'll start fresh tomorrow," Beth said, her voice soft beneath the steady rhythm of the horses' hooves.

Miles nodded, his expression peaceful despite everything. "With God's help and good neighbors, we will."

Chapter 13

A gentle breeze carried the earthy scent of fresh-turned soil and sawdust across the clearing, mingling with the sharper tang of sweat as men worked in the strengthening morning sun. The rhythmic thud of hammers punctuated the steady hum of conversation, creating a symphony of renewal that stood in stark contrast to the devastating silence that had followed the tornado's fury. Miles breathed it all in, finding strange comfort in these sounds of hope replacing the destruction.

"Hand me that beam, would you?" Frank called, wiping sweat from his brow despite the early morning hour. "If we get this corner post set today, we can start framing the smithy by tomorrow."

Sheriff Braddock hefted the rough-hewn timber onto his shoulder and carried it across the muddy yard to where Frank stood beside the newly cleared foundation. A dozen men worked around the Donovan property, some clearing more debris, others measuring and marking for reconstruction. The buzz of activity had started at dawn, the community of Hope Springs rallying around one of their own.

Miles crouched nearby, examining the stone foundation of his former smithy with Virgil beside him, pointing to various sections with a practiced eye.

"This corner's still solid," Miles observed, running his hand along the stacked limestone. "We can build up from here without starting fresh."

"The Whole south wall held up pretty well," Virgil agreed, scratching his grizzled chin.

Miles ran his hand over the limestone block, its rough surface familiar under his calloused palm. The unasked-for charity surrounding him both warmed and chafed at his spirit. A blacksmith shaped things, fixed things—he wasn't meant to be the broken thing others mended. His father's voice echoed in his memory: "A Donovan stands on his own two feet." Yet here he stood, surrounded by the generosity of near-strangers, his independence as shattered as his home.

Beth stood a few yards away with Eleanor and Alice, the wagon's shade offering meager relief from the morning sun that had already promised a scorching day. She watched Miles work, his movements purposeful and measured despite the dark circles shadowing his eyes. Sleep had been elusive in his apartment. She'd heard his footsteps late into the night, pacing the wooden floors as his daughters slept. His resilience stirred something in her chest, an admiration tinged with a warmth. He hadn't once surrendered to despair, though she'd glimpsed moments when the weight nearly broke him—when he thought no one was watching.

"The train with the lumber should arrive tomorrow afternoon," Eleanor was saying, consulting a list in her hand. "Tim got confirmation by telegraph last night. The railroad's being quite generous."

"The Lord provides," Alice added with a gentle smile. "Often through the most unexpected channels."

The words hung in the morning air, simple yet profound. Beth's gaze drifted to the clear blue sky, unmarked by clouds—the same sky that had birthed such destruction days before. How quickly nature's face could change, from deadly to benevolent, just as human fortunes could turn from secure to desperate in the span of a heartbeat.

Eleanor nodded, glancing toward where Clara and Ellie sat playing with several other children under the watchful eye of Harriet. "Those poor children. At least they seem to be adjusting. Especially little Ellie."

"They're surprisingly resilient," Beth said, her gaze drifting back to Miles. "All three of them."

Alice followed her line of sight, her expression knowing. "Indeed."

Reverend Weatherly approached the group. "We've made excellent progress this morning. I believe we should discuss the most pressing needs while we're all gathered."

Frank nodded, driving a stake into the ground to mark a corner post. "Smithy first, that's clear. Miles needs to work. We can get Miles and Virgil set up to work behind the livery today."

"That's settled then," Reverend Weatherly said. "I'll stay here with the men and continue clearing and doing what we can and prepare for the lumber arrival tomorrow. Meanwhile, Virgil, Miles, and Frank can establish the temporary forge."

"What about clothing and household goods?" Alice asked. "The Donovan's lost nearly everything."

Eleanor turned to Beth and the other women. "I suggest we return to town and begin sewing. The girls need proper dresses, not just the few salvaged items and hand-me-downs."

"I have plenty of fabric at the shop," Beth offered. "And patterns for children's clothing."

"I could start helping right away," Harriet added, joining their circle. "I'll keep my bookstore closed for the rest of the day, and I'm handy with a needle."

"I have some of my boys' outgrown things that might fit Clara until proper dresses are made," Eleanor added.

"That's very kind," Miles said as he joined the group, looking somewhat uncomfortable at accepting so much assistance. "But I can't ask you ladies to—"

"You didn't ask," Eleanor interrupted firmly. "We offered. There's a difference, Mr. Donovan."

Miles inclined his head with a small smile. "Yes, ma'am."

"It's decided then," Reverend Weatherly concluded. "The women will see to clothing and necessities." He glanced at the children. "And perhaps the little ones should go with the ladies. They've been quite patient this morning."

Beth walked over to where Ellie and Clara played. Clara was arranging small stones in patterns while Ellie watched, occasionally offering suggestions. Both looked up as Beth approached.

"Would you girls like to come back to town with me and the other ladies?" Beth asked. "We're going to start making some new dresses for you both."

Clara bounced to her feet. "New dresses? With pretty fabric?"

"The prettiest," Beth promised with a smile.

Ellie stood more slowly, brushing dirt from her dress. "Can I help sew?" she asked quietly.

"Of course you can," Beth assured her, touched by the request. "I think you'd be an excellent helper."

Miles joined them, kneeling to his daughter's level. "You be good for Miss Beth and the other ladies," he instructed. "I'll see you this evening."

"Are you coming home for dinner?" Clara asked, wrapping her arms around his neck.

Miles glanced briefly at Beth before answering. "Yes. I'll be there."

Beth felt a curious warmth at his reference to her apartment as "home," however temporary the arrangement might be.

"My temporary forge should be operational by tomorrow if all goes well," Miles told Beth as he stood.

"That's wonderful news," Beth replied. "We'll make sure to have a special dinner to celebrate."

"You don't need to—"

"I want to," Beth interrupted gently. "Let people help, Miles. It's what communities do."

He held her gaze a moment longer than strictly necessary, something unspoken passing between them. "Thank you. I truly appreciate it."

Eleanor's voice broke the moment. "Beth! We're ready to depart if you are."

"Coming!" Beth called back, then smiled at Miles. "We'll see you this evening."

As Beth helped the girls into Eleanor's wagon, she caught Harriet watching her with a barely suppressed smile.

"What?" Beth asked as they settled on the wagon seat.

"Nothing at all," Harriet replied innocently, though her eyes sparkled with meaning. "Nothing whatsoever."

***

Beth's shop transformed quickly into a hive of activity. Tables were cleared to make workspace for cutting fabric. Chairs were arranged in a circle near the windows for optimal light. Eleanor, Alice, Harriet, and several other women from town—Maggie, Nellie, and Gussie—gathered around, sorting through fabric bolts and pattern pieces.

The scents of starch and fabric filled the air. Sunshine streamed through the large front windows. The rhythmic snip of scissors against cloth and the soft murmur of women's voices created a soothing cadence that belonged exclusively to gatherings such as these—a timeless ritual of community and care that transcended the harshness of frontier life.

"This blue calico would make a lovely everyday dress for Ellie," Eleanor suggested, holding up a length of fabric patterned with tiny flowers.

"And perhaps this yellow for Clara?" Alice added, indicating a sunshine-colored cotton. "It matches her cheerful disposition."

Clara, overhearing, clapped her hands in delight. "Yellow is my favorite! Like butter and sunshine!"

The women laughed, charmed by her enthusiasm.

"Then yellow it shall be," Beth agreed, beginning to measure and mark the fabric.

Beth smiled, remembering her own childhood delight in new fabric, a rare luxury on the frontier, where most children wore homespun or hand-me-downs until they were threadbare. Before the railway, such colorful calicos would have been precious indeed, transported by wagon trains across perilous miles. Even now, with the railroad bringing Eastern goods more regularly, a new dress remained something special, particularly for a child who had lost everything.

"We'll add some rickrack trim along the collar," Beth suggested, fingering the zigzag braid that had just arrived in her latest shipment from St. Louis. "And perhaps some covered buttons down the back. Very fashionable."

Clara's eyes widened at such finery. "Like in the Godey's Lady's Book pictures Mrs. Weatherly showed me?"

"Very similar," Beth confirmed, touched that the child aspired to such Eastern elegance, even here on the Nebraska prairie.

Ellie stood quietly beside Beth, watching the proceedings with solemn interest. Unlike her outgoing sister, she seemed overwhelmed by all the attention and activity.

Beth pulled a small chair close to her worktable. "Would you like to help me, Ellie? I need someone with careful hands to sort these buttons."

Relief crossed the child's face at being given a specific task. She climbed onto the chair and began methodically grouping the buttons by size and color.

"You have a knack for organization," Beth observed. "That's a valuable skill."

"Mama taught me," Ellie said, her voice soft but clear. Her small fingers moved deliberately, grouping pearl buttons separate from wooden ones, larger from smaller. "She said a place for everything and everything in its place makes a happy home." The child paused, a tiny brass button pinched between her finger and thumb, her dark eyes distant with memory. "She let me organize her sewing basket every Sunday after church. Said I had the best sorting hands in all of Iowa."

The pride in Ellie's voice made Beth's throat tighten. "Your mama was very wise. I wish I could have met her," she replied, carefully cutting along the marked lines of the pattern. "And she was right about your sorting hands. They're quite exceptional."

A ghost of a smile touched Ellie's lips—rare as a desert bloom and just as precious. "Papa says I have Mama's hands. Do you think that's true?"

Beth studied the child's slender fingers, so careful with each button. "I think we carry pieces of those we love with us always. Maybe you do have your mama's hands—her way of touching the world with care."

"Do you miss your mama and papa?" Ellie asked unexpectedly, looking up from her button sorting.

The question, so direct and innocent, caught Beth off guard.

"Yes," she answered honestly. "Every day. But it helps to keep busy and to remember the good things they taught me."

Ellie nodded, considering this with the seriousness of a much older person. "I miss Mama. But I'm glad we have you now."

Beth's hands stilled on the fabric, her heart swelling with emotion. "I'm glad to have you too, Ellie."

"Will you stay with us even when our new house is built?" Clara piped up, appearing suddenly at Beth's other side.

Before Beth could formulate a response to this loaded question, Harriet intervened smoothly. "Clara, come help me choose some ribbons for your new dresses. I've got blue ones and red ones and even some with little flowers."

As Clara skipped off with Harriet, Beth caught her friend's wink. She'd have to thank Harriet later for the timely rescue.

"Miss Beth?" Ellie's voice drew her attention back. "You didn't answer Clara's question."

Beth selected her words carefully. "When your new house is built, you and Clara and your papa will live there. But I'll still be right here in town, and you can visit me anytime you want."

Ellie's brow furrowed slightly. "But won't you be lonely in your apartment all by yourself?"

"I've lived alone for some time now," Beth said gently.

"But Papa smiles more when you're around."

Beth felt heat rise to her cheeks, acutely aware that Alice was watching them, though pretending to be absorbed in hemming a petticoat. "Your papa and I are friends, Ellie."

Ellie seemed to accept this, returning to her button sorting. "He needs more friends. And so do you."

From the mouths of babes, Beth thought, picking up her scissors again. The quiet wisdom in Ellie's observation lingered with her as she continued cutting the pattern pieces.

Across the room, Eleanor was regaling the group with news of her husband's latest farming venture. "Frank's convinced this new seed corn will yield double, but I told him not to count his kernels before they're planted. Men and their ambitious schemes!"

"Speaking of schemes," Nellie said, lowering her voice conspiratorially, "has anyone heard what Elijah Aldridge is planning? I saw strangers at his ranch yesterday, businessmen by the look of them."

Beth's ears perked up at the mention of Thomas's uncle.

"Railroad men, I heard," Maggie supplied, threading a needle with practiced ease. "Discussing some sort of arrangement about rights-of-way through his property."

"The man never misses an opportunity to profit," Eleanor said disapprovingly. "Not that there's anything wrong with honest business, but there's something about the way Elijah Aldridge operates that just doesn't sit right with me."

Beth kept her head down, focusing on her cutting. She'd had limited dealings with Elijah Aldridge over the years, but each encounter had left her unsettled. After Thomas disappeared on what should have been her wedding day, she'd avoided his uncle entirely since then.

"I think we should focus on our sewing," Alice suggested kindly, clearly sensing Beth's discomfort. "These children need proper clothing, and gossip never hemmed a skirt yet."

The women obediently returned to their work, though Beth could feel their curious glances. Her former engagement with Thomas Aldridge and his subsequent disappearance had been the subject of town speculation for months after it happened.

"Miss Beth," Ellie whispered, leaning closer, "are you alright? Your face went funny for a minute."

Beth managed a smile for the perceptive child. "I'm perfectly fine, sweetheart. Just concentrating on this tricky curve."

Ellie didn't look entirely convinced, but returned to her buttons without further comment.

By midday, significant progress had been made. Ellie's blue dress was cut out completely and partially assembled, and Clara's yellow one was well underway.

"We should break for some refreshment," Eleanor suggested. "I brought some ginger cookies and apple cider."

As the women paused in their work, Beth opened the shop door to let in fresh air. Main Street bustled with the usual midday activity. Wagons rolled past, townspeople moved between shops, and from the livery at the end of the street came the distant ring of metal against metal.

"Sounds like Miles and Virgil aren't wasting any time," Harriet observed, joining Beth in the doorway. Her shrewd eyes followed Beth's gaze toward the distant livery. "That's determination for you."

The rhythmic clanging carried in the afternoon air, each strike of hammer against anvil a declaration of resilience. Beth could almost picture Miles—shoulders set with purpose, strong hands guiding the metal, brow furrowed in concentration.

"Miles needs to work," Beth said simply, aware of Harriet studying her face with too much interest. "It's how he defines himself."

"Among other things," Harriet replied, nudging Beth gently with her elbow. "Like being a devoted father. And perhaps being an attentive friend?"

A nearby sparrow took flight from the shop awning, wings beating against the spring air, drawing Beth's eyes skyward—a welcome distraction from Harriet's knowing look. "Harriet."

"What?" Innocence dripped unconvincingly from Harriet's voice. "I'm merely observing that our blacksmith seems to have forged more than iron since arriving in Hope Springs." She lowered her voice, though the nearest women were well out of earshot. "And that certain shopkeepers have developed a sudden interest in metallurgy."

"You have an overactive imagination," Beth chided, though without heat.

"Do I?" Harriet's eyebrows rose with theatrical skepticism. "Then why did you rush to his property right after a tornado? Why did you offer your parents' apartment without hesitation? And why—" she paused for emphasis, "—do you blush every time his name is mentioned?"

"I do not—" Beth began, then stopped as she felt the telltale warmth in her cheeks. "You're impossible."

Harriet laughed softly. "I'm right, and you know it. There's nothing wrong with admitting you care for the man, Beth."

"It's complicated."

"Only because you're making it so," Harriet countered. "Heart matters are actually quite simple when you stop fighting them."

Clara bounded up to them, cookie in hand. "Can we go see Papa? I want to show him my new dress pieces!"

"Not yet, dear," Beth said. "We'll take it to him when it's done, and you can surprise him properly then."

"But I miss him," Clara insisted, crumbs falling from her cookie as she spoke. "Don't you miss him too, Miss Beth?"

Harriet's poorly suppressed a snort of laughter earned her another warning look from Beth.

"Your papa is working very hard," Beth told Clara, choosing to ignore the question. "We'll see him at dinner, remember?"

This seemed to satisfy Clara, who skipped back to join the other women. Harriet, however, remained insufferably smug.

"Out of the mouths of babes," she murmured.

"Oh, hush," Beth replied, unable to completely suppress her own smile.

The afternoon continued productively. By four o'clock, both girls' dresses were nearly complete, requiring only final details and pressing. Several additional garments had been cut out: night dresses, pinafores, and everyday play clothes that would see them through the coming weeks.

"I believe we've accomplished enough for one day," Eleanor announced, inspecting their work with satisfaction. "The girls will have some proper clothing by tomorrow, and we can continue with additional items throughout the week."

As the women gathered their belongings and prepared to depart, Alice lingered behind, helping Beth fold the remaining fabric and organize the patterns.

"You've taken on quite a responsibility," Alice said as she folded the remaining fabric with practiced hands.

"It's no trouble," Beth replied, carefully placing pins back in their cushion.

"Those children are becoming attached to you," Alice continued, her voice lowered to ensure privacy. "Clara quite openly, and Ellie in her more reserved way. Children who've known loss recognize safe harbors when they find them."

Beth's hands stilled, a pin suspended between her fingers. "They've been through so much. It's natural they'd seek security wherever they can find it."

"And you? Are you becoming attached as well?" Alice's question came softly, wrapped in compassion rather than judgment.

"Yes," she admitted. "More than is probably wise."

Alice patted her hand. "The heart rarely consults wisdom before choosing its path, my dear."

"But they've just lost everything, Alice," Beth said, her voice strained with the effort of articulating fears she'd barely acknowledged to herself. "Miles is struggling to rebuild his life and care for his daughters. The last thing he needs is..." Beth trailed off, uncertain how to finish the sentence without revealing too much of her guarded heart.

"Is what?" Alice prompted gently. "Companionship? Understanding? Perhaps even love?"

Beth felt heat rise to her cheeks at the last word. "It's too soon."

"For whom?" Alice asked shrewdly. "For Miles, or for you? Remember, Beth, his loss is not recent. It's been some time since Charlotte passed. And your heart has been shuttered since Thomas left. Perhaps it's not too soon at all. Perhaps it's precisely the right time."

Ellie appeared at her side. "Miss Beth? I finished sorting all the buttons." She held up several small fabric pouches. "I put them in these so they wouldn't get lost."

"That's very thoughtful, Ellie," Beth said, grateful for the interruption. "You're a wonderful helper."

Alice smiled at the child. "Would you like to come to the parsonage tomorrow, Ellie? I'm baking pies for Sunday services, and I could use an assistant."

Ellie's face brightened. "May I, Miss Beth?"

"If your papa agrees," Beth replied.

"And Clara too?" Ellie asked, showing unusual concern for including her sister.

Alice laughed. "Clara too, though I suspect she'll eat more pie filling than she'll help prepare."

With final goodbyes, Alice departed, leaving Beth alone with the girls in the suddenly quiet shop. The organized chaos of the sewing circle had given way to neat piles of nearly completed garments and carefully sorted notions.

"Can we go upstairs now?" Clara asked, clearly tired from the day's excitement. "I'm hungry."

"Yes, let's go prepare dinner," Beth agreed. "Your papa will be home soon."

There it was again—home. The word felt both right and slightly dangerous. This temporary arrangement wasn't meant to feel so... natural.

The thought disquieted her.

Upstairs in the apartment, Beth set the girls to simple tasks while she began preparing a hearty stew using vegetables from her garden and beef from the butcher. Clara chattered continuously, describing in elaborate detail how her yellow dress would be "the most beautifulest dress in all of Hope Springs." Ellie worked quietly beside Beth, carefully washing potatoes with concentration.

The domestic scene filled Beth with contentment. For so long, her evenings had been solitary affairs, quiet meals followed by mending or reading or account books. Now the surrounding space hummed with life and childish voices.

The sound of boots on the stairs broke into her thoughts, followed by Clara's excited squeal and the pattering of small feet racing to the door. Miles entered, his face brightening visibly at the sight of his daughters.

"There are my girls," he said, kneeling to embrace them both. His shirtsleeves were rolled up, revealing forearms streaked with soot, and his face bore smudges of the same, but his smile was wide and genuine. "Did you have a good day?"

"We made dresses!" Clara announced, bouncing on her toes. "Yellow for me and blue for Ellie!"

"Is that so?" Miles glanced up at Beth, still standing by the stove. "Productive day, then."

"Very," Beth confirmed. "How was the forge setup?"

"It went well," Miles replied, rising to his feet. "We're operational again and for that, I feel blessed."

"That's wonderful news."

Miles seemed to become aware of his disheveled state. "I should wash up before dinner. Don't want to get soot all over your furniture."

"There's hot water in the basin," Beth told him. "And I set out a clean shirt for you on the chair."

As he disappeared into the small washing alcove, Beth returned to her cooking, aware of a curious fluttering sensation in her stomach. This temporary arrangement was becoming altogether too comfortable, too natural.

"Miss Beth?" Clara tugged at her skirt. "Can I set the table? I know how. Mama taught me before she went to heaven."

"Of course you can," Beth replied, grateful for the distraction. "Ellie, would you like to help your sister?"

The girls worked together, carefully placing the plates and utensils on the table while Beth finished preparing the meal. By the time Miles returned, cleaned up and wearing the fresh shirt she'd laid out, the stew was bubbling merrily, and the table was set for four.

"Something smells delicious," Miles said, his hair still damp from washing, curling slightly at his temples.

"Beef stew," Beth explained, suddenly feeling self-conscious. "I thought you'd need something substantial after working all day."

Miles smiled. "You thought right. Thank you."

They settled around the table; the girls sitting opposite each other, while Beth and Miles took the remaining chairs. It struck Beth how quickly they'd established this routine, as if they'd been taking meals together for years.

Miles said grace, his deep voice steady as he thanked God for the food, for safety, for the generosity of neighbors, and—with a glance at Beth—for the kind hearts that opened their homes to those in need.

As they began to eat, Clara launched immediately into a detailed description of the sewing day, complete with colorful impersonations of the various ladies which had Miles struggling to maintain his composure.

"And then Mrs. Hanley said, 'Land sakes, child, you've got more energy than a grasshopper in July!'" Clara mimicked, dropping her voice comically low. "But she gave me a cookie, anyway."

Miles laughed, the sound rich and warm. "I hope you thanked her properly."

"I did," Clara assured him. "Miss Beth reminded me."

Beth smiled at the memory. Clara's enthusiasm had charmed even the most proper of the town ladies, including Eleanor Hanley, whose own children were long grown.

"And what about you, Ellie?" Miles asked, turning to his quieter daughter. "Did you enjoy the sewing day?"

Ellie nodded. "I sorted buttons. And Miss Beth says I have a knack for organization. That means I'm good at it," she added.

"You certainly are," Miles agreed. "You get that from your mother. Charlotte could find a place for everything, no matter how small our quarters."

"Mrs. Weatherly invited us to help make pies tomorrow," Ellie continued after a moment. "If it's alright with you, Papa."

"That sounds like an excellent opportunity," Miles replied. "You'll enjoy that, I think."

"Will you be working at the new forge?" Beth asked, passing him more stew.

Miles nodded. "I'll work until the lumber arrives on the train, and then I'll go assist the men and start on the house. Though word has it, the train will arrive before dawn, so I may not even make it to my temporary shop."

As they finished eating, Miles insisted on helping clear the table, despite Beth's protests. The girls were sent to wash up and prepare for bed while Beth and Miles worked side by side in the kitchen area.

"The ladies were very generous today," Beth said as she dried a plate. "Nearly a week's worth of clothing was cut and prepared. We should have several complete outfits for each of the girls soon."

"I should find a way to thank them," Miles replied, rinsing another dish in the basin.

"Your gratitude is enough," Beth assured him. "And seeing the girls in their new dresses will be thanks enough as well."

Miles handed her the last plate, then dried his hands on a towel. "And how do I thank you, Beth? For opening your home, for caring for my daughters, for..." he gestured around the kitchen, encompassing the domesticity they'd temporarily created, "...all of this?"

Beth placed the dried plate carefully on the shelf before answering. "You don't need to thank me, Miles. Having you and the girls here has been... nice. This apartment feels alive again."

"Still," Miles persisted, his blue eyes serious, "it's a significant disruption to your life. Your routine."

"A welcome one," Beth admitted.

Something shifted in Miles's expression—a softening around his eyes, a slight parting of his lips as if words were forming that he hadn't planned to speak. The space between them seemed suddenly charged with unspoken possibility, like the air before a lightning strike. Beth felt her pulse quicken, aware of the dampness of the dish towel in her hands, the lingering scent of beef stew, the gentle tick of the clock on the mantel marking seconds that seemed mysteriously elongated. Miles took a half-step closer, close enough that she could see the flecks of gold in his irises, the day's stubble along his jaw, and the small scar above his right eyebrow she'd never noticed before.

"Beth, I—" His voice had dropped to a register that seemed to resonate directly in her chest rather than her ears.

"Papa! We're ready for our story!" Clara called.

Miles's smile turned apologetic. "Duty calls."

"Go ahead. I'll finish up here."

As Miles disappeared into the bedroom, Beth leaned against the counter, steadying herself. What had just happened? Or almost happened? The intensity of that unspoken moment lingered, making her heart beat a little faster than normal.

She pressed a hand to her cheek, finding it warm to the touch. From the bedroom came the gentle cadence of Miles's voice reading a story. The familiar words of "Jack and the Beanstalk" carried on the evening air. Clara's excited interruptions punctuated the tale, while Ellie's occasional thoughtful questions revealed a child trying to make sense of a world where giants could fall and boys could triumph.

Beth moved to the window, drawing back the curtain to gaze at the darkening street below. Lamps were being lit in windows across

Hope Springs, each golden square representing another family, another home. For years, she'd watched those lights from her solitary perch, content in her independence—or so she'd told herself. Now, with the sounds of family life filling the rooms behind her, she wondered if contentment had simply been a more comfortable word for loneliness.

The question that had been circling her mind all day returned with newfound urgency: what would happen when Miles and the girls no longer needed this temporary haven? When their home was rebuilt and their lives restored? The thought of returning to her quiet existence made something constrict painfully in her chest.

"Foolish woman," she whispered to her reflection in the glass, the words barely disturbing the air. "Guard your heart more carefully."

But even as she formed the admonition, she knew it might already be too late.

Chapter 14

The sharp crack of hammers echoed across the Donovan property as men swarmed over the blacksmith shop's emerging frame like industrious ants. Sawdust hung in the air, golden motes dancing in shafts of sunlight, while the tang of fresh-cut pine mingled with the earthy smell of turned soil and honest sweat. Beth balanced three heavy plates of cornbread in her arms, their warmth seeping through her sleeves as she navigated between bustling workers, each step calculated on the uneven ground of new beginnings.

"Watch your step there, Miss Bartlett!" Sheriff Braddock called, gesturing toward a pile of lumber scraps. "Frank's crew is moving faster than we can clear away."

Beth deftly sidestepped the obstacle. "At this rate, you'll have the whole building up before dinner."

"That's the plan," Frank responded from atop a ladder, hammer in hand. "Rails sent twice the lumber we expected. No sense wasting daylight."

Hope Springs had turned out in full force for the building effort. Nearly every able-bodied man in town worked on either the blacksmith shop or the house foundation. Women had established a cooking area beneath canvas tarps where cast-iron pots bubbled with stew and beans while children darted between workers delivering water, nails, and messages.

Eleanor appeared beside Beth, relieving her of two cornbread plates. "Josiah Miller says they'll have the forge platform ready by midday. Miles can set his anvil before sundown if all goes well."

Beth nodded, scanning the property until she located Miles working alongside Reverend Weatherly. They were setting a massive beam that would support the smith's bellows, Miles's shoulders straining beneath his sweat-dampened shirt as he guided the heavy timber into place. Something tightened in Beth's chest—a sensation both pleasant and painful. How quickly he'd become a fixture in her thoughts, in her daily rhythms. How dangerous that might prove to be, when nothing about their arrangement was permanent. She tucked the feeling away, like a letter too precious to read yet too important to discard.

"Looking for someone in particular?" Eleanor asked, her voice innocently sweet.

Beth turned her attention back to arranging food. "Just checking progress."

"Of course," Eleanor replied, not bothering to hide her smile. "The progress."

Clara's excited voice rose above the construction noise as she ran toward them, Ellie following more sedately behind. Both girls wore their new dresses, Clara's sunshine yellow and Ellie's cornflower blue, completed by Beth and the sewing circle.

"Miss Beth! Papa says our house will have a real glass window in each room!" Clara exclaimed, practically bouncing. "And Ellie's going to have a garden spot, just like you do!"

Beth bent down to Clara's level. "That sounds wonderful. Have you decided what you'll plant in your garden, Ellie?"

Ellie nodded seriously. "Flowers for Mama. And herbs like in your garden."

Beth's heart squeezed. The child's quiet determination to create something beautiful amidst their loss spoke volumes about her resilience.

"I think that's perfect," Beth said, straightening. "Now, would you girls like to help serve lemonade to the workers? They must be thirsty."

The girls eagerly took up their new responsibility, Clara announcing their "lemonading mission" loudly enough to draw chuckles from nearby workers. Beth watched them move through the crowd, offering cups with careful concentration.

"Those children have taken to you remarkably," Alice Weatherly observed, joining Beth at the food table. "Especially Ellie. She's blossoming under your attention."

Beth arranged biscuits on a platter. "They're wonderful children. They have been raised well."

Alice nodded toward where the blacksmith had paused in his work, wiping his brow while accepting lemonade from his daughters. His face broke into a wide smile at something Clara said, his laughter visible even from a distance.

"He seems lighter today," Beth commented. "More hopeful."

"There's power in community," Alice said. "And perhaps in other things as well." She patted Beth's hand before moving away to help Maggie with a heavy pot.

Throughout the morning, Beth worked alongside the other women, serving food, replenishing water barrels, and occasionally stopping to admire the rapidly progressing structures. What had been merely stone foundations and scattered lumber at sunrise now showed definite shape—the blacksmith shop's post-and-beam frame fully erected, mortise and tenon joints locked together without a single nail, the house foundation prepared for its floor joists. Men moved with the coordinated precision that came from generations of barn-raisings and community building, their knowledge passed from father to son in the practical education of frontier life.

A hot wind swept across from the open prairie beyond the town's boundary, carrying the scent of sun-baked grass and distant wildflowers. Beth paused to wipe perspiration from her forehead with her apron, watching a red-tailed hawk circle lazily overhead, riding the thermal currents in an effortless dance against the endless Nebraska sky.

Shortly before noon, Frank's voice rose above the general clamor. "Let's set that center beam! Miles, where do you want it exactly?"

Miles conferred briefly with Frank, pointing toward specific spots on the smithy frame where the heavy timber would need to be notched and secured. Several men gathered, positioning themselves beneath the massive ridge beam that would crown the structure and bear the weight of the roof.

"Ready now! All together on my count!" Frank called, his voice carrying the authority of a man who'd directed dozens of such raisings. "One... two... heave!"

The men strained in unison, muscles cording in their necks and forearms as they lifted the heavy beam skyward. Inch by laborious inch, the timber rose. A precarious moment followed when the beam wavered slightly, threatening to slip from sweaty grips. Beth held her breath, suddenly aware of how quickly celebration could turn to catastrophe.

Miles and Virgil guided the beam with sure hands and steady voices, calling directions as it reached shoulder height, then overhead. With a final coordinated push, the timber settled into the precisely cut notches, waiting to receive it, fitting home with an audible thunk of wood against wood. A spontaneous cheer erupted when it locked into place, the sound rising like a prayer of thanksgiving toward the clear Nebraska sky.

"The Highest beam is in place!" Frank announced. "That's the backbone of your new smithy, Donovan!"

Miles stood for a moment, staring at the emerging structure with an expression Beth could only describe as reverent gratitude. He removed his hat, wiping sweat from his forehead as he turned to survey the workers.

"I can't thank you all enough," he called, his deep voice carrying across the property. "Not just for today, but for everything since the storm. My family and I..." His voice caught slightly. "We're blessed to call Hope Springs home."

"Hear, hear!" Sheriff Braddock responded, which was met with approving nods and murmurs.

Beth felt a swell of pride, not just for Miles's gracious words, but for her town. This was Hope Springs at its best, neighbors supporting neighbors without hesitation.

"Food's ready!" Eleanor announced. "Come, while it's hot!"

Men set down tools and made their way to the food tables, where women were ladling stew into bowls and cutting generous slices of cornbread. Beth served Miles when he reached the front of the line.

"This is remarkable progress," she said, filling his bowl.

"Thanks to everyone here," Miles replied, his blue eyes meeting hers. "And to you."

"I'm just serving food," Beth deflected.

Miles shook his head. "You know it's far more than that."

"Papa! Jimmy says they're going to put the door on soon. Can I watch?" Clara asked.

Miles smiled down at his daughter. "Yes, sprite."

As the meal continued, Beth circulated among the workers, refilling drinks and ensuring everyone had enough food. The atmosphere was festive despite the hard work, with jokes and stories flowing freely.

***

"Miss Beth!" Ellie called, waving from beneath a large oak tree at the edge of the property. "Papa saved you some shade."

Beth made her way toward them, carrying her plate of food. Miles sat with his back against the oak's trunk, both girls flanking him. He shifted to make room as she approached.

"You should rest a moment," he said. "You've been working non-stop."

Beth settled onto the grass beside them. "Says the man who's been lifting timbers since dawn."

Miles chuckled, the sound warm and relaxed. "Different kind of work."

They ate in companionable quiet for several minutes, watching the activity across the property.

"Papa made mama a special gate with roses on it for her garden. I hope we have one like it here," Ellie said eventually, leaning against her father's arm.

"Is that so?" Beth smiled at Miles. "I didn't know you were artistic as well as practical."

A faint flush colored Miles's cheeks. "Charlotte liked roses. I worked iron roses into the gate hinges for her birthday one year."

"That must have been a beautiful gift," Beth said.

Miles nodded, his eyes taking on a distant quality. "She deserved beautiful things. She brought so much light into our lives." He glanced down at his daughters. "Still does, through these two."

Clara, apparently bored with the conversation, spotted Jimmy nearby and scampered off to play. Ellie remained, quietly arranging pebbles in a pattern beside her.

"Do you miss Iowa?" Beth asked, noticing how Ellie's hands stilled at the question, her small fingers hovering over her arranged pebbles like a pianist paused mid-measure.

Miles considered this, his calloused thumb absently tracing the rim of his tin cup. "Not the place so much," he said finally. "The soil was good, the neighbors were kind. But there were memories there that sometimes felt too heavy to carry, too precious to leave behind."

"Good ones, though," Beth said, understanding the weight of cherished recollections that both comfort and haunt.

"Yes." Miles straightened slightly, his voice lowering to match the rustling leaves overhead. "The hardest part of leaving was feeling like I was abandoning those memories. Charlotte's favorite places. The church where we married, where she'd squeeze my hand during prayers." His eyes took on a faraway look. "The meadow where we picnicked, where Clara took her first steps."

Beth nodded, twisting the fabric of her skirt between her fingers. "As if leaving might mean forgetting. As if distance could erase what the heart has written."

Miles looked at her with surprise, the shadow of the oak leaves dappling his face. "Exactly that. How did you know?"

"Because I've stood at that same crossroads," Beth admitted softly. "Afraid to move forward, terrified of leaving the past behind."

"The memories came with us, though. They're inside, not tied to places."

"That's what Reverend Weatherly told me after my parents died," Beth admitted, absently brushing a fallen leaf from her skirt. "When I was afraid to change anything in their apartment because it felt like erasing them somehow."

"Is that why you kept it untouched?"

Beth nodded, surprising herself with her candor. "Partly. And partly because facing it alone seemed too difficult."

"Not being alone makes many things easier," Miles said quietly.

The silence stretched, comfortable yet charged with possibility, like the moment before a seed decides to push through resistant soil toward sunlight.

"Papa?" Ellie's small voice broke the moment. "Is Miss Beth sad about her mama and papa like we're sad about Mama?"

Miles placed his hand gently on Ellie's shoulder. "Everyone's sadness is their own, sunshine. But yes, I think Miss Beth understands our sadness very well."

Ellie nodded, absorbing this concept. She picked up one of her carefully arranged pebbles, a smooth white stone, and held it out to Beth. "For remembering," she said simply.

Beth accepted the small stone, emotion tightening her throat. "Thank you, Ellie. I'll keep it safe."

A call from the smithy drew their attention. "Miles! We're ready for your expertise on the door frame!"

Miles rose to his feet, brushing grass from his trousers. "Duty calls." He offered his hand to Beth, helping her up. The brief contact sent warmth spreading up her arm.

They walked together toward the smithy, where several men were positioning the heavy door frame. Clara rejoined them, bouncing with excitement.

"Papa's door is SO big!" she announced. "Jimmy says it's because Papa is a giant."

Miles laughed, ruffling Clara's hair. "Not quite a giant sprite. The door needs to be large enough to move big pieces of iron and equipment through."

For the next hour, Beth watched as Miles directed the placement of his smithy door, explaining to his daughters the importance of proper alignment and sturdy hinges. His knowledge and confidence were evident in every instruction, every movement.

"He's in his element now," Reverend Weatherly commented, pausing beside Beth. "A man needs purpose. Miles finds his in providing for his daughters and practicing his craft."

"He's very skilled," Beth agreed.

"In many ways," the reverend said meaningfully. "Not least in recognizing what, and who, truly matters." With a gentle smile, he moved away to help with the next task.

By mid-afternoon, the smithy structure was nearly complete, lacking only roofing and interior fittings. The house had progressed remarkably as well, with wall frames ready to be raised. The atmosphere remained energetic despite hours of labor.

Beth was arranging a plate of gingerbread when Eleanor approached, fanning herself with her handkerchief.

"I believe we've earned a celebration when this is finished," Eleanor declared. "Perhaps a dinner at the church."

"That's a wonderful idea," Beth agreed. "The Donovans should be properly welcomed as permanent residents of Hope Springs."

"Indeed." Eleanor's eyes twinkled with gentle mischief. "Though some welcome them more than others."

Beth felt heat rise to her cheeks. "Eleanor!"

"Oh, don't look so scandalized, dear. It's obvious to anyone with eyes that you and Miles Donovan share something special." Eleanor patted Beth's arm. "And about time, too. You've kept your heart locked away long enough."

Beth opened her mouth to protest when something—a shift in the air, a premonition—made her glance toward the road. Later, she would wonder if some hidden part of her soul had known, had felt the approaching disruption before her eyes confirmed it.

Chapter 15

Beth turned toward the road where a wagon was approaching, dust rising behind it in a golden plume against the afternoon sky. Something in the set of the driver's shoulders, the way he handled the reins—familiar as a half-remembered dream—sent a jolt of recognition through her before her mind could name what her body already knew.

The wagon drew closer, and Beth's heart stuttered in her chest, then hammered painfully against her ribs. Her hands went numb, the plate of gingerbread tilting precariously in her suddenly clumsy grip.

Thomas.

Thomas Aldridge, whose face she had once known better than her own. Thomas, who had disappeared without explanation two years ago on what should have been their wedding day, leaving her standing alone in her mother's altered wedding dress, clutching wilting wildflowers while whispers rippled through the waiting congregation. Thomas, whose abandonment had shattered her trust and locked her heart away behind walls she'd believed impenetrable—until Miles.

The wagon stopped at the edge of the property. Thomas set the brake and jumped down with the same fluid grace she remembered. His eyes locked on Beth as if the crowded construction site contained no one else. The surrounding sounds muffled, as though she'd suddenly been submerged underwater.

"Who's that man looking at you, Miss Beth?" Clara asked, appearing at Beth's side, her yellow dress bright as a canary against the dusty ground.

Beth couldn't answer. Her throat had closed, her pulse thundering in her ears, as Thomas began walking toward her with purposeful strides that ate up the distance between them. A distance she had once thought would remain forever.

Miles materialized beside them, wiping sawdust from his hands with a rag. His casual movements stilled when he registered Beth's expression, his body instantly alert like a hound catching an unfamiliar scent. "Beth? What's wrong?"

His eyes tracked to where she stared, narrowing slightly as they assessed the approaching stranger. Almost imperceptibly, Miles shifted his stance, angling his broad shoulders between Beth and the newcomer, one hand dropping to rest protectively on Clara's shoulder. The gesture wasn't possessive—it was instinctive, the movement of a man accustomed to standing between his family and potential harm.

Thomas was close enough now that Beth could see the details of his face, older, more weathered than she remembered, but unmistakably him. His eyes never left hers as he approached.

"Beth!" he called, his voice sending a jolt through her like an electric current.

Miles tensed beside her, his hand moving protectively toward his daughters. "Beth? Who is this?"

Before she could respond, Thomas reached them, stopping a few feet away. His eyes darted from Beth to Miles and the girls, then back to Beth, confusion evident in his expression.

"Beth," he said again, softer. "I've been searching everywhere for you."

Beth finally found her voice, though it emerged as barely more than a whisper.

"Thomas."

The name hung in the air between them, loaded with two years of questions, pain, and unanswered prayers.

Miles's body grew rigid beside her.

Thomas took another step forward, his hand half-raised as if to touch her, before dropping back to his side.

"I need to speak with you," Thomas said urgently, his voice the same timber and cadence that had once promised her forever. "It's important. More important than you know."

Beth felt the ground shift beneath her, two years of carefully constructed defenses threatening to crumble like drought-parched soil. The noise of the construction site receded, the busy workers fading into the background until all she could see was Thomas's face. All she could feel was Miles's solid presence beside her, warm and real against the ghost from her past.

Two men.

Past and present.

The life she had expected and the one that now beckoned unexpectedly from a different direction. Her fingertips tingled with a peculiar numbness.

"I think you should leave," Miles said, his voice low and controlled, but with an undercurrent that reminded Beth he was a man who shaped unyielding metal with his bare hands.

Thomas's jaw tightened, a muscle flickering beneath his tanned skin. "This doesn't concern you." The words came clipped, dismissive.

"It concerns Beth," Miles countered, not raising his voice but somehow filling more space than before. "And Beth seems uncomfortable with your appearance." He didn't touch her, didn't claim her with words or gestures, but his stance conveyed a clear message: she wasn't alone.

"Uncomfortable?" Thomas challenged, his eyes moving between them with growing comprehension, reading the invisible threads connecting Beth to this stranger. "I see I've interrupted something."

Ellie pressed against Beth's skirts, sensing the tension crackling in the air like the static before a prairie storm. Clara stared openly at the stranger, unusually quiet, her small hand finding Beth's. Beth squeezed it gently, the contact anchoring her when she felt in danger of floating away on a tide of shock.

"Why are you here, Thomas?" Beth finally managed, her voice steadier than she felt.

"To explain." Thomas's expression softened. "To tell you the truth about why I left. It wasn't my choice, Beth. It was never my choice."

The words she had longed to hear for two years now landed with devastating impact. If not his choice, then whose? And why now, when she had finally begun to heal, to hope, and to open herself to the possibility of loving again?

Thomas took another step closer. "Please, just give me a chance to explain everything."

Beth felt Miles shift beside her, the tension radiating from him in waves. She glanced up, meeting his eyes briefly. What she saw there, concern, confusion, and something deeper, something more vulnerable, and it nearly undid her.

"I think," Beth said carefully, looking back at Thomas, "that we should speak privately."

Thomas nodded, relief evident in his posture.

"Beth," Miles began, his voice low.

"It's alright," she assured him, though she felt anything but assured herself. "I need to hear what he has to say."

Thomas looked pointedly at Miles. "My uncle's home? We could talk there."

"No," Beth replied firmly. "The church. It's neutral ground."

As Beth stepped toward Thomas, Clara called out, "Miss Beth! Are you coming back for supper?"

The innocent question hung in the air, highlighting the domestic rhythm that had developed between Beth and the Donovan's. Thomas's eyebrows rose slightly.

"Yes, Clara," Beth replied, forcing a smile that didn't reach her eyes. "I'll be back."

She didn't look at Miles as she spoke, couldn't bear to see what might be written on his face—concern, confusion, or worst of all, the first shadows of betrayal. The promise to return felt simultaneously like truth and deception as she walked away with Thomas, her past literally taking her by the arm to lead her away from her tentative future.

With each step, Beth felt the weight of Miles's gaze following her, like a physical touch across her shoulders. The construction sounds faded behind her, replaced by the thudding of her heart and Thomas's voice beginning, "Beth, you have no idea what I've been through to find you..."

Her fingers closed around Ellie's small white stone in her pocket, its smooth surface warming against her skin as she walked toward answers she'd once desperately craved and now knew were too late.

Chapter 16

Miles stood frozen, watching Beth walk away with the stranger. The half-raised wall frames of his new smithy cast long shadows across the turned earth, like the skeletal ribs of some great beast. A heaviness settled in his chest that had nothing to do with the day's labor, the weight of it making the leather suspenders dig into his shoulders. The girls pressed against his legs, Clara tugging at his canvas work pants with questions he barely registered over the distant clang of hammer on nail. The mournful call of a prairie dove from the eaves of a nearby building.

"Papa? Who was that man? Why did Miss Beth look scared?"

He couldn't answer. How could he explain what he himself didn't understand? The comfortable rhythm they'd established over these past days seemed suddenly fragile, threatened by this man's unexpected arrival.

"Miles." Harriet appeared at his side, her usually cheerful face somber. She touched his arm lightly. "Come away from the crowd. We should talk."

He nodded mutely. "Ellie, take your sister to help Mrs. Hanley with the lemonade," he instructed, his voice sounding distant even to his own ears.

"But Papa—" Clara began.

"Please, Clara." Something in his tone must have conveyed the seriousness of the moment, for Clara simply nodded, allowing Ellie to lead her toward the refreshment table.

Harriet guided him toward the shade of the large oak tree where he, Beth, and the girls had shared lunch just an hour before.

"You're wondering who that was," Harriet said once they were out of earshot of the workers, who had tactfully resumed their tasks despite the obvious drama unfolding.

"Yes." Miles wiped a hand across his brow, leaving a smudge of sawdust. "Beth called him Thomas."

"Thomas Aldridge," Harriet confirmed, settling onto a tree stump. "Beth's former fiancé."

The words hit Miles with such force that he actually took a half-step backward, his hand instinctively reaching for the oak tree's trunk to steady himself. "Fiancé?" The word came out hoarse, as if his throat had suddenly constricted. The taste of sawdust seemed bitter now as he swallowed hard.

Harriet nodded grimly. "They were engaged to be married two years ago. The wedding was planned, the church decorated, guests assembled..." She paused, her expression darkening. "Thomas never arrived. No note, no explanation. He simply disappeared."

Miles felt his jaw tighten. "He abandoned her at the altar?"

"Yes." Harriet's fingers worried the edge of her apron. "It nearly destroyed Beth. One day planning her future with the man she loved, the next facing a church full of pitying faces and no explanation whatsoever."

"God above," Miles muttered, staring in the direction Beth had gone. Understanding washed over him, her careful reserve, her hesitation to trust, her reluctance to acknowledge what had been growing between them. "Did anyone know why?"

"No one," Harriet replied. "Thomas had seemed completely devoted. Their courtship lasted nearly two years. Everyone in town expected them to marry, have children, and build a life together." She sighed. "His uncle, Elijah Aldridge, claimed Thomas had second thoughts and couldn't face Beth, so he simply left. Elijah seemed almost pleased about it, which struck many of us as odd."

Miles paced a few steps, processing this information. "And now he's back. After two years of silence. He seemed desperate to explain himself."

Harriet stood, brushing dust from her skirt. "Beth deserves answers, certainly. But I'm worried about her. The wound of Thomas's abandonment ran deep, Miles. Deeper than most realize. It came before her parents fell ill, and I sometimes think facing both losses in such quick succession is what caused her to..." She trailed off, searching for the right words.

"To wall herself away," Miles finished softly.

"Yes." Harriet studied his face. "You understand her better than I expected."

Miles looked down, suddenly aware of how much he had come to care for Beth in their short acquaintance. How natural it had felt to have her in his life, in his daughters' lives. The thought of her pain angered him, but something else nagged at his mind.

"This uncle—Elijah Aldridge. You said he seemed pleased about Thomas's disappearance?"

Harriet's expression hardened. "Elijah Aldridge is not well-liked in Hope Springs, despite his wealth. Or perhaps because of how he acquired it. He owns considerable land south of town and has a reputation for questionable business dealings."

"What's his connection to Thomas?"

"Thomas was orphaned young and raised by Elijah. They never seemed particularly close, but Thomas worked for his uncle's various enterprises." Harriet sighed. "After Thomas disappeared, Elijah expanded his businesses significantly. Some whispered he'd used Thomas's inheritance to do so, but nothing was ever proven."

Miles processed this information, pieces falling into place. "And Beth never heard from Thomas at all during these two years?"

"Not a word." Harriet's gaze drifted toward town. "It nearly broke her, Miles. Not just the abandonment, but the complete absence of explanation. She blamed herself for months, wondering what she'd done wrong, what flaw he'd discovered that made him flee."

Anger flared hot in Miles's chest.

"Rejection without reason leaves terrible wounds, Miles. Especially for someone like Beth, who cares deeply for everyone," Harriet said.

Miles glanced back toward the construction site, where his daughters were now helping distribute cookies to the workers. Ellie looked up, her solemn eyes finding his across the distance. Even from here, he could see her concern.

"What will you do?" Harriet asked quietly.

Miles turned back to her. "Do?"

"About Beth. About...whatever has been growing between you."

Miles felt heat rise to his face. Was it so obvious to everyone? "I don't know that there's anything to do. Beth needs to resolve her past. I have no right to interfere."

Harriet studied him with shrewd eyes. "That's very noble, Miles Donovan. And very foolish."

"Pardon?"

"Beth cares for you," Harriet stated bluntly. "More than she's cared for anyone since Thomas left. I've watched her walls crumble a little more each day you and your daughters have been in her life." She stepped closer, her voice lowering. "But Beth's been hurt terribly by a man she trusted completely. She won't easily trust those feelings again, even if Thomas's explanation proves legitimate."

Miles ran a hand through his hair, discomfort and uncertainty warring within him. "This isn't my place, Harriet. Beth and I... we've been thrown together by circumstance. By the tornado. Her kindness in taking us in doesn't mean—"

"Oh, for heaven's sake," Harriet interrupted, exasperation clear in her tone. "Are all men this blind? It's not about the tornado or the living arrangements or her kindness. It's about the way she looks at you when she thinks no one notices. The way she smiles more in your presence than she has in a very long time. The way you and your daughters have brought light back to her eyes."

Miles stared at her, speechless.

"And it's about the way you look at her," Harriet continued, undeterred. "Like she's the sunrise after a long, dark night."

He couldn't deny it. Beth Bartlett had become essential to him in ways he hadn't fully acknowledged, even to himself. Her quiet strength, her gentle way with his daughters, her unwavering faith despite her losses—all had worked their way into his heart.

"I didn't expect this," he admitted quietly. "After Charlotte... I never thought I'd feel this way again."

Harriet's expression softened. "The heart doesn't always warn us before it decides to heal, Miles."

Clara came running over. "Papa! Mr. Hanley says they're going to put up the first wall of our house now! Come watch!"

Miles forced a smile, pushing his troubled thoughts aside for his daughter's sake. The irony wasn't lost on him—the walls of his new home rising just as the fragile foundations of his hopes with Beth threatened to crumble. Charlotte's face flashed in his memory, her kind eyes seeming to urge him forward, to trust again despite the risk.

"Of course, sprite. Let's go see."

As Clara tugged him back toward the construction site, he glanced once more in the direction of the church where Beth had gone with Thomas. Questions swirled in his mind, but one certainty emerged: whatever explanation Thomas offered, whatever history they shared, Miles would respect Beth's choice. Even if that choice broke his newly healing heart.

Allowing himself this one moment of weakness, Miles silently prayed. Not for any specific outcome, but for Beth to find the peace she deserved—and for the strength to accept whatever that meant for him.

Chapter 17

The air inside the church hung heavy. The wood cross on the altar catching the colored light that filtered through the simple stained-glass windows. The hard oak pew creaked as Beth perched on its edge, her hands clasped so tightly in her lap that her knuckles showed white against her skin. Thomas's boots made hollow sounds against the plank floor as he paced before her, each footfall echoing in the empty sanctuary like the ticking of some relentless clock.

"I don't know where to begin," he said, running a hand through his sandy hair, a gesture so achingly familiar it made Beth's chest hurt.

"The beginning would be customary," she replied, striving for composure when her insides felt like churning water. "Why did you leave, Thomas? Without a word?"

He stopped pacing and faced her. "I never wanted to leave you, Beth. You must believe that."

"Must I?" The words came out sharper than she intended. Two years of unanswered questions hardened her voice. "You disappeared. No explanation. No goodbye. Just...gone."

Thomas moved to sit beside her, then seemed to think better of it, settling instead in the pew across the aisle. "I was forced to leave."

"Forced?" Beth's eyebrows rose. "By whom?" The skepticism in her voice was unmistakable.

"My uncle." Thomas's face darkened, his fingers curling into fists before deliberately relaxing. "Elijah orchestrated everything." He leaned forward, eyes earnest. "He came to me the night before our wedding with fabricated documents showing the business was failing. He claimed he'd mortgaged everything, including the family property, to cover debts I knew nothing about. He said if I married you, we'd be destitute within months."

Beth noted how his voice changed when speaking of finances—the same urgent tone he'd used when discussing business opportunities during their courtship. Some things, it seemed, hadn't changed.

Beth stared at him in disbelief. "And you believed him? Without question?"

"He had papers, Beth. Banknotes with signatures—forged, I now know. Documents showing massive losses." Thomas leaned forward, his eyes pleading. "He told me he'd arranged passage for me on the midnight train to Denver, where a business associate would offer me work to pay off the debts. He said once I'd earned enough, I could return to you without shame."

"And you couldn't have told me this before leaving?" Beth's voice trembled with hurt. "You couldn't have trusted me enough to face it together?"

Thomas looked away. "He threatened you, Beth. You and your family." He swallowed hard. "I couldn't risk that. Not when I believed I could fix everything and return."

Beth closed her eyes, memories washing over her. The wedding dress hanging in her bedroom, the flowers arranged in the church, her father's proud smile as he prepared to walk her down the aisle. All turned to ash.

"What happened in Denver?" she asked finally, opening her eyes.

"There was no business associate," Thomas replied bitterly. "Just a foreman at a mining operation who'd been paid to keep me there with the promise of good wages. Every letter I tried to send back to Hope Springs was intercepted. When I finally saved enough to return, I learned Elijah had spread the story that I'd fled from commitment, that I'd abandoned you willingly."

"Why would he do this?" Beth asked, struggling to comprehend. "What could he possibly gain?"

"Control," Thomas said simply. "And my inheritance. My parents left a substantial sum in trust that I could only access after marriage or my thirtieth birthday. By preventing our wedding and keeping me away, Elijah maintained control of those funds as my guardian. He's been using that money to expand his holdings these past two years."

Beth's mind reeled. The story seemed incredible, yet it explained so much. Elijah's lack of concern after Thomas vanished, his expansion of business interests, his subtle hints that Thomas had found Beth lacking somehow.

"How did you discover all this?" she asked.

"Martin Clarke, my parents' former solicitor, tracked me down in Denver." Thomas's expression grew earnest. "He'd returned from back East and was shocked to learn I'd abandoned you and disappeared. He knew something was wrong—he'd helped draft my parents' will and knew the terms of my inheritance. Once he explained everything, I realized how thoroughly Elijah had deceived me."

Beth stood suddenly, needing movement to process these revelations. She paced down the aisle, past the altar where they were to have exchanged vows.

"Two years, Thomas," she said quietly. "Two years of wondering what I'd done wrong. Of questioning every moment of our courtship, looking for signs I'd missed." She turned to face him. "Two years of rebuilding my life."

"I know." He remained seated, giving her space. "I can't imagine what you've endured. Your parents passing, and the store to manage alone…" He hesitated. "I should have found a way back sooner. Should have questioned Elijah's story from the beginning."

"Yes," Beth agreed, unable to soften the truth. "You should have trusted me enough to tell me what was happening."

Silence stretched between them, filled with the weight of time and choices and consequences.

"I want to make this right, Beth," Thomas finally said. "I've confronted Elijah. With Mr. Clarke's help, I'm reclaiming my inheritance, filing legal charges for the fraud. But more importantly…" He stood, taking a step toward her. "I want to know if there's any chance for us. If you could find it in your heart to forgive me."

Beth felt suddenly light-headed. This moment—Thomas returning, explaining, asking forgiveness—had featured in her dreams for months after he disappeared. But now, facing the reality, she found her feelings complicated by the life she'd built in his absence.

And by Miles Donovan.

The thought of Miles sent an unexpected pang through her chest. His steady presence, his gentle strength, his daughters who had somehow worked their way into her carefully guarded heart. What had been growing between them these past weeks was new, undefined, yet undeniably real. She could almost smell the comforting scent of wood smoke and iron that clung to his clothes, feel the steady assurance of his calloused hand helping her down from a wagon. The memory of Clara's laughter and Ellie's solemn eyes seemed more vivid than the man sitting across from her now—a man who had once been her entire future.

"What you've told me... it changes everything I believed about why you left. But it doesn't erase these past two years."

Thomas nodded, disappointment clear in his expression, though he tried to hide it. "I understand. I have no right to expect immediate forgiveness."

Beth touched the small white stone in her pocket, the one Ellie had given her "for remembering." The simple gift from a child who understood loss had somehow become an anchor in this turbulent moment.

"I should go," she said.

"Of course." Thomas moved aside, allowing her clear passage to the church door. "May I call on you tomorrow? Perhaps after church? We have much more to discuss."

"No."

As she stepped out of the church into the late afternoon sunlight, Beth felt disoriented, as if she'd stepped into someone else's life. Thomas had returned with an explanation that absolved him of the callous abandonment she'd believed in for two years. Yet, the hurt remained, the hurt of his lack of trust, of opportunities lost, of a future diverted.

And now there was Miles, whose quiet strength had begun to heal parts of her she'd thought permanently broken. Miles and his daughters, who needed her in ways Thomas never had.

Beth closed her eyes briefly against the sun, a prayer rising from her confused heart. *Lord, show me the way forward. Help me see Your plan in all of this.*

With measured steps, she began the walk back to the Donovan property, uncertain of what awaited but knowing she couldn't delay facing it.

Chapter 18

The sun hung low in the western sky by the time Beth returned to the building site, the golden light softened by wisps of cloud that had gathered on the horizon. A cooling breeze had begun to stir, carrying the scent of sun-warmed grass and the promise of evening dew. The day's work was winding down, with a good deal of townspeople already departed and others gathering tools and supplies.

Beth hesitated at the edge of the property, her fingertips tingling with nervous energy. A dull ache had settled behind her temples, the tension of the day manifesting physically. She scanned the remaining workers for Miles, her breath catching slightly when she spotted him by the smithy, deep in conversation with Frank and Sheriff Braddock. His shoulders were set in a tense line she hadn't noticed earlier, his stance somehow both guarded and vulnerable.

Clara spotted her first, breaking away from where she'd been helping Eleanor fold table linens. "Miss Beth! You came back!" she called, running across the yard with boundless energy despite the long day.

Beth knelt to receive the child's enthusiastic embrace, Clara's small arms wrapping tightly around her neck. "Of course I came back. I promised I would."

"Papa was worried," Clara informed her matter-of-factly, pulling back to examine Beth's face. "He kept looking at the road."

Beth glanced toward Miles again and found him watching them, his expression unreadable from this distance.

Ellie approached more slowly, her blue eyes serious. "Are you alright, Miss Beth? You look sad."

Beth managed a smile for the perceptive child. "I have much on my mind, but I'm fine, Ellie."

"Who was that man?" Clara asked, bouncing slightly in her curiosity. "Is he your friend? He looked at you funny."

"Clara," Ellie scolded quietly. "Papa said not to ask about the man."

Beth sighed, realizing she couldn't avoid explanations. "He is someone I knew a long time ago. He needed to talk to me about something important."

"Important like when Papa talks to Reverend Weatherly?" Clara pressed, undeterred by her sister's warning.

"Something like that," Beth replied, rising to her feet as Miles approached.

He moved carefully, as if uncertain of his welcome. "You're back," he said simply.

"Yes." Beth wished suddenly they were alone, without curious eyes, watching their every move. "I said I would be."

Miles nodded, his blue eyes studying her face with concern. "The girls and I were about to head back to town. Most of the work is done for today."

"I can see that." Beth glanced around at the remarkable progress. "The buildings are really taking shape."

"Yes. Frank estimates another three days of work before they're habitable. Basic, but sound." Miles hesitated, then added quietly, "You don't have to explain anything now, Beth. It's been a long day."

His consideration nearly undid her. "Thank you," she managed, grateful for the reprieve.

Clara tugged at Miles's pants leg. "Can Miss Beth make us pancakes for supper? Please, Papa?"

The simple request broke some of the tension, and Miles's mouth curved slightly. "I think Miss Beth might be tired, little one. We can make do with—"

"I'd be happy to make pancakes," Beth interrupted, suddenly desperate normalcy. "If you'd like that."

Miles's eyes met hers, something grateful in his gaze. "Are you certain?"

"Yes." Beth reached out to take Ellie's offered hand, drawing comfort from the child's trusting gesture. "Let's go home."

Home. The word slipped out unintentionally, yet felt right despite its complications. The apartment above her store had truly become home these past days—not because of the physical space, but because of the people who filled it with life and laughter and care.

They walked back to town mostly in silence, Clara's occasional chatter the only respite from their thoughts. Beth was hyperaware of Miles beside her, the careful distance he maintained, and the way he glanced at her when he thought she wouldn't notice.

As they entered the apartment, the familiar domestic rhythm resumed despite the underlying tension. Beth set about gathering ingredients for pancakes while Miles helped the girls wash up. Clara's excited voice drifted from the washroom, recounting the day's construction progress in elaborate detail to anyone who would listen.

"And then Mr. Hanley let me hammer a nail! A real one, in the wall of our house! Papa said I did it perfect."

Beth smiled despite her troubled thoughts, measuring flour into a bowl with practiced movements. She heard Miles's patient responses, his deep voice a comforting counterpoint to Clara's exuberance and Ellie's quieter additions.

She was stirring batter when he entered the kitchen area, sleeves rolled up after washing.

"Can I help?" he asked, keeping his voice low.

Beth nodded toward the cupboard. "Plates and cups, if you would."

They moved around each other in the small space, the domesticity of the scene both soothing and painful given the uncertain future. Beth noticed Miles watching her as she poured the batter onto the heated griddle, concern evident in his gaze.

"I'm alright," she assured him.

"Are you?" He set plates on the table, his movements deliberate. "You don't have to pretend for my sake, Beth."

The simple statement, so characteristic of his straightforward compassion, made her throat tighten. "I know," she managed. "I'm still sorting through everything." She poured another circle of batter onto the griddle, watching it spread and bubble.

Miles nodded, understanding in his eyes. "Whenever you're ready to talk, I'm here to listen. No expectations."

The girls bounded into the room, Clara delighted by the promise of pancakes for dinner, and Ellie arranged the silverware on the table with careful precision. Within moments, they were settled around the table.

Miles said grace, his deep voice steady as he thanked God for the day's blessings, for shelter, for community, and for safety.

As they ate, Clara dominated the conversation with tales of the day's construction adventures, while Ellie quietly observed the adults with knowing eyes beyond her years.

"Miss Beth, can we read a story tonight?" Clara asked as they finished eating, her expression hopeful. "The one about the bear family?"

"Of course," Beth replied, grateful for the simple request. "After you help clear the table."

The evening routine continued, dishes washed, floors swept, and bedtime preparations made with practiced efficiency. Beth read to the girls while Miles sat nearby in the rocking chair, his presence a steadying force despite everything left unspoken between them.

When the girls finally drifted to sleep, Beth quietly closed the book and rose from the edge of their bed. Miles followed her from the bedroom, careful to leave the door slightly ajar, as was their custom.

Beth walked to the window, looking out at the darkened street below. Stars dotted the night sky, unchanged despite the earth-shifting revelations of the day.

"Harriet told me about Thomas," Miles said, his voice soft but clear.

Beth nodded without turning. "I thought she might have. She's protective of me."

"She cares about you. As do many people in this town." Miles remained across the room, giving her space. "She told me he left without explanation."

"Yes." Beth turned to face him, needing to see his expression. The lamplight cast half his face in shadow, making him seem both familiar and unknowable at once.

Miles's face remained carefully neutral, though a muscle worked in his jaw. "And now?"

Beth sighed, moving to sit in the armchair by the hearth. Her fingers absently traced the worn pattern in the upholstery—circles within circles, endless loops with no beginning or end. "Thomas claims he was manipulated by his uncle. Forced to leave under false pretenses." She briefly outlined Thomas's explanation, watching Miles's expression grow increasingly troubled.

"Do you believe him?"

"I don't know." Beth twisted her hands in her lap.

Miles nodded, understanding in his eyes. "It's a difficult position you're in."

"Two years lost," Beth said. "Two years of pain that could have been avoided with more trust and more courage."

"What will you do?" Miles asked, echoing Harriet's earlier question to him.

Beth looked up, meeting his steady gaze. "Thomas wants... he hopes..." She couldn't bring herself to say the words.

"He wants to resume your engagement," Miles supplied, his voice carefully neutral. "To pick up where you left off."

"Yes." Beth's voice wavered slightly. "And two years ago, that's all I wanted. To understand why he left, to have him return, to continue the life we'd planned."

"And now?" The question hung in the air between them, loaded with implications neither had openly acknowledged.

Beth stood, needing movement. "Now everything is different. I'm different. My life is different." She hesitated, then added softly, "You and the girls are here."

Miles's breath caught audibly. "Beth—"

"I don't expect anything," she hurried to add. "These past days, having you all here, it's been... wonderful. For all of us, I think. But

I know it's temporary. I know you'll soon have your own home again, and your own life to rebuild."

"Is that what you think this is?" Miles asked, taking a step toward her. "Just temporary convenience? A shelter during a storm?" His voice remained soft, but she heard the hurt beneath the carefully measured words.

Beth looked away, suddenly vulnerable. Her fingers twisted a loose thread on her sleeve. "Isn't it? You never planned to come here, to have your life intertwined with mine. It was circumstance, nothing more."

"Circumstance may have brought us together," Miles said quietly, "but what's grown between us is something else entirely." He paused, then added, "God's plans often look like accidents to those not paying attention."

Her heart beat faster at his words, at the gentle certainty in his tone. "Miles..."

"I'm not asking for promises, Beth. Not now, with everything unsettled." He moved closer. "But I need you to know that what I feel for you... what my daughters feel for you... it isn't temporary. It isn't convenient. It's real."

Beth's breath caught in her throat.

"Take the time you need," Miles said, though she could see the effort it cost him in the tightness around his eyes, the careful control of his breathing. "Sort through your past with Thomas. Understand what happened, find the closure you deserve." He hesitated, then added, "Whatever you decide, Beth, know that I want your happiness above all else. Even if that happiness lies in a direction I might wish were different."

Something broke loose inside Beth's chest. Tears welled in her eyes before she could stop them, one escaping to trace a warm path down her cheek. She turned slightly away, fingers pressed against her lips.

That this man—who had held his dying wife, who had traveled hundreds of miles with grieving children to start anew—could stand before her offering freedom instead of demands, understanding instead of ultimatums, left her breathless.

"You should go and get some rest," he said gently. "Tomorrow will bring its own challenges."

Chapter 19

Beth paced the floorboards of her little bedroom. Moonlight painted silver rectangles on the wooden floor through her bedroom window, casting the familiar furniture into ghostly silhouettes.

She paused at the window, staring down at the darkened street. Hope Springs slept peacefully while her mind churned with turbulent thoughts. Thomas's unexpected return had ripped open wounds she'd thought long scarred over, leaving her raw and exposed.

"He was forced to leave," she whispered to herself, testing the words in the darkness. "He was lied to, and yet he abandoned me willingly without every speaking to me about the situation his uncle presented to him."

The explanation should have brought relief, vindication of her initial trust in Thomas. For months after his disappearance, she'd agonized over what she might have done wrong, what flaw he might have discovered that sent him fleeing. Now she knew it hadn't been her fault at all.

Beth turned from the window, memories of their courtship filtering through her consciousness. Thomas bringing wildflowers to the store every Thursday afternoon. His earnest proposal. Planning their modest wedding, his steady reassurances when she fretted over details.

She'd imagined their wedding day countless times, standing before Reverend Weatherly, exchanging vows, beginning their life together in the small house Thomas had been preparing. The image that had once brought aching pain now seemed oddly muted, like viewing a daguerreotype of strangers rather than her own shattered dreams.

Beth sank into the chair by her bed, fingers idly tracing the pattern of the quilt her mother had made. Why didn't these memories evoke stronger emotions now? Shouldn't Thomas's explanation have rekindled all those old feelings?

Instead, her thoughts kept returning to Miles, his quiet strength, and his gentleness. The way his laugh transformed his solemn face when Clara said something particularly outlandish.

Her feelings for Miles weren't abstract memories or faded hopes. They were vivid, present, and undeniably real. The warmth that spread through her when he entered a room. The way her heart quickened when his fingers accidentally brushed hers. The profound sense of rightness she felt watching him with his daughters.

"I never felt this way with Thomas," she said. "Not once in two years of courtship."

Her feelings for Thomas had been comfortable affection, a fondness cultivated through shared church socials and casual conversations. Fitting together like adjacent puzzle pieces, not because they were made for each other, but because they seemed the logical match in a small frontier town.

With Miles, something elemental shifted inside her. Something deeper and more profound than she'd experienced before. Not the safe, expected match of compatible personalities, but something that resonated in her very core. It was like returning to a home she hadn't realized she'd been homesick for—familiar and yet entirely new.

Beth pressed her hands to her face. Had her feelings for Thomas ever been this intense? This clarifying? She couldn't remember experiencing this fierce protectiveness, this overwhelming tenderness, this bone-deep certainty with him.

And then there was trust.

Thomas hadn't trusted her enough to tell her about his uncle's threats. He'd made the decision alone, believing she was unable to handle the truth or participate in finding a solution. Even with his explanation, that fundamental fact remained unchanged.

Miles, by contrast, had trusted her with his most precious treasures, his daughters. He'd allowed her to witness his vulnerability after the tornado destroyed their home. He'd been honest about his grief for Charlotte, transparent about his struggles as a single father.

Trust.

Such a simple word for something so foundational.

Beth ran her fingers along the edge of her desk, feeling the worn smoothness of wood that had belonged to her father. He had always told her that trust was like the cornerstone of a building—once laid properly, everything else could be built upon it, but if it was flawed or missing, even the grandest structure would eventually crumble. Thomas had removed that cornerstone without warning, and no explanation, however sincere, could restore the foundation to its original integrity. With Miles, the cornerstone had been placed from their first interaction—solid, honest, and true.

She picked up the white pebble Ellie had given her "for remembering" and rolled it between her fingers as clarity began to solidify in her mind.

She took out a sheet of paper and dipped her pen in ink, needing to organize her tangled thoughts. At the top, she wrote "Thomas" and below it, "Miles."

Under Thomas's name, she hesitated, then wrote: "History. Familiarity. Unresolved past."

Under Miles's name, her pen moved with greater certainty: "Present. Future. Trust. Home."

The last word caught her by surprise. Home. Not the physical structure Miles and the townspeople were building, but the feeling his presence created. Security. Belonging. Acceptance. The very things she'd been missing since her parents' deaths.

With sudden clarity, Beth understood that her heart had already made its choice, perhaps from the moment Miles and his daughters had entered her life. Thomas represented her past, a past that needed resolution and forgiveness, but not revival.

Miles, with his quiet strength and gentle heart, had awakened possibilities she'd never dared imagine.

She blew out the lamp and returned to the window. The moon had traveled its nightly path, soon to give way to dawn. She would have to face Thomas at some point and would need to speak difficult truths. The prospect no longer filled her with dread, but with a sense of necessary closure.

The floorboard outside her room creaked softly—barely perceptible, but enough to alert her to another's wakefulness. She wasn't the only one finding sleep elusive tonight. Then came a soft knock, hesitant and considerate.

"Beth?" Miles's concerned voice came through the door, barely above a whisper. "I heard movement. Are you alright?"

"I'm fine," she called. "I'm having a hard time sleeping tonight."

"I wasn't sleeping well either. Would you like some tea? I put the kettle on," he said.

The simple thoughtfulness of the gesture touched her deeply. "That would be nice. Perhaps so we don't wake the girls. Let's meet downstairs in my shop and we can talk."

***

Beth sat waiting in the dimly lit shop as Miles descended the stairs, two cups of tea in hand. Outside, a gentle pre-dawn breeze had risen, occasionally rattling the shop's sign and making the window frames whisper. The air held that peculiar stillness that comes just before sunrise, when the world seems to collectively hold its breath in anticipation of the new day—fitting, Beth thought, for a conversation that felt like the threshold of something new.

"Couldn't sleep?" he asked, sliding her cup across the table.

Beth wrapped her fingers around the warm porcelain. "Too many thoughts."

Miles nodded, settling across from her. "Understandable, given the circumstances."

"I need to talk to Thomas at some point," she said, the decision firm now that she'd spoken it aloud. "I need to give him a proper answer."

"You don't need to explain your decision to me, Beth."

"I know." She met his gaze, drawing strength from the steadiness she found there. "But I want to. You deserve an explanation."

He waited, giving her space to find her words.

"When Thomas left, I thought it was because I wasn't enough," Beth said, her voice low but sure. "That he'd discovered some fundamental flaw in me that made him flee. For two years, I've carried that belief."

Miles's jaw tightened. "That was never true."

"I know that now. But the damage was done." She took a careful sip of tea. "Thomas wants to return to where we were, to reclaim our engagement, our plans. As if we could simply erase these past two years."

"And you can't," Miles supplied gently.

"No. Not just because we've both changed, but because the foundation was flawed from the beginning." Beth set her cup down with quiet determination. "He didn't trust me enough to share his burdens, to face challenges together. That's not the partnership I want for my life."

Miles remained silent, his eyes never leaving her face.

"The truth is," Beth continued, her voice steadying with each word, "what I feel for you in these few weeks is more real, more profound than anything I felt for Thomas in two years of courtship. I didn't realize how much was missing until..."

"Until what?" Miles asked softly when she faltered.

"Until you showed me what trust really means. Until your daughters showed me what family could be." Beth met his gaze directly. "Until you all made the apartment upstairs feel like home again."

Miles reached across the table, his calloused hand covering hers. "Beth..."

"I know our timing is complicated," she acknowledged. "Your life has been upended, and I'm only now finding closure with my past. But I needed you to know where my heart stands before I speak with Thomas."

Miles's fingers tightened around hers, his blue eyes reflecting a cautious hope. "Where does it stand, Beth?"

"With you," she said simply.

The stillness between them held an infinite possibility, a moment balanced on the edge of transformation.

Miles's other hand came up to cradle hers between both of his. "I thought I'd never feel this way again after Charlotte," he said, his voice deep with emotion. "Never imagined my heart could heal enough to love someone new. But you, Beth—you've brought light back into our lives in ways I never thought possible."

Tears pricked at Beth's eyes. "Is that a yes?"

A smile broke across Miles's face, genuine and unguarded. "It's a thousand yeses. For me and for my daughters, who already love you dearly."

Beth felt a weight lift from her shoulders, replaced by a lightness she hadn't experienced in years. "I need to speak with Thomas tomorrow. To give him the closure he deserves and to move forward with a clear conscience."

"Of course." Miles squeezed her hand gently. "Take whatever time you need. I'm not going anywhere."

The simple promise, delivered with such quiet certainty, warmed Beth from within.

They finished their tea, the silence between them comfortable, filled with shared understanding rather than unspoken questions.

"We should try to get some sleep," Beth said eventually. "Tomorrow will be challenging enough without exhaustion."

"Will you be alright?"

"Better than I've been in a very long time," she answered truthfully.

"Beth?" His voice had softened to a near whisper.

"Yes?" She looked up, finding his gaze steady on hers.

"Thank you for trusting me with your heart."

She reached across and briefly touched his wrist. "Thank you for being worthy of that trust," she replied, the simple words containing volumes of meaning between them.

"Good night, Beth." He remained seated. "If you don't mind, I wish to sit here a bit longer." The request held a vulnerability that touched her—a man accustomed to strength admitting his need for quiet contemplation.

"Good night, Miles." She paused at the foot of the stairs, her hand resting lightly on the bannister. "And yes, stay as long as you need. Sometimes we all need quiet moments to truly hear what our hearts are saying."

Chapter 20

B eth's boots thumped softly against the packed dirt of Hope Springs' main street as she hurried toward the white clapboard church, her navy Sunday dress sweeping at her ankles. The rising sun, on the eastern horizon, painted the town in soft amber light that filtered through a thin veil of morning mist rising from the distant creek. Streets typically bustling with wagons, shopkeepers setting out their wares, and townspeople exchanging the week's news lay quiet in the early morning stillness, giving Beth the solitude she craved. Only the distant crowing of a rooster and the occasional whinny from the livery stable broke the hush.

Reverend Weatherly had always left the church unlocked, believing God's house should remain open to those seeking refuge—a practice some found foolish but which had served the community well. Beth climbed the worn wooden steps, the familiar creak of the third board announcing her presence to the empty building. Beneath her gloved hand, the brass doorknob felt cool, its once-shiny surface dulled by years of faithful hands seeking entrance. The heavy oak door swung open under her touch, its iron hinges protesting slightly with a sound that echoed in the sacred silence.

Inside, the sanctuary welcomed her with cool, still air. Dust motes danced in beams of colored light streaming through stained-glass windows. Empty pews stretched before her, polished wood gleaming in the morning sun. The silence wrapped around her like a familiar shawl, comforting in its constancy, broken only by the distant cooing of mourning doves nesting in the church eaves.

Beth moved down the center aisle, her footsteps echoing softly. She slid into the front pew, folding her hands in her lap. Today would test her resolve, her conviction in the choice she'd made. She needed strength beyond her own.

Beth bowed her head, hands clasped so tightly her knuckles whitened. Unlike her previous prayers filled with turmoil and questioning, this morning she felt a quiet resolve.

"Lord," she whispered, her breath barely disturbing the stillness, "grant me wisdom and courage today. Help me speak truth with compassion. Guide my words and actions."

The words of Proverbs 3:5-6 came to her mind, verses her father had often quoted during difficult times: Trust in the Lord with all your heart, and lean not on your own understanding; in all your ways acknowledge Him, and He shall direct your paths.

Beth repeated the verse several times, drawing strength from its familiar cadence. Her decision wasn't made in haste or emotion, but in thoughtful consideration of truth. Thomas had returned, but her heart had moved forward.

The distant sound of a door opening pulled Beth from her prayers. She turned to see Alice Weatherly entering with a basket of fresh flowers for the altar.

"Beth!" Alice exclaimed softly, surprise evident in her gentle features. "You're here early, dear."

Beth rose, smoothing her skirts. "I needed some quiet time to prepare for today."

Understanding softened Alice's expression. "News of Thomas's return has spread quickly. I imagine today and the days to come will be challenging for you."

"Yes," Beth acknowledged. "But I'm at peace with what I must do."

Alice set her basket on a pew and approached Beth, taking her hands. "Whatever you decide, remember that God walks with you."

"He truly does."

Alice squeezed her hands before releasing them. "Would you like to help me arrange these flowers? I've always found working with God's creation soothing to a troubled spirit."

Beth nodded gratefully, welcoming the distraction. They worked together, placing fragrant blooms in crystal vases on the altar. The simple task steadied Beth's hands and focused her mind.

As they finished, Alice stepped back to assess their work. "Beautiful," she declared. "Just like new beginnings."

The meaningful glance Alice gave her wasn't lost on Beth. "You understand, don't you? About Miles and me?"

Alice's eyes crinkled with gentle wisdom. "I've seen the way you look at each other. The way his children have blossomed under your care. Some things don't need words to be understood."

Beth felt her cheeks warm. "It's new and... unexpected."

"The best gifts often are," Alice replied. "Benjamin and I married after knowing each other for just a few weeks. Forty years later, I've never regretted that leap of faith."

The church door opened again, admitting early parishioners. Alice squeezed Beth's arm. "Remember, dear—God doesn't always lead us along expected paths, but His direction is always true."

As she returned to her pew, Beth felt calm settling over her. People filed in steadily, many nodding or smiling in her direction. Some glanced curiously, whispering behind prayer books. She heard Thomas's name more than once, confirming Alice's observation about town gossip.

The murmurs increased noticeably when the Donovans entered. Miles guided his daughters in their new dresses, Clara bouncing in sunshine yellow calico, and Ellie moving with quiet dignity in a lavender floral print calico. His eyes found Beth immediately, and his subtle nod conveyed silent support.

Beth shifted slightly, making room on her pew. Clara spotted her and broke free from her father's grasp, hurrying down the aisle.

"Miss Beth! Miss Beth!" she stage whispered loudly enough for several rows to hear. "My new dress is pretty for church!"

Beth couldn't help smiling as she welcomed Clara beside her. "You look beautiful, Clara. Very proper for church."

Ellie followed more sedately, sliding next to her sister. "Thank you for our new dresses, Miss Beth," she said quietly. "Papa says we look like proper young ladies."

Miles joined them, his Sunday suit freshly pressed, his hair neatly combed. "Good morning," he said, his deep voice pitched for her ears alone. "You left early."

"I needed some time alone here in the church," Beth explained.

Understanding crossed his features. "Are you alright?"

Before she could answer, a ripple of whispers spread through the congregation. Beth turned to see Thomas entering, dressed in a fine dark suit, his confident stride carrying him down the aisle. His gaze locked on Beth, taking in her proximity to Miles and his daughters with a slight furrow between his brows.

Thomas nodded politely to several parishioners before taking a seat directly behind Beth. The weight of his presence sent a prickle up her spine, making her shoulders tense involuntarily. She found herself leaning imperceptibly toward Miles, his solid form beside her providing an anchoring counterbalance. The scent of his freshly laundered shirt—soap and starch and something uniquely him—steadied her racing pulse.

"Miss Beth," Clara whispered, oblivious to the tension, "can we pick berries after church? Jimmy says there's lots by the creek."

"Hush, Clara," Ellie admonished softly. "Church is starting."

Reverend Weatherly approached the pulpit as the pianist began the opening hymn. Beth rose with the congregation, grateful to focus on worship rather than the complicated dynamics surrounding her.

Miles's rich baritone joined the singing beside her, the vibration of his voice somehow steadying. Beth found herself drawing strength from his presence, from Clara's small hand slipping trustingly into hers during prayers, from Ellie's solemn attention to every word of the service.

When Reverend Weatherly announced his text for the morning sermon, Beth felt a jolt of recognition.

"Today," he began, "we examine Proverbs, chapter three, verses five and six. 'Trust in the Lord with all your heart, and lean not on your own understanding; in all your ways acknowledge Him, and He shall direct your paths.'"

Beth glanced up sharply. The very verses she'd been praying earlier. Coincidence? Or divine confirmation?

"In frontier life," the reverend continued, "we often face circumstances beyond our understanding. Crop failures despite diligent planting. Illness despite careful precautions. Loss despite fervent prayers."

His gaze swept across the congregation, momentarily connecting with Beth's.

"Our human understanding is limited, friends. We see only what stands before us, not the broader landscape of God's plan. When we lean on our own understanding alone, we build on shifting sand."

Beth felt the words resonating in her chest. For two years, she'd tried to understand Thomas's abandonment, to make sense of seemingly senseless pain. Even now, with his explanation, full understanding remained elusive.

"God calls us instead to trust," Reverend Weatherly's voice strengthened, resonating through the wooden beams overhead. "Not blind faith without thought, but trusting acknowledgment that His wisdom exceeds our own. That His paths, though sometimes steep or winding, lead to green pastures."

Miles shifted beside her, his elbow lightly touching hers—the contact brief but electric. She glanced up to find him already looking at her, the furrow between his brows softening. Something passed between them, unspoken but profound; they were both hearing a message that seemed to part the veil between heaven and earth, speaking directly to their situation.

"When we acknowledge God in all our ways—our decisions, our relationships, our daily work—we invite divine direction. The Hebrew word for 'direct' here suggests smoothing or making straight. God doesn't remove all obstacles, but He smooths our path as we walk in faith."

Beth's fingers tightened around her Bible until the leather binding creaked softly. The gilt-edged pages blurred as tears threatened. Her path had seemed anything but smooth these past years—a rutted wagon trail of disappointment and loss—yet, looking back, she could trace God's guiding hand even through the darkest valleys. A tear slipped down her cheek, quickly wiped away with a gloved finger before anyone could notice.

"Brothers and sisters," Reverend Weatherly concluded, "whatever decisions you face this day and in the days to come, trust not in your own limited understanding, but in God's infinite wisdom. Acknowledge Him in every choice, and your paths—though perhaps unexpected—will be directed by the Master's hand."

As the congregation bowed for the closing prayer, Beth felt clarity crystallizing within her. She'd sought understanding of Thomas's actions for too long. Now, she needed to trust God's direction toward a future she couldn't fully see, but felt with certainty was right.

The service concluded with a final hymn and benediction. As parishioners rose to socialize, a crescendo of conversation filled the previously reverent space. Beth felt tension coiling between her shoulder blades, winding tighter with each passing second. The moment she'd been preparing for had arrived—inevitable as the changing seasons.

Miles leaned close, his breath warm against her ear. "We can leave quickly if you prefer. The side door is clear."

Beth drew herself up straighter, gathering strength from the sermon still echoing in her mind. She shook her head. "No. This needs to be done. Some paths, though difficult, must be walked."

Clara tugged at Beth's sleeve. "Can we get cookies now? Mrs. Prescott brought a basket."

"In a moment, Clara," Miles answered for Beth, his hand briefly touching the small of her back in silent support.

"Beth." Thomas's voice came from behind her, confident and familiar.

She turned slowly, facing him directly. His handsome features were arranged in an expression of pleasant anticipation, as if their conversation at the church had settled everything.

"Thomas," she acknowledged.

He extended his arm toward her. "May I walk with you to the picnic? We have much to discuss about our future."

The hushed conversations nearby quieted as people noticed the interaction. Beth felt rather than saw the collective breath being held, the curious gazes, the expectant stillness.

"No, Thomas," she said, her voice clear and steady in the sudden quiet.

His confident smile faltered. "Beth, surely after my explanation—"

"Your explanation helped me understand what happened," Beth interrupted, her tone gentle but with an underlying firmness like river water flowing over bedrock. "But understanding isn't the same as restoring."

Thomas's arm dropped to his side, his brow furrowing. Confusion flickered across his face, followed by something that looked almost like indignation. "What do you mean? I was forced to leave. I had no choice, Beth."

"There are always choices, Thomas," Beth replied, keeping her voice even despite the public setting and the weight of staring eyes. "You chose not to trust me with the truth. You chose to assume I couldn't weather difficulty. You chose to make decisions that affected both our lives without consulting me, as if I were a child rather than your intended wife."

Around them, a circle had formed, not close enough to seem intrusive, but near enough to hear. Beth was acutely aware of Miles standing slightly behind her, a solid presence but not interfering.

Thomas's expression hardened slightly. "I was protecting you."

"By breaking my heart?" The words emerged more sharply than Beth intended, and she took a steadying breath. "Protection without trust isn't protection at all, Thomas. It's control."

A murmur rippled through the onlookers. Beth hadn't wanted this confrontation to be public, but perhaps there was a purpose in the community witnessing her standing firm.

Thomas stepped closer, lowering his voice. "Beth, be reasonable. We were to be married. We can still have that life. I've returned for you."

"Miss Beth!" Clara's voice pierced the tension, her small form suddenly wedging between Beth and Thomas, her petticoats rustling against the adults' Sunday best. "Jimmy says the wild blackberry bushes by Silver Creek are all purple now! Mrs. Cooper says we could pick enough for a cobbler if we hurry! Can we go see? Please?"

Beth blinked, momentarily thrown by the innocent interruption. Clara stood looking up at her, completely unaware of the charged exchange she'd interrupted, her yellow dress bright as sunshine against the somber tones of adult Sunday attire.

Something about Clara's artless intrusion cleared Beth's mind like a fresh breeze through a stuffy room. This child—this present reality of yellow dresses and berry bushes and simple joys—reflected where her heart truly belonged now.

Beth smiled at Clara, then looked back at Thomas, her voice gentle but firm. "You broke my trust, Thomas. That's not something easily mended, no matter the explanation." She placed a hand on Clara's shoulder. "I forgive you for what happened, but I can't return to the past. My life has moved forward."

Thomas's gaze shifted to Miles, then to the girls—lingering on Clara's small hand clutching Beth's skirt. The color drained from his face, leaving two bright spots on his cheekbones. His jaw worked silently for a moment, and he took a half-step backward as though physically struck.

"I see," he said stiffly, his voice tight as a new violin string. His gloved hand clenched at his side, the fine leather creaking. "I've come too late."

"Perhaps," Beth acknowledged softly. "Or perhaps we were never meant to walk that path at all."

She turned slightly toward Miles, who stood with Ellie at his side, his expression carefully neutral despite the obvious tension. "Clara would like to see the berry bushes," she said, her voice steadier than she felt. "Shall we?"

Miles nodded, his eyes conveying far more than his simple response. "The berries await, then."

With gentle pressure on Clara's shoulder, Beth guided the girls toward the church door, Miles stepping in beside her. She felt Thomas's gaze on her back, and sensed the curious eyes of the congregation, but each step forward lightened something within her.

"Did I do something wrong?" Clara whispered, looking up with sudden concern. "That man looked sad."

"No, sweetheart," Beth assured her, smoothing a hand over the child's blonde curls. "You did nothing wrong at all. Sometimes grown-ups have difficult conversations."

"Is he your friend?" Clara persisted, as they stepped outside into bright sunshine.

Beth considered how to answer truthfully, yet appropriately. "He was a long time ago. Now we're going different ways."

This seemed to satisfy Clara, who immediately returned to her excitement about berries, skipping ahead down the church steps. Ellie, however, looked up at Beth with quiet perception.

"You chose us," she said simply.

Beth felt her throat tighten with emotion at the child's insight. "Yes, Ellie. I do."

The little girl nodded solemnly, then took Beth's hand with unusual demonstrativeness. "I'm glad."

As they crossed the churchyard toward the path leading to Silver Creek, Beth glanced up to find Miles watching her with an expression that made her heart flutter.

"Are you alright?" he asked quietly as the girls moved ahead, Clara already pointing out the distant berry bushes to her sister.

"Better than I expected," Beth admitted. "It needed to be done."

Miles nodded, then cleared his throat. "That was... brave. Speaking your truth in front of everyone."

Beth felt her cheeks warm. "I didn't plan for an audience. But perhaps it's for the best that there's no room for misunderstanding."

They walked a few paces in silence, the sounds of church socializing fading behind them.

"You said something back there," Miles ventured carefully, his voice hesitant in a way Beth had rarely heard from this steadfast man. His Adam's apple bobbed as he swallowed. "About your life moving forward."

Beth slowed her steps slightly, allowing more distance between them and the girls. "Yes."

"Did you mean that?" His voice had dropped lower, uncertainty making the question vulnerable.

Beth stopped walking entirely, turning to face him. The morning sun caught in his dark hair, highlighting strands of copper she'd never noticed before. His eyes, so steadily blue, watched her with careful hope.

"Every word," she said firmly. "I've spent too long looking backward, Miles. Wondering why things happened, trying to understand. But understanding isn't always possible, and it isn't always necessary."

A smile tugged at the corner of his mouth. "Leaning not on your own understanding?"

"Exactly," Beth confirmed, returning his smile. "I'm choosing to trust the path forward, even if I can't see where it leads."

Miles's expression sobered. "Beth, I want you to be certain. What's between us... it's still new. I don't want this to be a hasty decision you might regret."

The concern in his voice only confirmed what she already knew—this was a man who valued her happiness above his own desires.

"Miles Donovan," she said, reaching to take his hand, marveling at how natural the gesture felt despite its public boldness. "Choosing you is not a hasty decision. You're the most carefully considered choice I've ever made."

His fingers curled around hers, warm and strong, calloused from honest work. His eyes searched hers with an intensity that made her breath catch. "Really?"

"Really," she affirmed. "When we met a few weeks ago, I never imagined we'd be standing here like this. But sometimes the unexpected path is exactly the right one."

"Papa! Miss Beth!" Clara called from ahead. "Hurry! The berries are waiting!"

Miles chuckled, his thumb brushing over Beth's knuckles before releasing her hand. "We're being summoned."

As they resumed walking, Beth felt a profound rightness settle in her chest. Behind them lay Thomas and the past; ahead waited Clara's berries and whatever future God had planned. Beth felt completely aligned with her path.

"She's something else, isn't she?" Miles said fondly, watching Clara demonstrate berry-picking techniques to a patient Ellie. The morning sun filtered through the leaves, dappling the girls in patterns of light and shadow.

"They both are," Beth agreed, a warmth spreading through her chest that had nothing to do with the summer heat. "Each in her own way." She looked from the girls to Miles, then back to the church spire visible through the trees behind them—her past and future in one sweeping glance.

Chapter 21

Clara shrieked with delight as her berry-stained fingers missed Jimmy by inches. The children darted between picnic blankets and quilts spread across the grass near the creek, their game of tag transforming the Sunday gathering into a playground of laughter and scattered napkins. Like hummingbirds among flowers, they flitted from group to group, trailing joy and mild chaos in their wake.

"Clara Donovan!" Beth called, trying to sound stern despite her smile. "Mind Mrs. Prescott's pie table!"

The yellow-dressed whirlwind pivoted just in time, narrowly avoiding disaster as Nellie Prescott guarded her apple pies with mock severity.

"Sorry, Mrs. Prescott!" Clara called without slowing, her curls bouncing as she changed direction.

Beth shook her head while seated on a quilt beneath the sprawling oak tree. "That child has more energy than a steam locomotive."

"And about as much ability to stop once she gets going," Miles agreed, settling beside her with two glasses of lemonade. His fingers brushed hers as he handed her a glass.

"Ellie seems to be enjoying herself," Beth observed, nodding toward where the quieter Donovan daughter sat with several girls her age, carefully weaving daisy chains under Mrs. Weatherly's guidance.

Miles followed her gaze, his expression softening. "She's coming out of her shell more each day. I worried when we first arrived that she might never."

"Children are remarkably resilient," Beth said when he didn't finish. "Given time and stability."

"And love," Miles added quietly, his eyes meeting hers.

Beth felt her cheeks warm under his gaze.

"The picnic committee outdid themselves again," she said, gesturing toward the abundance spread across tables and blankets. "Eleanor will be insufferable with pride."

Miles chuckled, the sound rumbling pleasantly. "Deservedly so. I haven't eaten this well since..." He paused, then finished honestly, "Since your pancakes last week."

"Flatterer," Beth accused lightly, but pleasure bloomed in her chest at the compliment.

"Papa!" Clara materialized beside them, breathless and flushed. "Jimmy says there's a frog-jumping contest by the creek! Can I go watch?"

Miles raised an eyebrow. "Watch only? Or participate?"

Clara's expression turned calculating. "Well, if a frog happened to need someone to help him jump better..."

Beth bit back a laugh as Miles sighed dramatically.

"You may go watch," he conceded. "But stay where adults can see you. And no getting wet."

Clara was off before he finished speaking, calling for Ellie to join her.

"That was optimistic," Beth remarked. "No getting wet at a frog-jumping contest?"

"A father can dream," Miles replied with a rueful smile. "Though I brought an extra dress along, just in case."

"Wise man."

They ate in easy companionship, occasionally commenting on the surrounding activities. Sheriff Braddock engaged Reverend Weatherly in an animated chess match on a portable board. Harriet and Tim sat close together near the lemonade table, their heads bent in conversation. Josiah Miller helped Jimmy organize the frog contestants, while children cheered each amphibian athlete.

"I've been meaning to ask," Miles said, setting aside his empty plate. "What made you decide to become a seamstress? Was it always your plan to run the store?"

Beth considered the question, appreciating that he'd asked about her choices rather than assuming. "Not exactly. I always enjoyed sewing, my mother taught me from a young age. But I had dreams of teaching school when I was younger."

"What changed?"

"My father's health began failing when I was sixteen. Mother needed help in the store, so I put aside thoughts of teaching." Beth smoothed her napkin, memories surfacing. "After a while, I discovered I had a talent for design and fabric selection that brought customers from neighboring towns. By the time my parents fell ill, the business had become mine in all but name."

Miles nodded thoughtfully. "You speak of it with pride."

"I do love it," Beth admitted. "Creating something beautiful and functional from simple cloth. Watching a bride's face when she tries on her wedding dress. Seeing children grow through the clothes they need." She smiled self-consciously. "That sounds rather fanciful, doesn't it?"

"Not at all," Miles countered. "It's how I feel about blacksmithing. There's something... sacred about transforming raw materials into something useful. Something that will last."

Beth felt a rush of connection at his understanding. "Exactly. Though I doubt my needle and thread will endure as long as your ironwork."

"I wouldn't be so certain," Miles said. "Good stitchery outlasts most things made by human hands."

The genuine respect in his voice touched her deeply. Thomas had never truly understood her work, viewing it as a temporary occupation until marriage rather than a calling in its own right.

Their conversation flowed easily to other topics—books they'd enjoyed, memories of childhood, hopes for the coming future. Beth felt herself relaxing fully for the first time since Thomas's return.

A cloud briefly shadowed the sun, sending a ripple of cooler air across the picnic grounds. The momentary dimming of light seemed to presage a change, and Beth felt the hairs on her arm rise slightly—not from cold, but from some instinctive awareness of shifting circumstances.

A shadow fell across their blanket, breaking the moment.

"Beth."

She looked up to find Thomas standing before them, his expression carefully composed. Gone was the confident expectation of the morning, replaced by a more subdued demeanor.

Miles tensed beside her, but remained seated, his steady presence a comfort.

"Thomas," Beth acknowledged, keeping her voice even. "Would you like to sit?"

He hesitated, then nodded, settling on the edge of the blanket at a respectful distance. The three of them formed an awkward triangle, watched with poorly disguised interest by nearby picnickers.

"I've been thinking about what you said this morning," Thomas began, his fingers working the brim of his hat. "About trust and choices."

Beth waited. The distant laughter of children playing by the creek filled the silence between them.

"You were right." Each word seemed to cost him something. "I should have trusted you with the truth, regardless of my uncle's threats. I convinced myself I was protecting you, but perhaps—" He stopped, swallowed. "Perhaps I was protecting myself from having to face a difficult situation together."

The honesty of his self-assessment surprised Beth. "Thank you for saying that."

Thomas glanced briefly at Miles, then back to Beth. "I came back hoping to reclaim what we had. To continue as if those two years never happened." He shook his head ruefully. "But they did happen. We both changed. You built a life without me, as you had every right to do."

"Yes," Beth agreed. "I did."

"I can see that now." Thomas's gaze drifted to where Clara and Ellie played by the creek, their laughter carrying across the picnic grounds. "Those girls adore you."

Beth felt her heart swell at the observation. "They're remarkable children."

"They need a mother," Thomas said simply. "And you need a family who appreciates your strength." He turned to Miles directly. "You're a fortunate man, Donovan."

Miles met his gaze steadily. "I'm well aware of that, Aldridge."

Something passed between the men, not quite friendship, but a measure of mutual respect. Thomas nodded once, then turned back to Beth.

"I won't pretend this is easy," he said. "Seeing you with someone else when I'd hoped..." He trailed off, then squared his shoulders. "But I want your happiness, Beth. I always did, even when I made poor choices that hurt you."

Beth felt a wave of compassion for him. Despite everything, Thomas had been an important part of her life, and his pain was genuine. "What will you do now?"

"Return to Denver, initially. I have unfinished business with my uncle's fraud that needs addressing through proper legal channels." His expression hardened briefly before clearing. "After that, I'm not certain. The West has many opportunities for a man willing to work."

"I hope you find what you're looking for," Beth said sincerely.

Thomas rose to his feet, brushing grass from his trousers. "I should take my leave."

Beth stood as well, Miles rising beside her. "Safe travels, Thomas."

Thomas extended his hand to Miles first. "Take care of her, Donovan. She deserves nothing less than complete devotion."

Miles clasped his hand firmly. "On that, we agree completely."

Thomas turned to Beth, hesitating before speaking. His eyes lingered on her face, as if memorizing it one last time. "I am truly sorry for the pain I caused you, Beth." His voice caught slightly. "I hope someday you can remember our time together with some fondness, despite how it ended. We were... we were good once, weren't we?"

The question held more vulnerability than anything Thomas had ever shown her—a crack in the confident facade he'd always maintained.

"We were young," Beth answered gently. "And yes, there was much good. That hasn't disappeared, Thomas. It just belongs to a different chapter."

He nodded, something like acceptance finally settling in his expression. "Goodbye, Beth."

"Goodbye, Thomas."

They watched as he made his way across the picnic grounds, stopping briefly to speak with Reverend Weatherly before continuing toward the road that led to town. His figure grew smaller against the backdrop of prairie grass and distant cottonwoods until he seemed to merge with the horizon—the past receding where it belonged.

The picnic continued around them, life flowing onward like the nearby creek. Mrs. Prescott rang the small bell that signaled desserts were being served, and children abandoned their games to dash toward the promise of sweets.

"Are you alright?" Miles asked when Thomas had gone from view.

Beth considered the question carefully. "Yes. I truly am. It feels like closing a book I've been trying to finish for too long—one whose ending I kept avoiding because I wasn't ready to put it away. But now I'm eager to start a new story."

Miles's hand found hers, his calloused fingers entwining with her smaller ones. "You handled everything with remarkable grace."

"As did you," she replied, squeezing his hand gently. "Thank you for not interfering and for letting me speak my mind. My heart has chosen its path forward. With you and your daughters, if you'll have me."

His blue eyes darkened with emotion. "If I'll have you? Beth, you've brought light back into our lives when I thought darkness might be all we'd ever know again."

Beth felt tears prick behind her eyes at the raw honesty in his voice. "Then we're agreed."

"We are," he confirmed, his thumb tracing a gentle pattern on her palm.

"Papa! Miss Beth!" Clara's voice broke the moment as she raced toward them, Ellie following at a more dignified pace. Both girls had mud splattered across their dresses.

"Look what we found!" Clara thrust forward, cupped hands containing a small green frog. "His name is Hopper, and he jumps higher than ALL the other frogs!"

Beth laughed, the sound bubbling up from a place of pure happiness. "That's quite an accomplishment, Hopper."

Miles sighed dramatically at their muddy state. "I see my instructions about staying dry were taken as mere suggestions."

"It wasn't our fault, Papa," Ellie explained seriously. "Hopper jumped in the mud puddle, and we had to rescue him."

"Of course you did," Miles agreed, his stern expression melting into affection. "A very noble rescue mission."

Clara looked between Beth and Miles, her sharp eyes missing nothing. "Were you holding hands?"

Beth felt her cheeks warm as Miles cleared his throat. "Yes, sprite, we were."

Clara's face split into a wide grin. "Does that mean Miss Beth is going to stay with us forever? Even when our new house is finished?"

The directness of the question hung in the air between them. Beth looked at Miles, uncertain how he wanted to handle such a forward inquiry from his daughter.

Miles knelt at Clara's level, careful not to disturb her amphibian friend. "Miss Beth and I care for each other very much. But proper things take proper time. Do you understand?"

Clara's brow furrowed in concentration. "Like when you're making something at the forge? You can't rush it or it breaks?"

"Exactly like that," Miles agreed, shooting Beth an appreciative glance. "Good things are worth waiting for."

Ellie, who had been quietly observing, stepped closer to Beth. "But you will stay near us, won't you?" she asked, her voice carrying a hint of vulnerability that tugged at Beth's heart.

"I promise I will always be near you, Ellie. No matter what happens."

The solemn child studied her face for a moment, then nodded, apparently satisfied with what she found there. "Good. Because Clara can't sew on buttons, and Papa always pricks his fingers when he tries."

The matter-of-fact statement broke the emotional tension, sending them all into laughter.

"Well, we can't have that," Beth agreed, rising to her feet. "Now, I believe I spotted Mrs. Hanley cutting some chocolate cake. Shall we investigate?"

"Yes!" Clara exclaimed, carefully transferring Hopper to one hand so she could grab Beth's with the other. "But Hopper needs cake too."

"I don't believe frogs care for chocolate," Beth explained gently. "Perhaps we should return him to the creek first?"

As they made their way toward the creek and then the cake table, Beth felt Miles's hand brush against hers, a brief, warm touch that carried promise. Around them, the picnic continued in full swing, but the curious glances and whispers that had followed her all day seemed to have subsided, replaced by accepting nods and warm smiles.

Reverend Weatherly caught her eye as they passed his chess game, offering a subtle nod of approval. Alice, arranging cake slices with Eleanor, winked knowingly. Even Sheriff Braddock raised his lemonade glass in a small salute.

Beth felt a wave of gratitude for this community that had witnessed her heartbreak, supported her through loss, and now celebrated her newfound happiness without judgment. The path forward might still hold challenges, but walking it with Miles, his daughters, and the people of Hope Springs beside her felt absolutely right.

As if reading her thoughts, Miles leaned close as they reached the cake table. "Happy?" he asked simply.

Beth looked at Clara excitedly, pointing out the biggest cake slice, at Ellie carefully arranging napkins for everyone, and finally at Miles himself, his blue eyes reflecting all she felt in her heart.

"Completely," she answered truthfully. The word felt almost too simple to contain what filled her heart—this sensation of pieces falling into their proper places after years of being scattered. Spring's hope had finally bloomed into summer's fullness, and Beth knew with certainty that whatever seasons lay ahead, they would weather them together.

Epilogue

The hammer's rhythmic tap-tap echoed through the late afternoon air as Miles secured the final shingle on the porch roof. Late November sunshine bathed the freshly painted homestead in warm amber light, glinting off the polished windows Beth had wiped to perfection just yesterday. Miles sat back on his heels, surveying his handiwork with satisfaction. The weather vane, his own design featuring a blacksmith's anvil, turned gently in the fall breeze above the main roof, marking another completed project on his seemingly endless list.

"Is it fixed, Papa?" Clara called from below, her yellow dress bright against the russet and gold foliage scattered across the yard.

"Tight as a drum," Miles replied, gathering his tools into the leather pouch strapped to his belt. "No leaks when winter comes."

"Good," Clara declared with the authority of her almost-five years. "Because Mama says rain makes everything damp, and damp isn't good for babies."

Miles smiled at her matter-of-fact repetition of Beth's words. In the months since their wedding, Clara had attached herself to Beth completely, soaking up every bit of maternal wisdom as if making up for lost time. She now proclaimed herself ready to be "the best big sister in all of Hope Springs" to the baby due to arrive in late March.

"Papa! Mr. Braddock is coming!" Ellie called from where she'd been gathering kindling at the edge of the yard. She pointed toward the road where the sheriff's horse approached at an unhurried pace.

Miles climbed down the ladder with ease, his boots making a solid thump as they hit the packed earth. Sheriff Braddock dismounted before the picket fence Miles had installed last month, Beth's special request, something she'd always dreamed of having.

"Afternoon, Donovan. Your homesteads looking better and better each time I see it," Braddock called, removing his hat as he approached.

"Afternoon, sheriff, and thank you. It's been a labor of love."

And it had been, in every sense. The town's initial building effort after the tornado had provided the basic structure, but Miles had spent every spare moment these past months adding the finishing touches that transformed a house into a home. The wide, wraparound porch Beth had mentioned admiring in a magazine. The custom-built cabinets in the kitchen with their wrought iron hinges. The rose trellis outside the main bedroom window, waiting for spring planting.

"Beth inside?" Braddock asked, shifting a small package in his hands.

"She's resting," Miles said. "Doc Reynolds suggested she take an afternoon rest now that she's—" He caught himself, still slightly self-conscious discussing Beth's condition, though her gently rounded figure made it increasingly obvious to everyone in town.

Braddock's weathered face creased in understanding. "Eleanor thought she might be tired these days. Asked me to deliver this on my rounds." He held out the package. "Some special tea Eleanor swears helped her through all four of her pregnancies."

Miles accepted the gift with genuine gratitude. "That's extraordinarily kind. Please thank her for us."

"Will do. Any more trouble with that broken fence on your southern boundary?"

Miles shook his head. "None since you spoke with Elijah Aldridge's foreman. Cattle have kept to their proper pasture."

The mention of Elijah Aldridge still brought a slight tension, though the man himself had largely withdrawn from town affairs since Thomas's revelations about his fraudulent business practices. Legal proceedings were underway, but such matters moved slowly on the frontier.

"Good to hear," Braddock nodded. "Well, I won't keep you. Give my regards to Beth."

As the sheriff rode away, Miles turned back toward the house with the package in hand. His house. Their home. The thought still amazed him sometimes. After Charlotte died, he'd never imagined finding such happiness again, certainly not so completely, so perfectly suited to him and his daughters.

"Can we go inside now, Papa?" Ellie asked, her arms full of kindling.

"Of course," Miles smiled, lifting Clara onto his shoulders with practiced ease. "Let's see what your mama is doing."

Inside, the house welcomed them with the scent of apple spice and warmth from the hearth. The main room, with its river stone fireplace and comfortable furniture, reflected both Beth's careful eye for color and Miles's craftsmanship. Handmade curtains framed windows that looked out over the property. Bookshelves held volumes from both their collections, now merged into one family library. A quilt pieced by Beth's mother draped across the back of the rocking chair where

Beth often sat in the evenings, sewing tiny garments for the coming baby.

But the chair was empty now.

"Mama?" Clara called, wriggling to be let down from Miles's shoulders.

"In here," Beth's voice answered from the kitchen, followed by the clatter of pans. "I'm just taking the bread from the oven."

Miles crossed to the kitchen, the girls racing ahead of him. The sight of Beth, her blond hair gathered in a loose knot at the nape of her neck, her figure draped in a soft blue dress that emphasized her softly rounded middle, made his breath catch as it always did. Five months of marriage hadn't dimmed the wonder of seeing her in his home, of knowing she was his wife.

"You're supposed to be resting," he admonished gently, setting the package on the table.

Beth turned, her cheeks flushed from the oven's heat, a loaf of golden bread in her hands. "I was resting. Then I had the sudden urge to bake bread." She smiled ruefully, setting the loaf on the cooling rack. "These peculiar demands from within me are quite insistent."

"Mama!" Clara tugged at Beth's apron. "Can I have a piece? It smells like heaven!"

"After it cools," Beth promised. "And after you wash up. You look like you've been rolling in the yard again."

"I was helping Jimmy build a fort after school," Clara explained, displaying her dirt-streaked hands as evidence of her industry. "We need a good fort before winter comes."

"Indeed you do," Beth agreed solemnly, though her eyes danced with amusement as they met Miles's over the child's head. "Now go wash, both of you. Dinner will be ready soon."

Miles watched his daughters scamper off to the washroom. When they were alone, he crossed to Beth, sliding his arms around her from behind, his hands resting gently on the swell of her belly.

"Truly, are you feeling well?" he murmured, pressing a kiss to her neck.

Beth leaned back against him, her hands covering his. "I'm perfectly fine," she assured him. "Doc Reynolds said walking and light activity are good for me. It's only heavy lifting and overtiring myself I need to avoid."

"Just the same, I'd prefer you let me handle the heavy work," Miles said. "That's what husbands are for."

Beth turned in his arms, her green eyes bright with mischief. "Is that all husbands are for? Heavy lifting?"

"Well," Miles pretended to consider, pulling her closer. "Perhaps a few other things."

He kissed her then, a tender meeting of lips.

A loud splash and Clara's indignant cry from the washroom separated them, both laughing softly.

"I should supervise," Beth said, reluctantly pulling away. "Clara's washing often resembles a pitched battle with water as the enemy."

"Wait." Miles reached for the package on the table. "Sheriff Braddock brought this. It's from Eleanor... some special tea she thought might help with your fatigue."

Beth's expression softened as she accepted the package. "How thoughtful. This town... they've become such a family to us both."

"They love you," Miles said simply. "As do I."

Beth's eyes glistened slightly. "These tears at the slightest provocation," she laughed, wiping her cheek. "Another peculiarity of my condition, I'm afraid."

"I find every peculiarity utterly charming," Miles assured her, pressing another quick kiss to her forehead.

"Papa!" Ellie's voice called from the washroom. "Clara's gotten water everywhere!"

"Duty calls," Miles sighed dramatically. "I'll handle the flood."

"My hero," Beth teased, giving him a gentle push toward the washroom.

Miles found the washroom exactly as expected: Clara standing in a puddle of soapy water, her dress soaked to the knees, while Ellie tried valiantly to contain the spillage with a towel. He rolled up his sleeves with exaggerated determination.

"I see we have a situation that requires a master craftsman's touch," he announced, making both girls giggle.

By the time they'd restored order to the washroom and dressed Clara in dry clothes, the bread had cooled enough for Beth to slice it. They gathered around the sturdy oak table Miles had crafted as a wedding gift, the late afternoon sun streaming through the kitchen windows.

Beth served vegetable stew, the savory aroma mingling with the freshly baked bread. As Miles said grace, his deep voice steady and sure, he felt a profound sense of thanksgiving for these simple moments surrounded by his family.

"And the teacher said my drawing was the best in the class," Ellie explained, carefully buttering her bread. "She put it on the wall for everyone to see."

"That's wonderful, sunshine," Miles praised, genuine pride warming his voice. "You've always had a good eye for detail."

"May I see it?" Beth asked.

Ellie retrieved the drawing from the sideboard where she'd carefully placed it. She unfolded it with reverence, presenting it for Beth's inspection.

Beth gasped softly as she took in the carefully rendered image. Ellie had drawn their family standing before their home. Miles tall and strong, Clara exuberant with arms outspread, Ellie herself standing neatly between them, and Beth with a pronounced curve to her middle. Even their cat, Hopper (named by Clara in honor of the frog they'd found at the picnic months ago), lounged in the foreground.

"Oh, Ellie," Beth whispered, tracing a finger over the figures. "It's beautiful. You've captured us perfectly."

"I made sure to draw the baby in your tummy," Ellie explained seriously. "So everyone would know our whole family."

Beth's eyes met Miles's across the table, love and gratitude shimmering between them at this child's simple acceptance of their blended family.

"It's perfect," Miles agreed, his voice slightly gruff with emotion. "We'll frame it for the mantelpiece."

Clara, not to be outdone, launched into a detailed explanation of her own artistic creation at school, a less recognizable but equally enthusiastic depiction of their family that included several imaginary horses she hoped to convince her father they needed.

As dinner progressed, the conversation flowed easily between them, the rhythm of family life Miles had once thought forever lost to him. He found himself watching Beth, the gentle way she encouraged Ellie to share more about school, her patience with Clara's boundless energy, and the unconscious way her hand occasionally rested on her growing belly.

They had married just five months ago in a simple ceremony at the church. Beth had worn a dress of white silk, carried wildflowers Ellie had gathered that morning, and promised to love not just Miles but his daughters as her own. Miles had stumbled over his vows, overcome with emotion when Beth's clear voice spoke of finding hope after darkness, of God's hand guiding them together.

The memory still brought a lump to his throat. The perfect rightness of that day, the blessing of beginning again with this remarkable woman.

"Miles?" Beth's voice broke into his thoughts. "You're a thousand miles away."

He blinked, focusing on her concerned expression. "Not away at all," he assured her. "Just remembering our wedding day."

Beth's face softened. "It was perfect, wasn't it?"

"One of many perfect days of my life," Miles replied.

"One of many?" Beth raised an eyebrow in question.

"Another perfect day is yet to come," he said, his gaze dropping meaningfully to her rounded middle. "When our family grows again."

Beth's hand moved instinctively to cradle her belly. "Not too much longer in the grand scheme of things. Doc Reynolds thinks perhaps late March."

"What's it like having a baby in your tummy, Mama?" Clara asked suddenly, her brow furrowed in curiosity. "Does it hurt?"

Beth considered the question with the seriousness it deserved. "Sometimes it's uncomfortable," she admitted. "But mostly it feels like carrying a miracle. Like being trusted with something precious."

"Does the baby know we're out here?" Ellie asked, her thoughtful nature evident in the question.

"I believe so," Beth said. "The baby can hear our voices now. When your papa speaks, I often feel movement, as if the baby recognizes him."

Miles felt his chest tighten with emotion. The thought of his child, formed from their love, already responding to his voice, was over-whelming.

"Can I talk to the baby?" Clara asked, bouncing slightly in her seat.

"Of course you can," Beth smiled. "After dinner, if you like."

Clara nodded solemnly, clearly taking this responsibility very seri-ously.

As they finished their meal, the girls helped clear the table, their assistance more enthusiastic than efficient, but Beth welcomed it with patient guidance. Miles watched the domestic scene with quiet con-tentment, remembering the days after Charlotte's death when such simple evening routines had seemed an impossible burden, weighted with grief and loss.

Now, the evening chores carried a different energy, the purposeful movement of a family working together, small tasks infused with love and belonging.

Once the kitchen was tidy, Beth settled in the rocking chair by the fireplace while Miles built up the fire to ward off the late fall evening chill. The girls arranged themselves at Beth's feet, Clara immediately placing her small hand on Beth's belly.

"Hello, baby," she whispered, her face inches from Beth's middle. "It's me, your big sister, Clara. I can't wait to meet you."

Ellie watched, fascinated, as Beth guided her hand to feel a particu-lar spot. "Wait," Beth instructed. "The baby's been active on this side today."

After a moment, Ellie's eyes widened. "I felt it! The baby moved!"

"Let me feel! Let me feel!" Clara demanded, shifting her hand to where Ellie's had been. When she felt the subtle movement, she squealed with such delight that Miles couldn't help laughing.

"The baby's saying hello to you both," Beth said, her expression radiant in the firelight.

Miles knelt beside them, placing his larger hand next to Clara's. The familiar flutter beneath his palm never failed to amaze him—new life, created from their love, growing stronger each day.

"What are we going to name the baby, Papa?" Ellie asked, leaning against his shoulder.

"Your mama and I have a few ideas," Miles answered, "but we thought perhaps you and Clara might like to suggest some names, too."

Clara's face lit up with excitement. "Can we name the baby Buttercup if it's a girl?"

Beth bit her lip, clearly suppressing a laugh. "That's certainly a cheerful name," she managed. "What if it's a boy?"

Clara considered this with comical seriousness. "Thunder," she decided finally. "Because boys are noisy."

This time, Beth couldn't contain her laughter, the sound mingling with Miles's deeper chuckle.

"I think we should name the baby after someone we love," Ellie offered quietly. "Like Mama Charlotte or Mama Beth's parents."

The simplicity with which Ellie referred to both women as "Mama" caught at Miles's heart. His older daughter had adapted to their blended family with remarkable grace, finding room in her heart for Beth without diminishing her memories of Charlotte.

"That's a lovely thought," Beth said softly, reaching to smooth Ellie's dark hair. "Your papa and I have discussed something similar. If it's a girl, perhaps Charlotte Rose, after your mother and my mother, whose middle name was Rose."

"And if it's a boy," Miles continued, "perhaps Timothy James, after Beth's father and my father."

"I think those are beautiful names," Ellie approved.

"But we could call her Buttercup for short," Clara persisted, making them all laugh again.

As evening deepened around them, the conversation shifted to plans for the coming winter. The final preparations needed for the house, supplies to be purchased in town, and projects for long winter evenings.

Though Beth had married Miles and moved to their new home, she hadn't abandoned her business. Instead, she'd trained Lydia Weatherly, the minister's granddaughter, to manage daily operations, visiting the shop several times a week to handle special orders and purchasing. The arrangement allowed Beth to maintain the business while embracing her new role as wife and mother.

"It's getting late, girls," Miles observed as Clara's animated chatter began to slow, her eyelids drooping slightly. "Time for bed, I think."

"But I'm not tired," Clara protested automatically, even as she stifled a yawn.

"Story first?" Ellie asked hopefully, already rising to fetch the book they'd been reading together.

"One chapter," Beth agreed. "Then sleep."

The bedtime routine had become one of Miles's favorite parts of the day. These quiet moments—so ordinary yet so precious—had once been shadowed by Charlotte's absence, his fumbling attempts at motherly tenderness, feeling inadequate. Now, watching Beth's natural grace with the girls, he felt not replacement but expansion, as if their family circle had widened to embrace both what was lost and what was found.

Tonight, Beth's voice was especially melodious as she continued the tale of a pioneer family making their way west, facing challenges with courage and faith. Miles watched his daughters' faces as they absorbed the story, Clara fighting sleep to hear just a little more, Ellie listening with quiet concentration.

When the chapter ended, both girls protested, but without real conviction, tiredness finally winning over curiosity about the story's continuation.

"Prayers," Miles reminded them gently.

The girls folded their hands dutifully, taking turns to thank God for specific blessings from their day. Clara's prayers tended toward the concrete—thanks for apple cake at lunch, for Jimmy sharing his marbles, for Hopper catching a mouse in the barn. Ellie's gratitude ran deeper—for her teacher's kindness, for the family being together, for the baby growing inside Beth.

Beth added her own quiet "Amen" when they finished, bending to kiss each girl goodnight, despite the awkwardness her growing belly created. Miles followed with his own kisses and the familiar reassurance that he would be just down the hall if they needed anything.

"Sleep well, my darlings," Beth whispered as they closed the door partway, leaving it open just enough for the hallway lamp's glow to reach the girls' beds.

Miles slipped his arm around Beth's waist as they walked to the main room, feeling her lean into him with comfortable familiarity. The quietness of the house settled around them, the crackling fire and ticking clock the only sounds.

"Tea?" Miles offered, guiding Beth back to her rocking chair. "We could try Eleanor's special blend."

"That would be lovely," Beth agreed, settling into the chair with a small sigh of contentment. "My ankles are reminding me I've been on my feet too much today."

Miles busied himself preparing the tea, another task that had once seemed insurmountable in his grief but now carried the easy rhythm of domestic affection. When the tea had steeped, he brought two cups to the fireside, placing Beth's on the small table beside her chair before settling in his own chair across from her.

"I finished the cradle today," he said, sipping the fragrant tea. "It just needs the final coat of polish."

Beth's eyes brightened. "May I see it?"

"It's meant to be a surprise," Miles protested mildly.

"I'm carrying your child. Surely, that earns me a preview of the cradle," Beth countered with a smile.

Miles chuckled, unable to deny her. "It's in the workshop. I'll bring it in tomorrow for your inspection."

"I'm sure it's beautiful," Beth said. "Everything you make is."

"I think it might be my finest work," Miles admitted. "Though I said the same about your hope chest, and the girls' beds, and the rocking horse I'm making for Christmas."

Beth laughed softly. "You always say that. Each new project is your masterpiece."

"That's because I pour a little more love into each one," Miles explained, his voice gentling. "Especially now, knowing these pieces will hold our family, our children, and the legacy we're building together."

Beth reached across the space between their chairs, offering her hand. Miles took it, enfolding her smaller fingers in his.

"I never thought I'd have this," Beth said softly, the firelight dancing across her features. "After my parents died, after Thomas left... I'd convinced myself I was meant for a solitary life. That God's plan for me was independence, not family."

"And I believed my chance at love died with Charlotte," Miles replied, his thumb tracing circles on the back of her hand. "That raising the girls alone was my path forward."

"How wonderfully wrong we both were," Beth smiled, a teasing light entering her eyes. "Though I must admit, when you first arrived in Hope Springs, romance was the furthest thing from my mind." Beth's eyes glistened with unshed tears at his words. "And now we've built a life together and a real home."

"With a white picket fence," Miles added, smiling at the fulfillment of her long-held wish.

"And a proper garden this spring for Ellie," Beth continued.

"And space for Clara's imaginary horses to become real ones someday," Miles chuckled.

"And a workshop where you can create beautiful things," Beth said.

"And a cradle for our baby," Miles finished softly, his gaze dropping to her rounded belly.

Beth rocked gently, her expression thoughtful. "I spoke with Harriet today," she said after a while. "She and Tim have set a wedding date for Christmas Eve."

"That's wonderful news," Miles replied. "They make a fine match."

"She credits us, you know," Beth smiled. "Says watching our happiness gave her the courage to accept Tim's proposal after hesitating for so long."

"I'm glad," Miles said sincerely. "Harriet deserves happiness. She was a true friend to you during difficult times."

"To both of us," Beth corrected.

Miles nodded, remembering Harriet's practical assistance and unwavering support in those early days. "We're blessed with good friends."

"We are," Beth agreed. "I was thinking we might host a dinner for Harriet and Tim before the wedding. A small celebration with just a few close friends."

"Whatever you wish," Miles assured her. "Though don't overtax yourself with preparations."

Beth made a soft sound of fond exasperation. "You're becoming as overprotective as Doc Reynolds."

"I'm concerned about your welfare," Miles defended himself. "And our child's."

"I know," Beth softened immediately. "And I love you for it. But I promise I won't do anything foolish. I'm being very careful."

Miles studied her face in the firelight, noting the healthy glow in her cheeks, the contentment in her expression. Pregnancy suited her, despite the occasional discomforts she mentioned. There was a radiance about her that transcended physical beauty, an inner light that seemed to grow stronger as their child developed within her.

"What are you thinking?" Beth asked, noticing his intent gaze.

"That you're the most beautiful woman I've ever seen," Miles answered truthfully.

Beth laughed softly. "Even with my waistline expanding daily and my ankles swollen?"

"Especially then," Miles insisted. "You're carrying our child, Beth. Creating life from our love. There's nothing more beautiful in this world."

Beth's expression turned tender. "You always know exactly what to say to make me feel cherished."

"Because you are," Miles said simply. "Cherished beyond measure."

The grandfather clock chimed nine, its resonant tones filling the room. Outside, the wind had picked up, rustling tree branches against the windows and adding an edge to the autumn chill.

"We should bank the fire for the night," Miles suggested, setting aside his empty teacup.

Beth nodded, making a move to rise, but Miles was already on his feet, offering his hand. "Allow me, Mrs. Donovan."

The title still brought a smile to Beth's lips. "Thank you, Mr. Donovan."

Miles helped her from the rocking chair, steadying her as she found her balance. Their bodies naturally moved closer, Beth's rounded belly pressing gently against him.

"Oh!" she exclaimed suddenly, her hand flying to her side.

"What is it?" Miles asked, alarmed.

Beth laughed, taking his hand and placing it where hers had been. "Someone is practicing their blacksmithing skills, I think. Feel this."

Miles waited, then felt it—a definite push against his palm, stronger than the flutters he'd felt before. "That's quite a kick," he marveled.

"He or she has been particularly active today," Beth said. "I think hearing your voice rouses the baby. It always—" She broke off with another small gasp as another movement rippled across her belly.

Miles knelt before her, both hands now cradling the swell that held their child. "Hello, little one," he said softly. "This is your papa. You should let your mama rest now."

As if in response, another push came against his hands, making both parents laugh.

"Stubborn already," Beth observed. "I wonder which of us that comes from?"

"Clearly you," Miles teased, rising to his feet again. "I'm known for my agreeable nature."

Beth raised an eyebrow skeptically. "Is that so? Then you won't mind when I tell you I've invited Eleanor and Frank to Sunday dinner next week?"

Miles groaned good-naturedly. "Frank will talk my ear off about his new farming equipment."

"As I said, completely agreeable," Beth laughed, patting his cheek affectionately.

Miles captured her hand, pressing a kiss to her palm. "For you, always."

Beth's laughter faded into a softer expression, her green eyes reflecting the firelight. "I love you, Miles Donovan. More than I ever thought possible."

"And I love you," Miles replied, drawing her close. "You've given me a second chance at happiness I never expected to find."

Their lips met in a kiss that began tenderly and deepened with the ease of those who had learned each other's rhythms.

When they separated, Beth's cheeks were flushed. "We should check on the girls before retiring," she suggested.

Miles nodded, banking the fire while Beth gathered their teacups. Together, they moved through their evening routine with the comfortable synchronization of a well-matched pair.

Checking on the girls revealed both sleeping soundly. Clara sprawled across her bed in typical fashion, Ellie neat and straight under her covers. Miles straightened Clara's blankets while Beth smoothed Ellie's hair back from her forehead, both parents lingering a moment to savor the peaceful sight of their children at rest.

In their bedroom, the nightly preparations continued in companionable quiet. Beth brushed out her hair at the dressing table while Miles turned down the bed. The room, with its handcrafted furniture and personal touches, reflected their merged lives—Beth's mother's quilt on the bed, the daguerreotype of Charlotte with infant Clara on the bureau alongside a portrait of Beth's parents, Miles's father's pocket watch on the bedside table.

"Our first Christmas as a family will be here soon," Miles observed, watching as Beth plaited her hair for the night. "The first of many."

Beth met his eyes in the mirror, her expression softening. "Many, many more to come."

When they finally settled into bed, Beth curled against his side as best her growing belly allowed, her head finding its familiar place on his shoulder. Miles's arm wrapped around her, his hand resting protectively over their unborn child.

"Are you comfortable?" he asked, adjusting the pillow behind her.

"Perfectly," Beth assured him, stifling a small yawn. "Though your son or daughter seems determined to practice somersaults all night."

"Sleep, little one," he murmured. "Your mama needs rest."

As Beth's breathing deepened toward sleep, Miles remained awake, savoring the weight of her against him, the subtle movements of their child, the profound peace that filled their bedroom. Through the window, he could see stars scattered across the black velvet of the night sky, countless points of light in the darkness.

So much like their journey, he reflected. What had begun in mutual loss and grief had transformed into something beautiful. Points of light emerging one by one until the darkness receded. Each small happiness, each shared moment of understanding, each challenge faced together, had brought them to this perfect culmination.

"What are you thinking about?" Beth murmured, not as asleep as he'd thought.

"That God's plans are indeed mysterious," Miles answered honestly. "That out of our deepest sorrows, He created this joy."

Beth's hand found his in the darkness, their fingers intertwining. "He makes all things new," she quoted softly, words from Revelation that had become something of a personal creed for them both.

"Yes," Miles agreed, feeling the truth of it settle in his bones. "All things new."

This was the life God had prepared for him, not despite his losses, but through them. This was the redemption of pain, the fulfillment of unspoken prayers, and the answer to questions he hadn't known to ask.

"I love you," he whispered to Beth, unsure if she was still awake to hear him.

Her fingers tightened slightly on his, her voice drowsy but clear. "And I love you. Always."

As sleep finally claimed him, Miles held those words close to his heart, a promise, and a prayer for all the days to come. Not just hope, but hope fulfilled. Not just springs of renewal, but the rich harvest of love that would sustain them through all seasons of their life together.

Together, they had found their way home.

Leave A Review

I f you enjoyed this book, please consider leaving an honest review on Amazon

Visit Our Website:

www.vivianbelle.com

Visit Our Amazon Author Page HERE

Find Us On Social Media:

Facebook

Facebook Author Page

Instagram